LONE WOLF 2100™

THE LANGUAGE OF CHAOS

Inspired by the classic manga
series **Lone Wolf and Cub** by
KAZUO KOIKE
and
GOSEKI KOJIMA

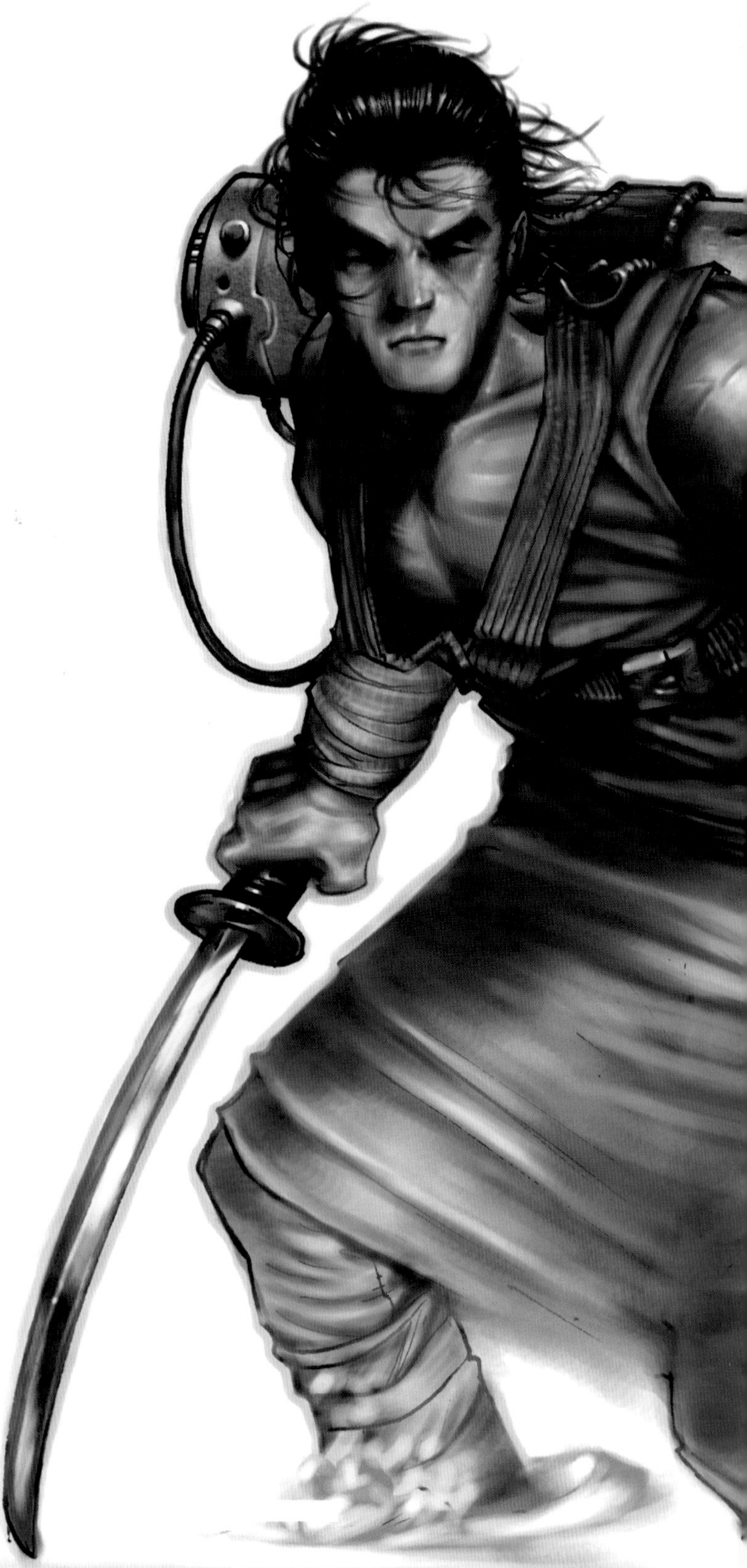

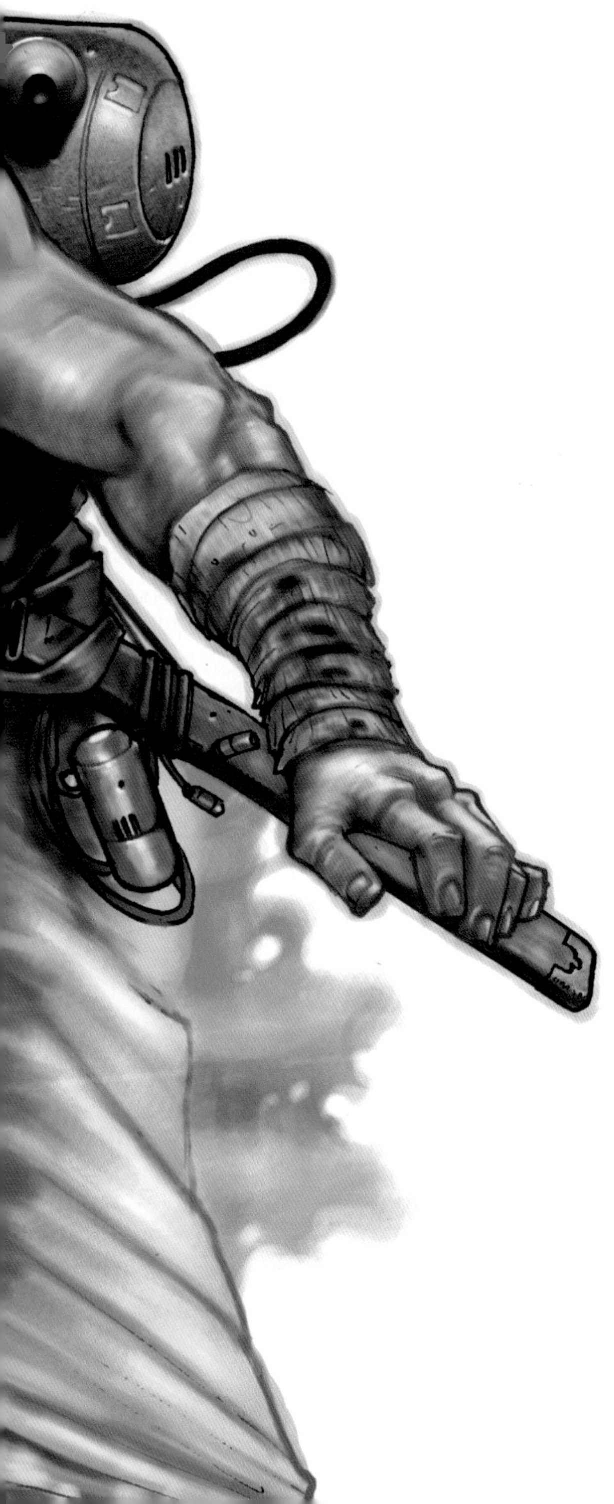

LONE WOLF 2100™

子連れ狼

THE LANGUAGE OF CHAOS

written by

MIKE KENNEDY

art by

FRANCISCO RUIZ VELASCO

with additional coloring by Studio F

lettering by

DIGITAL CHAMELEON,
SNO CONE STUDIOS,
& JASON HVAM

™

publisher

MIKE RICHARDSON

collection designer

DARIN FABRICK

art director

MARK COX

assistant editor

JEREMY BARLOW

editor

RANDY STRADLEY

LONE WOLF 2100 Volume 2—THE LANGUAGE OF CHAOS
Lone Wolf 2100™ copyright © 2002, 2003 Dark Horse Comics,
Inc., Koike Shoin, and Liveworks. Dark Horse Comics® is a
trademark of Dark Horse Comics, Inc., registered in various
categories and countries. All rights reserved. No portion of this
publication may be reproduced or transmitted, in any form or
by any means, without the express written permission of Dark
Horse Comics, Inc. Names, characters, places, and incidents
featured in this publication either are the product of the author's
imagination or are used fictitiously. Any resemblance to actual
persons (living or dead), events, institutions, or locales, without
satiric intent, is coincidental.

This volume collects issues five through eight
of the comic-book series, **Lone Wolf 2100**,
plus the short story "Dirty Tricks" from **Reveal.**

Published by
Dark Horse Comics, Inc.
10956 SE Main Street
Milwaukie, OR 97222

www.darkhorse.com

To find a comics shop in your area,
call the Comic Shop Locator Service toll-
free at 1-888-266-4226

First edition:
ISBN: 1-56971- 997-7

1 3 5 7 9 10 8 6 4 2
Printed in Hong Kong

GlobalNet Retrospective—4 March 2094

A container holding live virus samples of the War Spore was being secretly transported between two unknown locations by unknown parties. Investigations revealed that it arrived in Northern Taiwan via ship, where it was loaded onto a train headed for a port in Southern Taiwan. As the train passed through Sungshan, it was attacked by Coalition terrorists who were apparently aware of the shipment. During the altercation, the container was damaged and its contents were released. Forty-eight hours later, Sungshan was a festering, dying community.

The War Spore spread so quickly, debilitated so completely, and killed so mercilessly, that emergency workers could do nothing to contain it. Military forces sealed Sungshan, preventing anyone from leaving. The heads of the World Health Organization and the leaders of the Greater Asian 500 Commission decided to firebomb the region to stop the virus from infecting the entire island.

The city burned for eighteen days. Those who survived the fire were shot as they attempted to flee past Military barricades. On the nineteenth day, the last remaining flames were doused with a blanket of anti-viral flame retardant.

The World Health Organization surveyed the area and found no detectable trace of the virus. The area was declared a restricted zone and no salvage or cleanup was attempted.

Eight days later, the War Spore destroyed Kowloon.

子連れ狼 2100

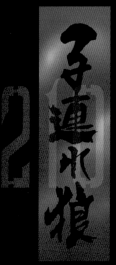

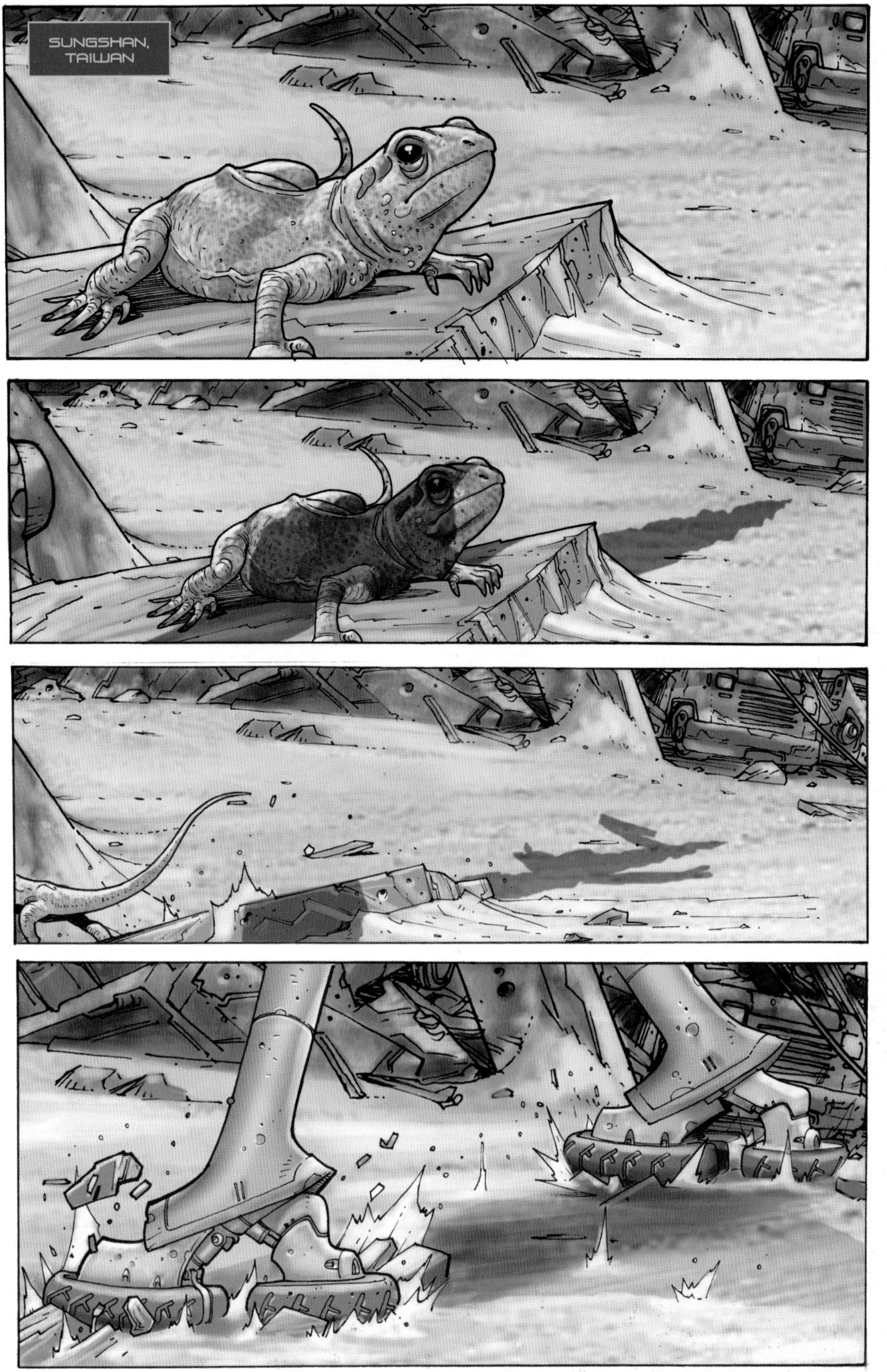
SUNGSHAN,
TAIWAN

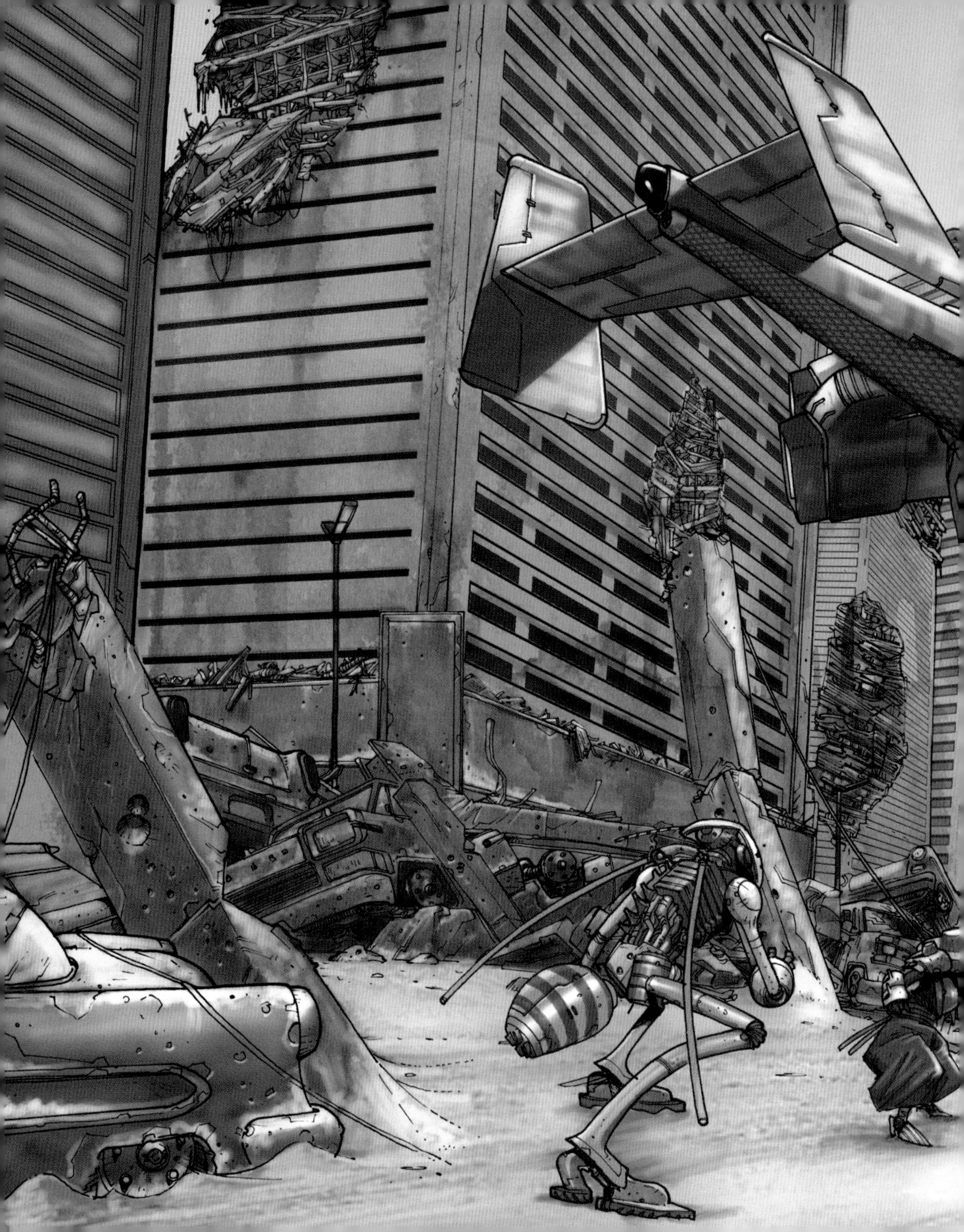

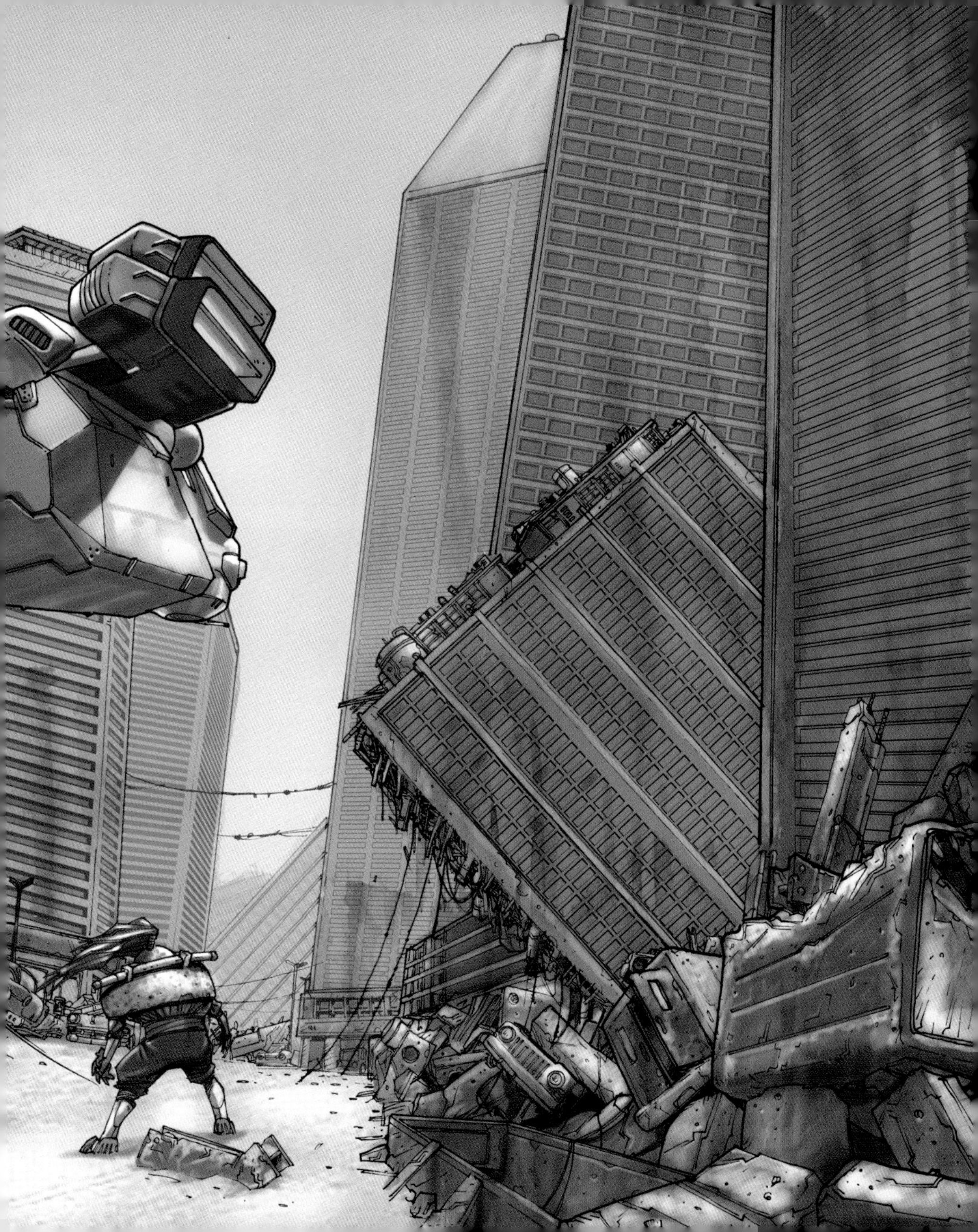

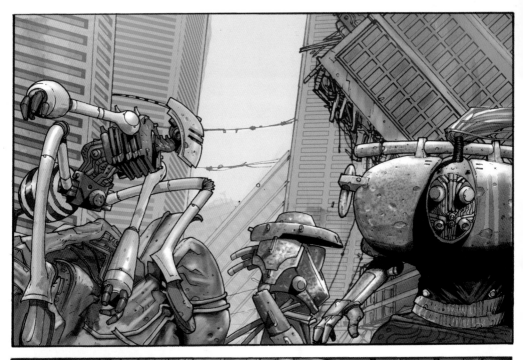

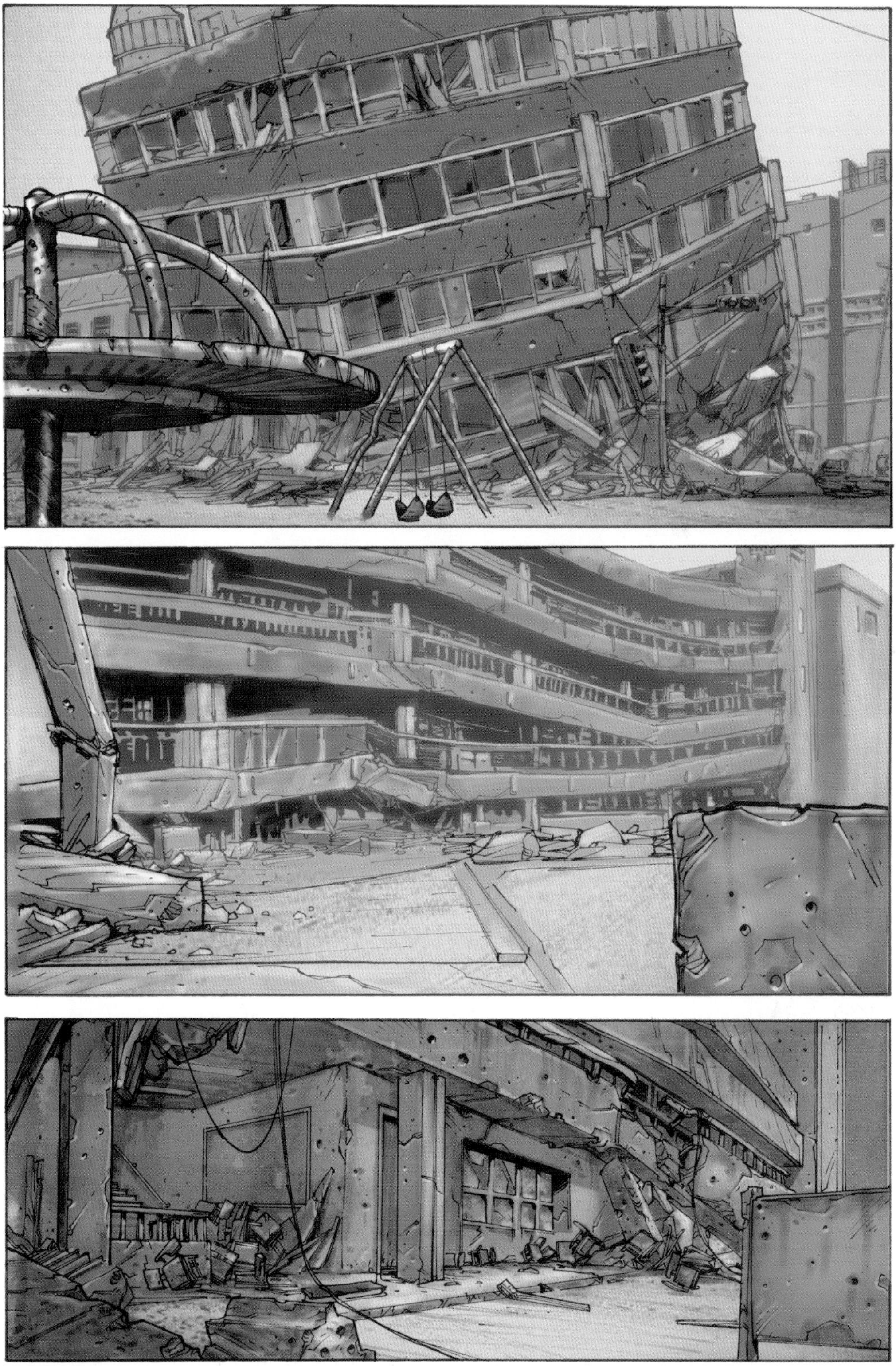

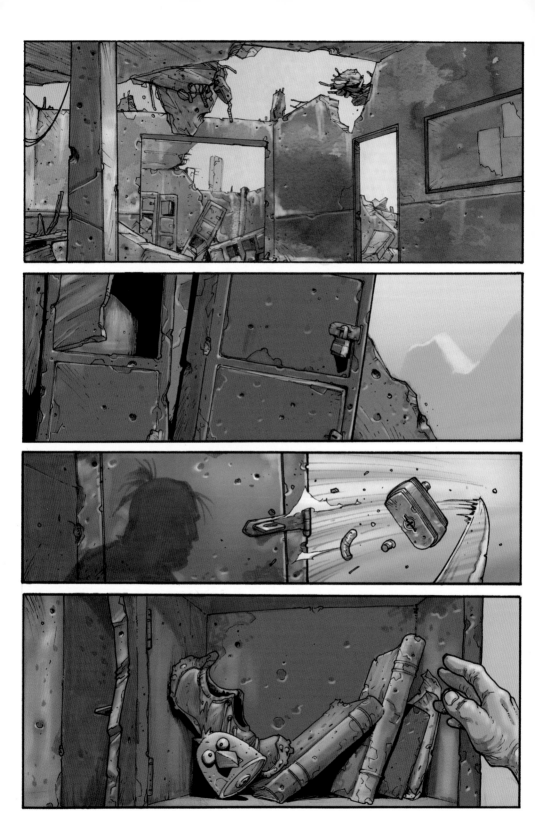

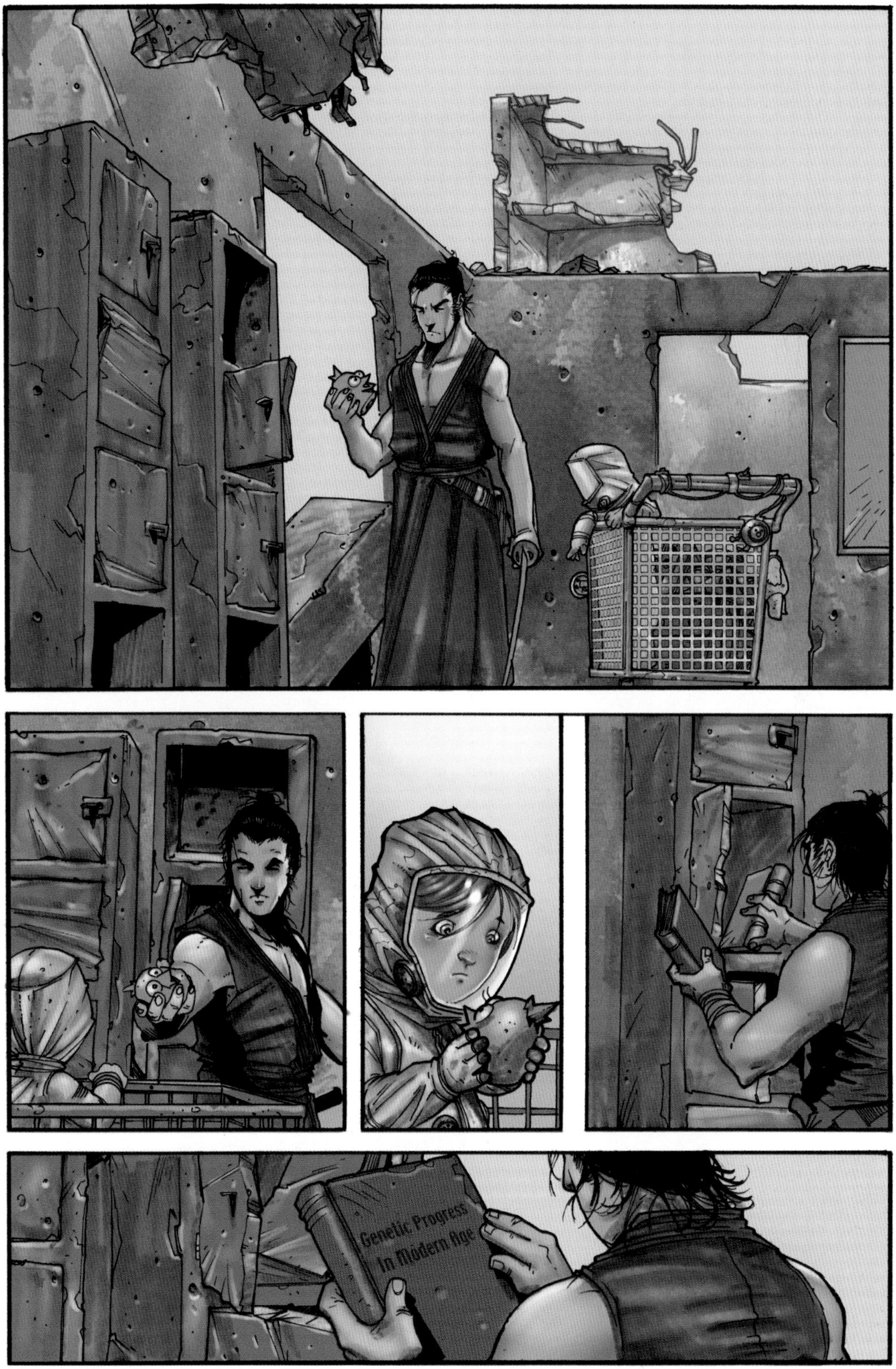
Genetic Progress
In Modern Age

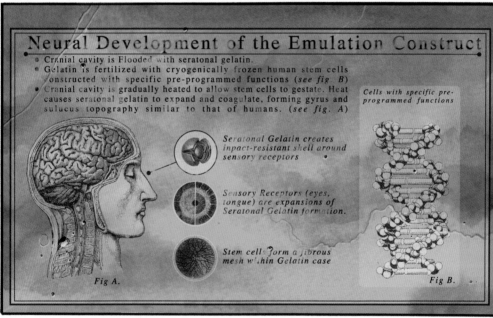

Neural Development of the Emulation Construct

- Cranial cavity is Flooded with seratonal gelatin.
- Gelatin is fertilized with cryogenically frozen human stem cells constructed with specific pre-programmed functions (*see fig B*)
- Cranial cavity is gradually heated to allow stem cells to gestate. Heat causes seratonal gelatin to expand and coagulate, forming gyrus and sulucus topography similar to that of humans. (*see fig A*)

Cells with specific pre-programmed functions

Seratonal Gelatin creates inpact-resistant shell around sensory receptors

Sensory Receptors (eyes, tongue) are expansions of Seratonal Gelatin formation.

Stem cells form a fibrous mesh within Gelatin case

Fig A.

Fig B.

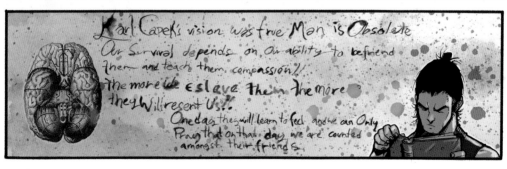

Karl Capek's vision was true Man is Obsolete
Our Survival depends on our ability to befriend
them and teach them compassion!
The more we eslave them the more
they will resent us!
One day they will learn to feel and we can only
Pray that on that day we are counted
amongst their friends

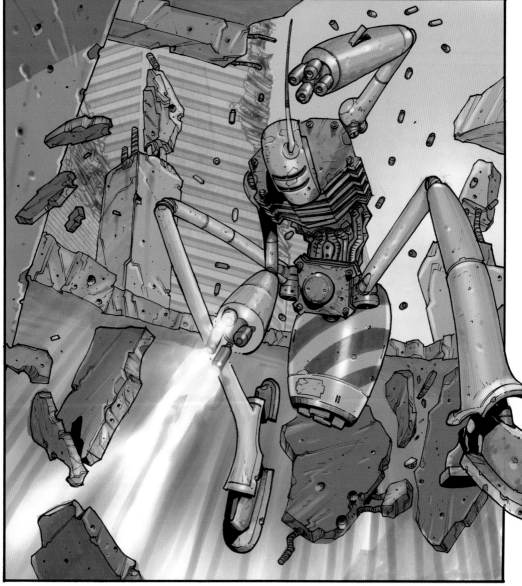

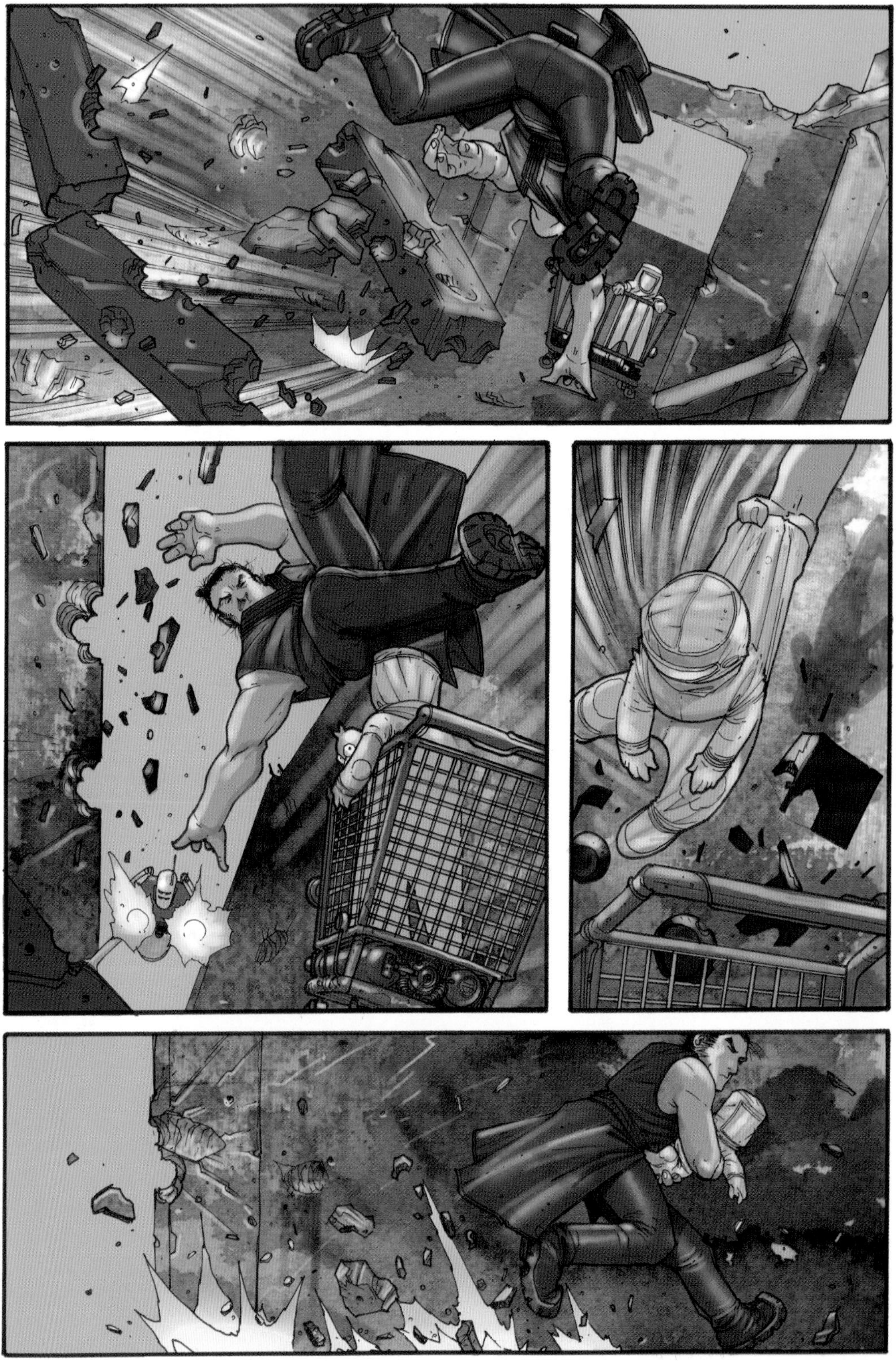

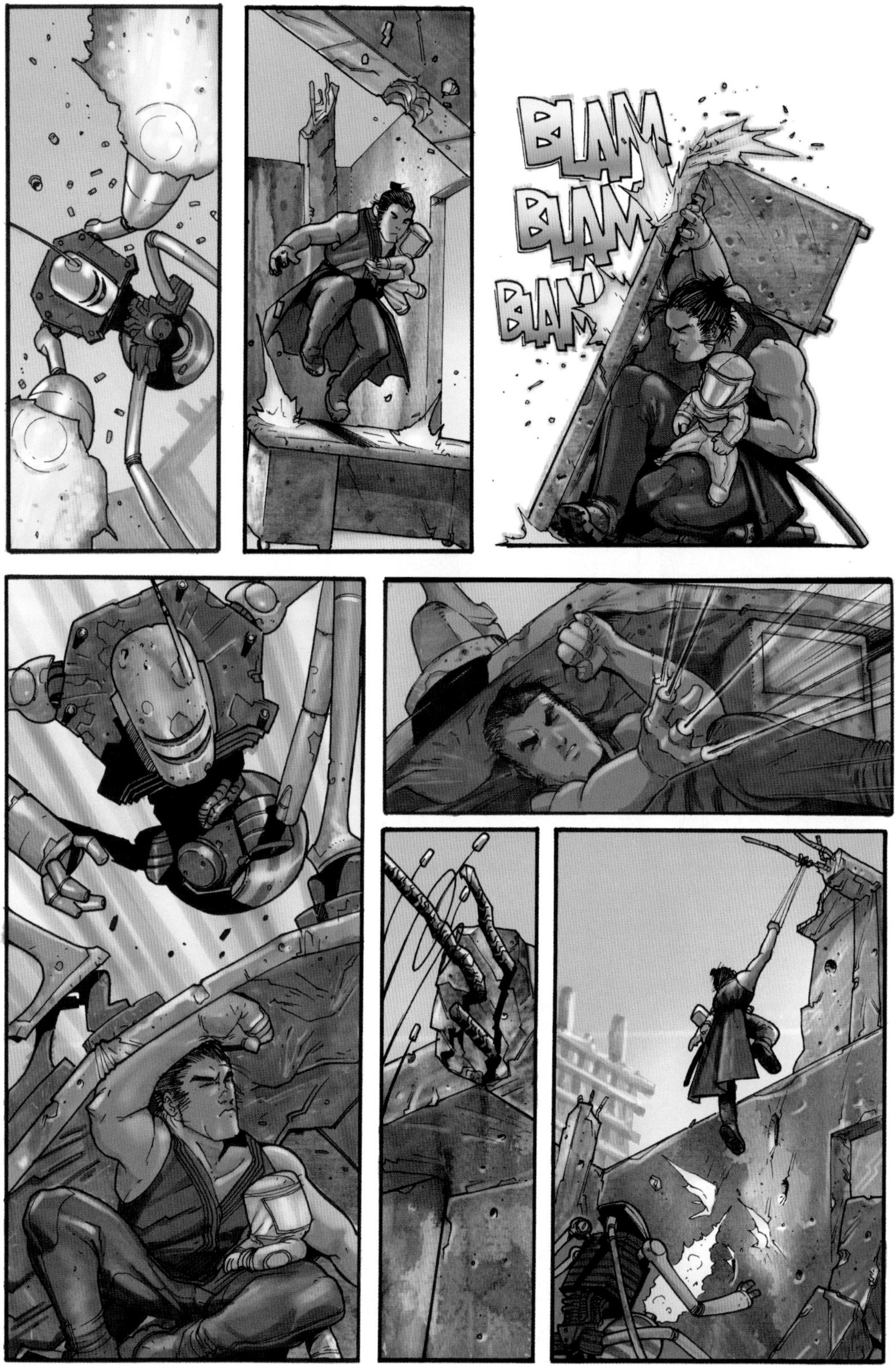
BLAM
BLAM
BLAM

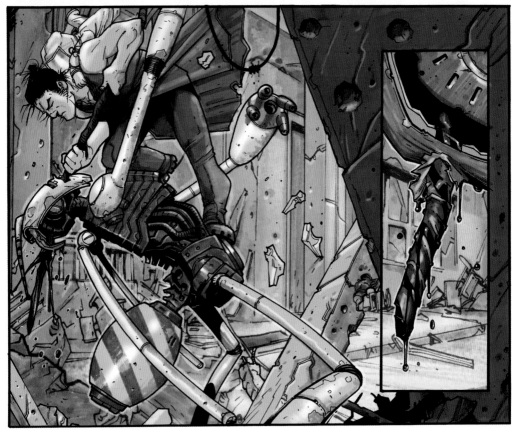

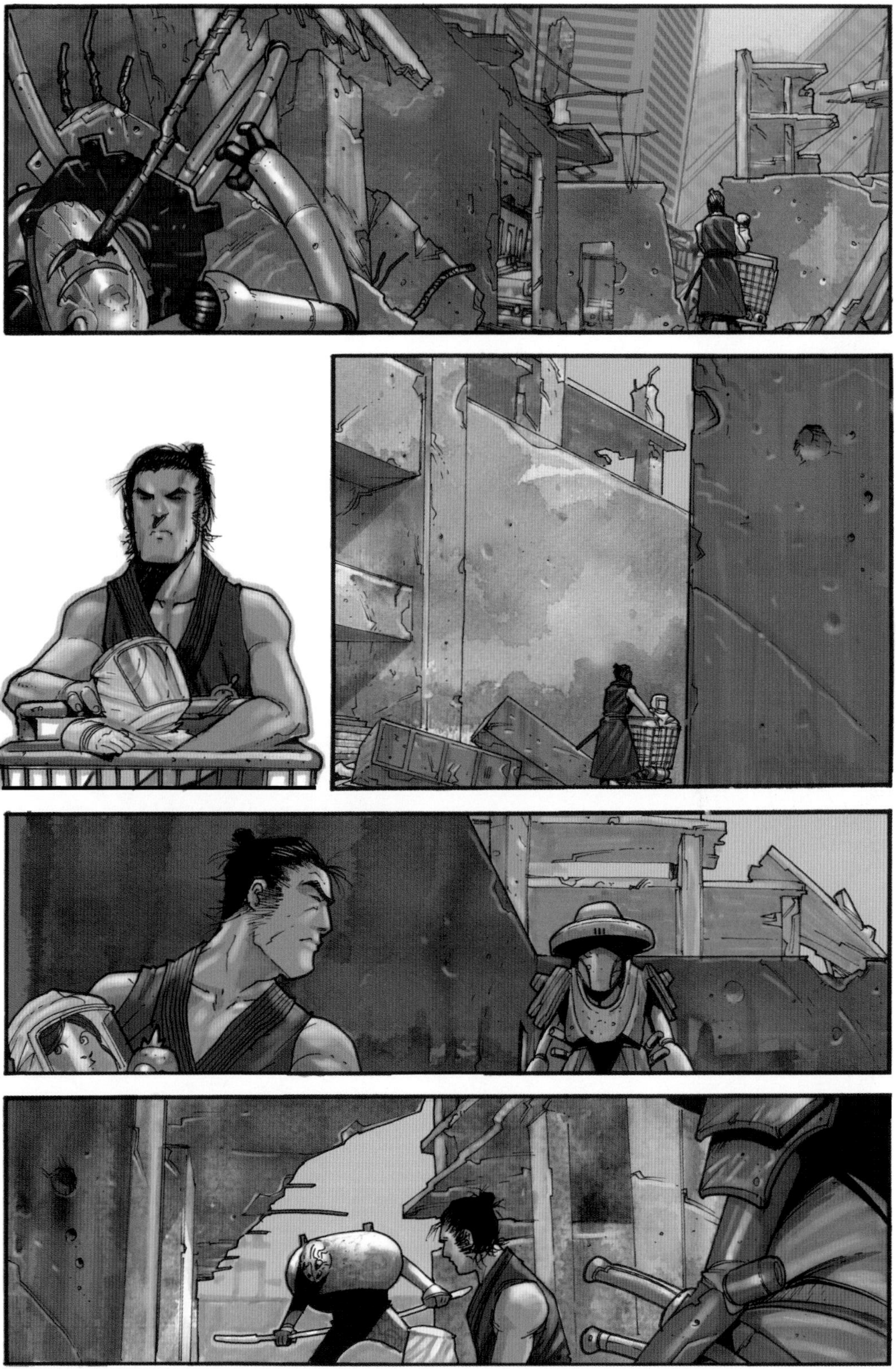

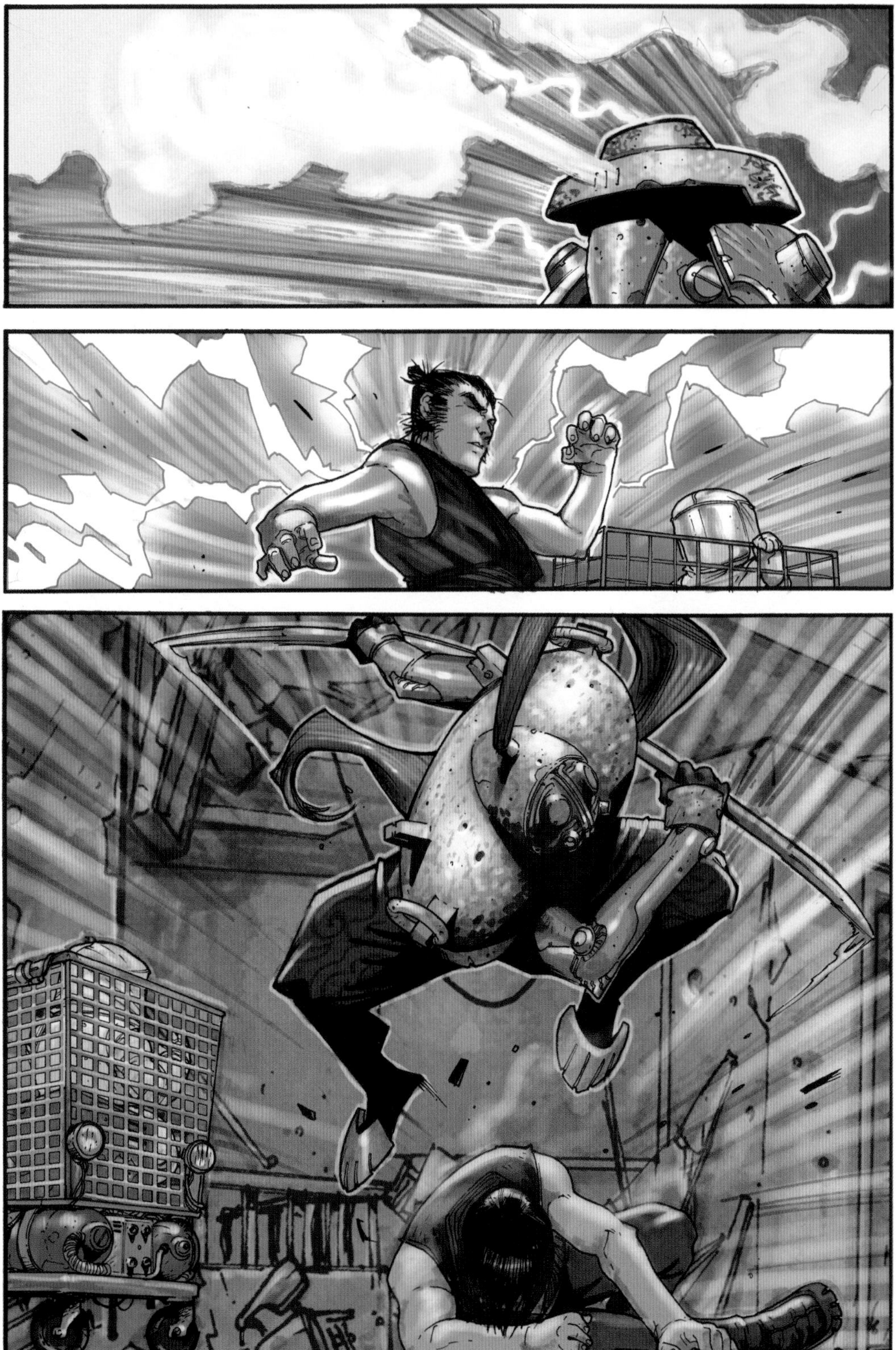

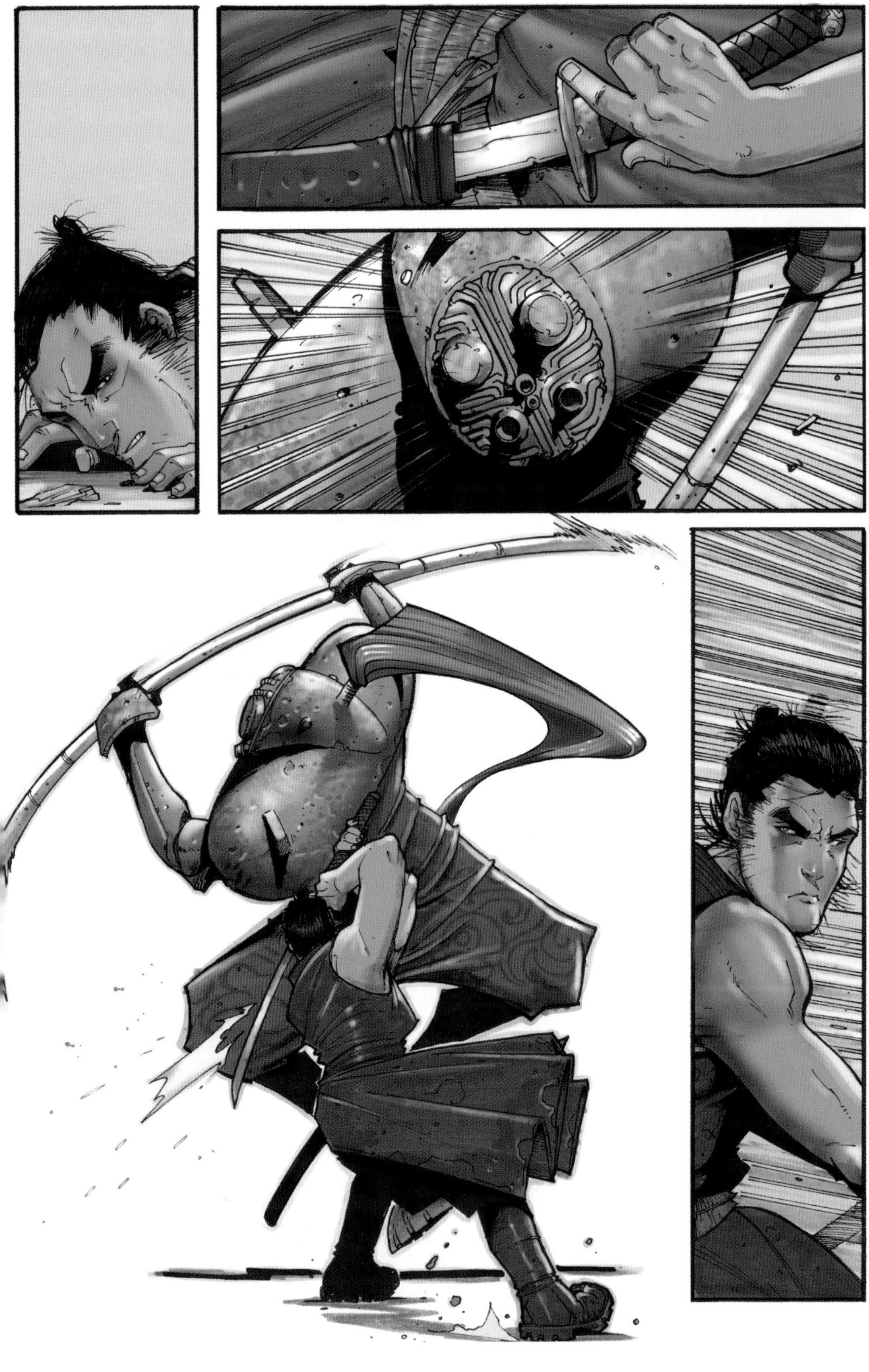

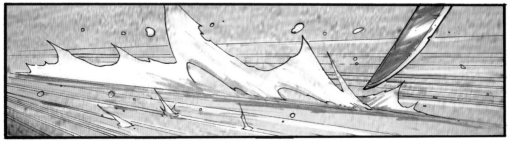

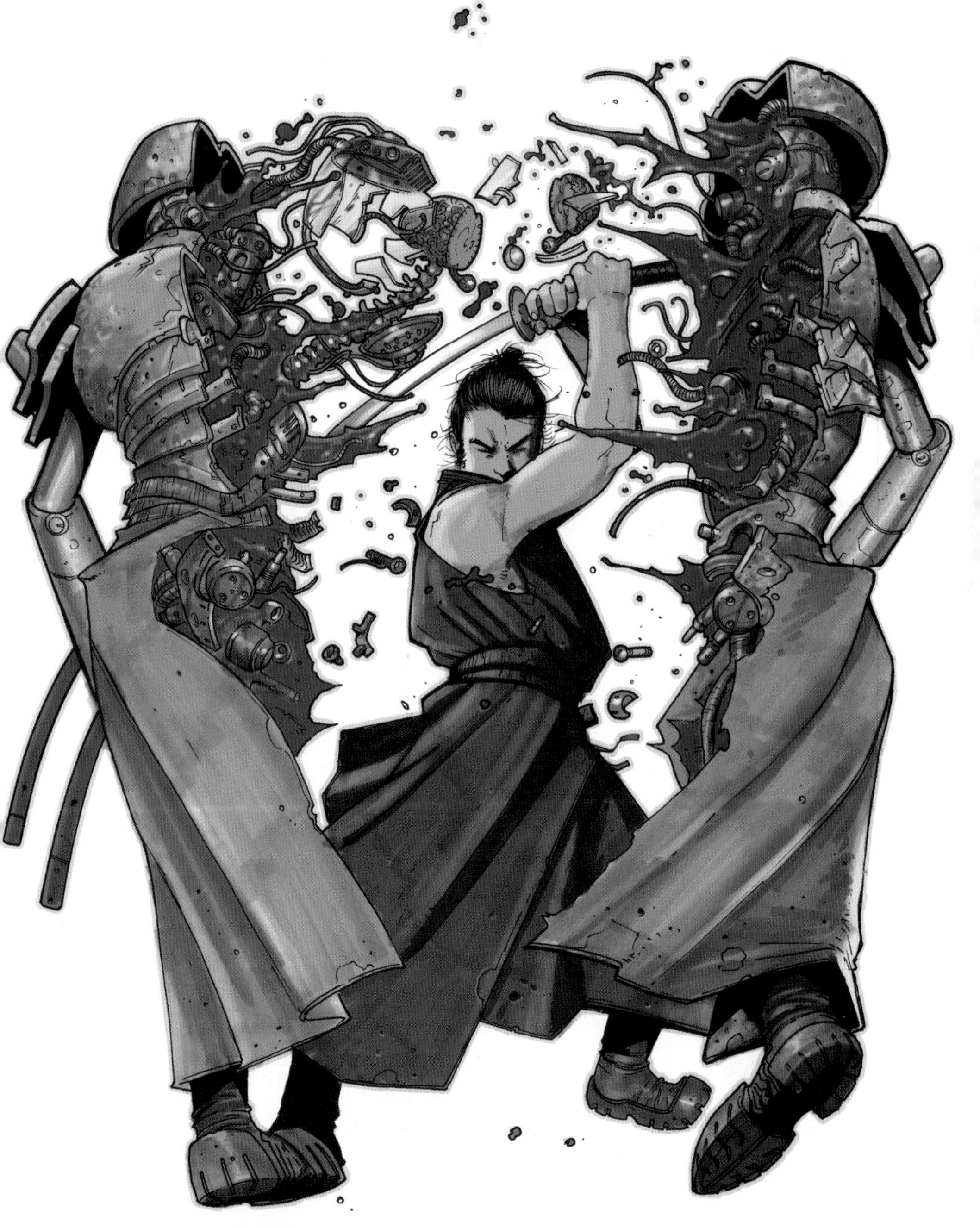

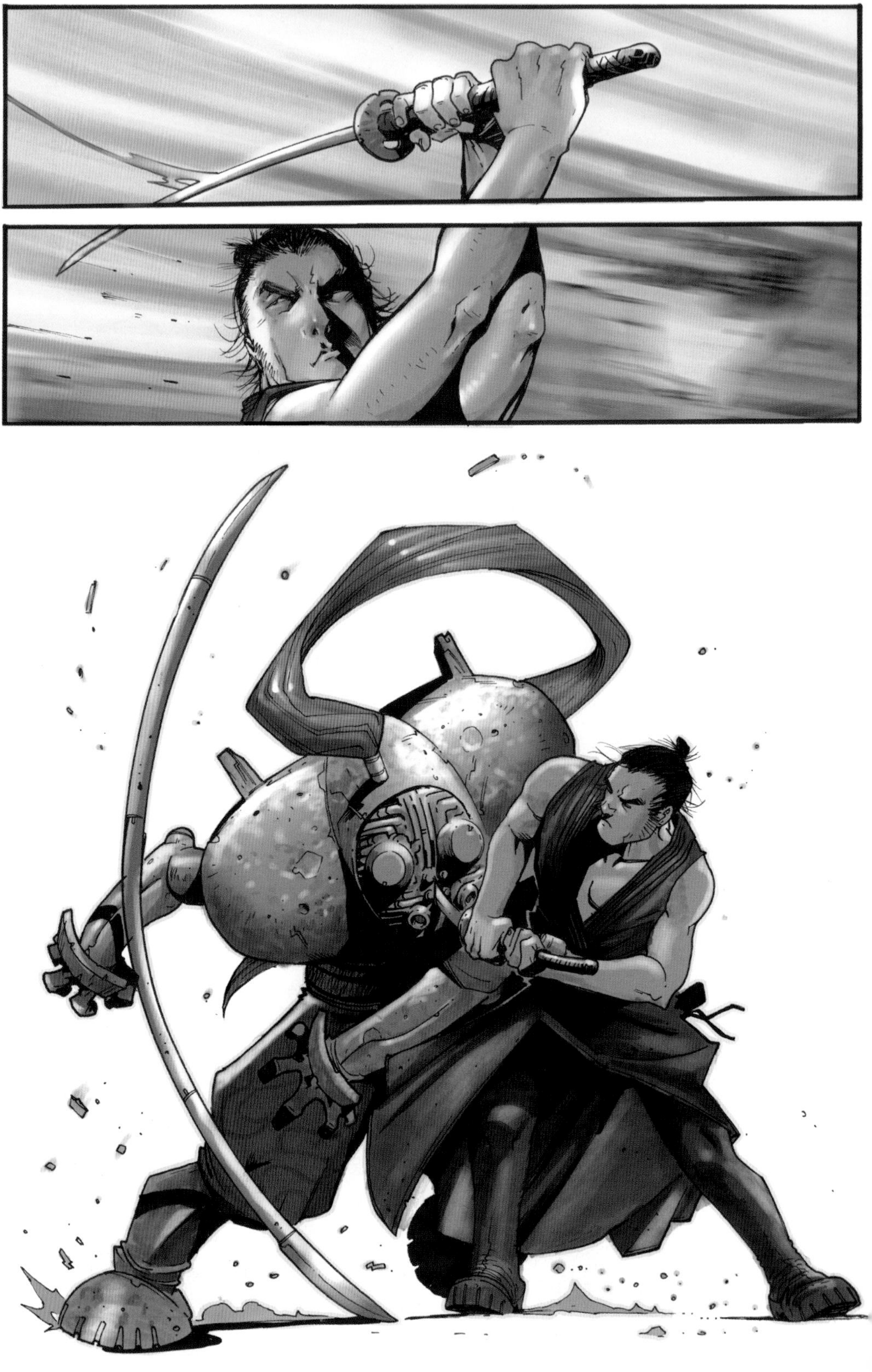

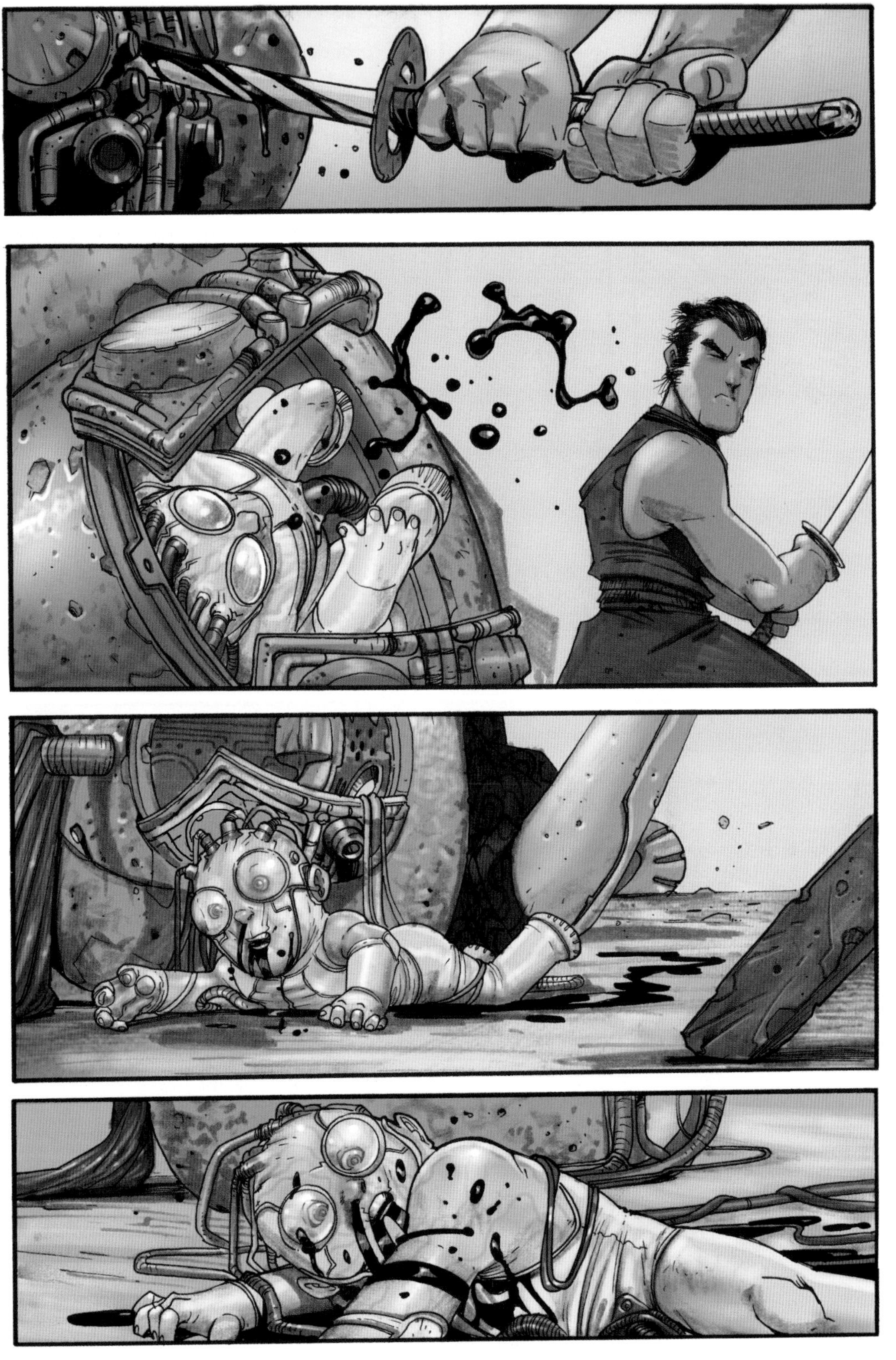

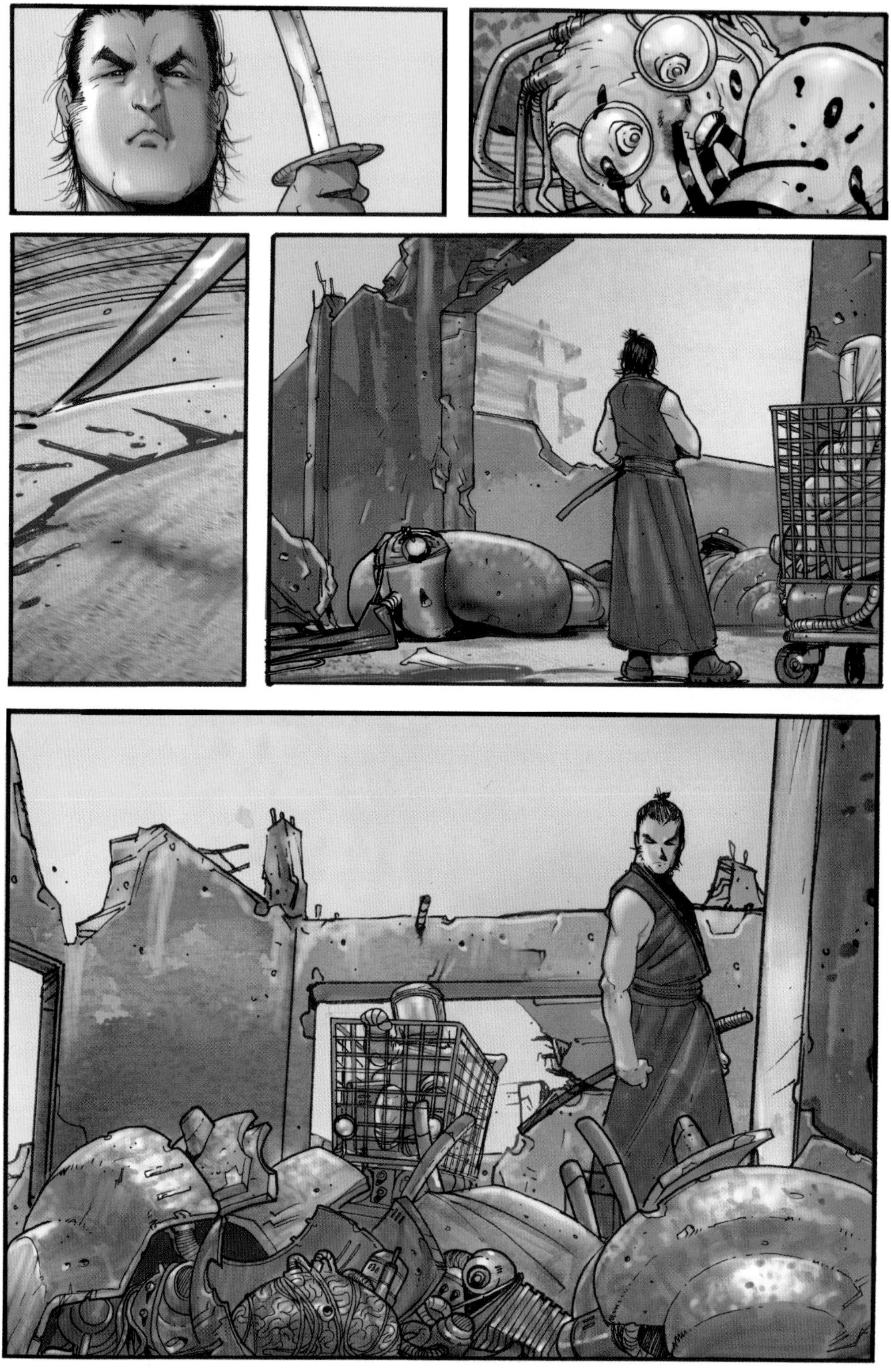

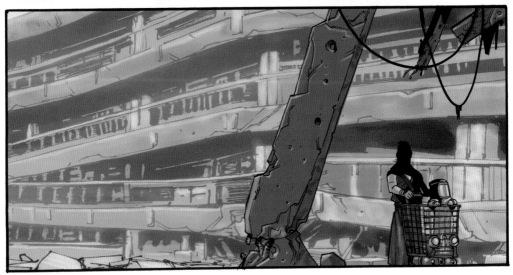

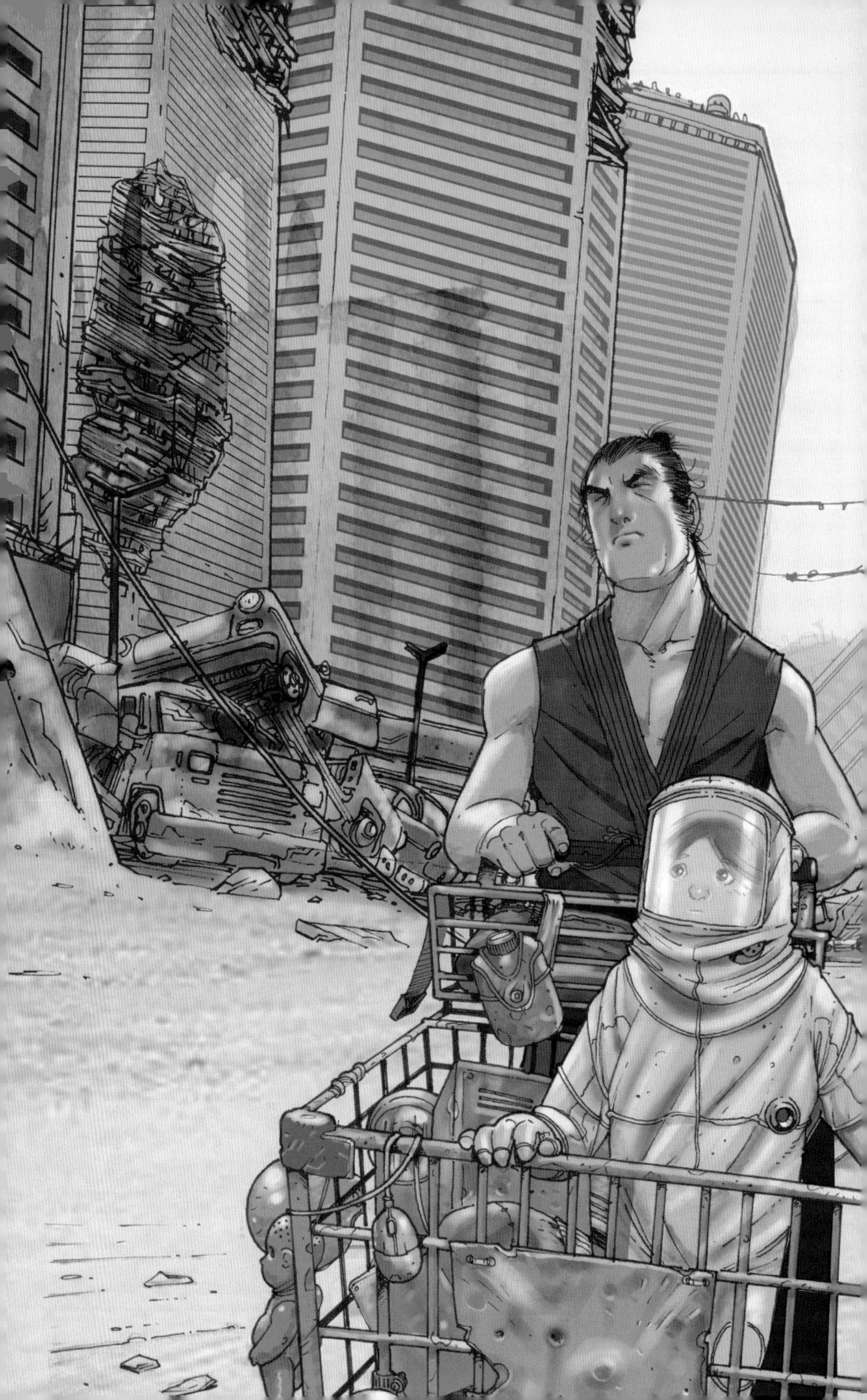

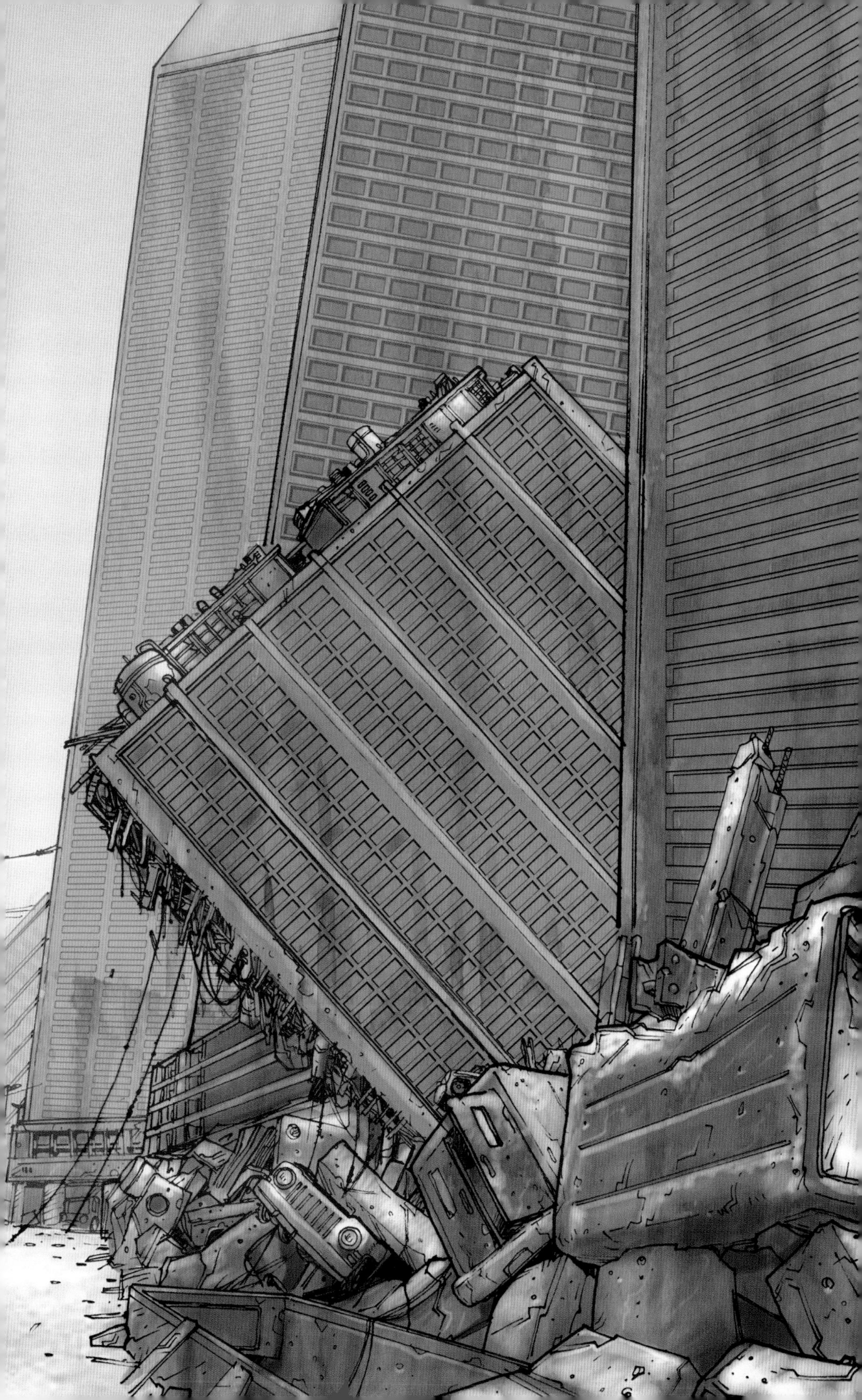

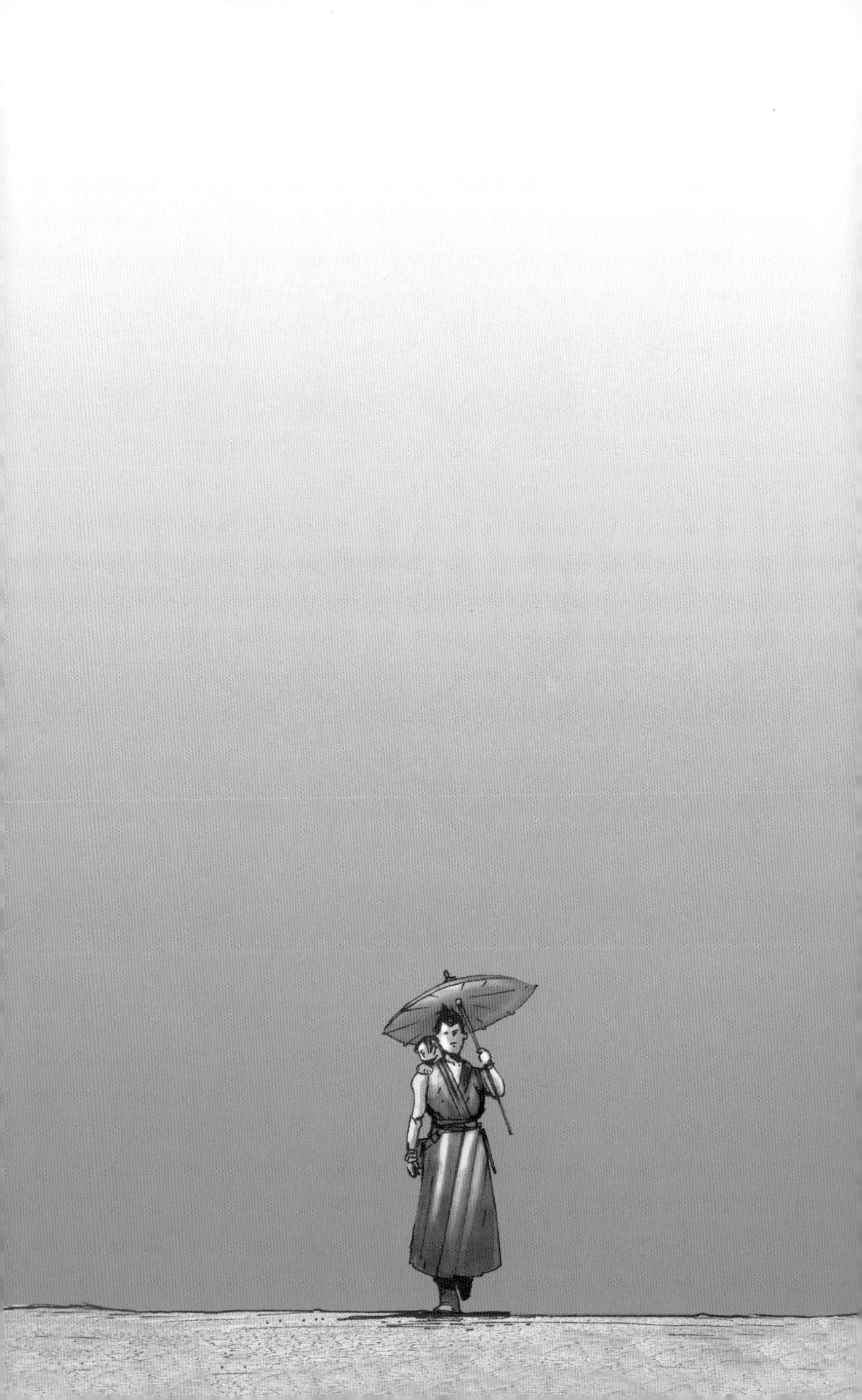

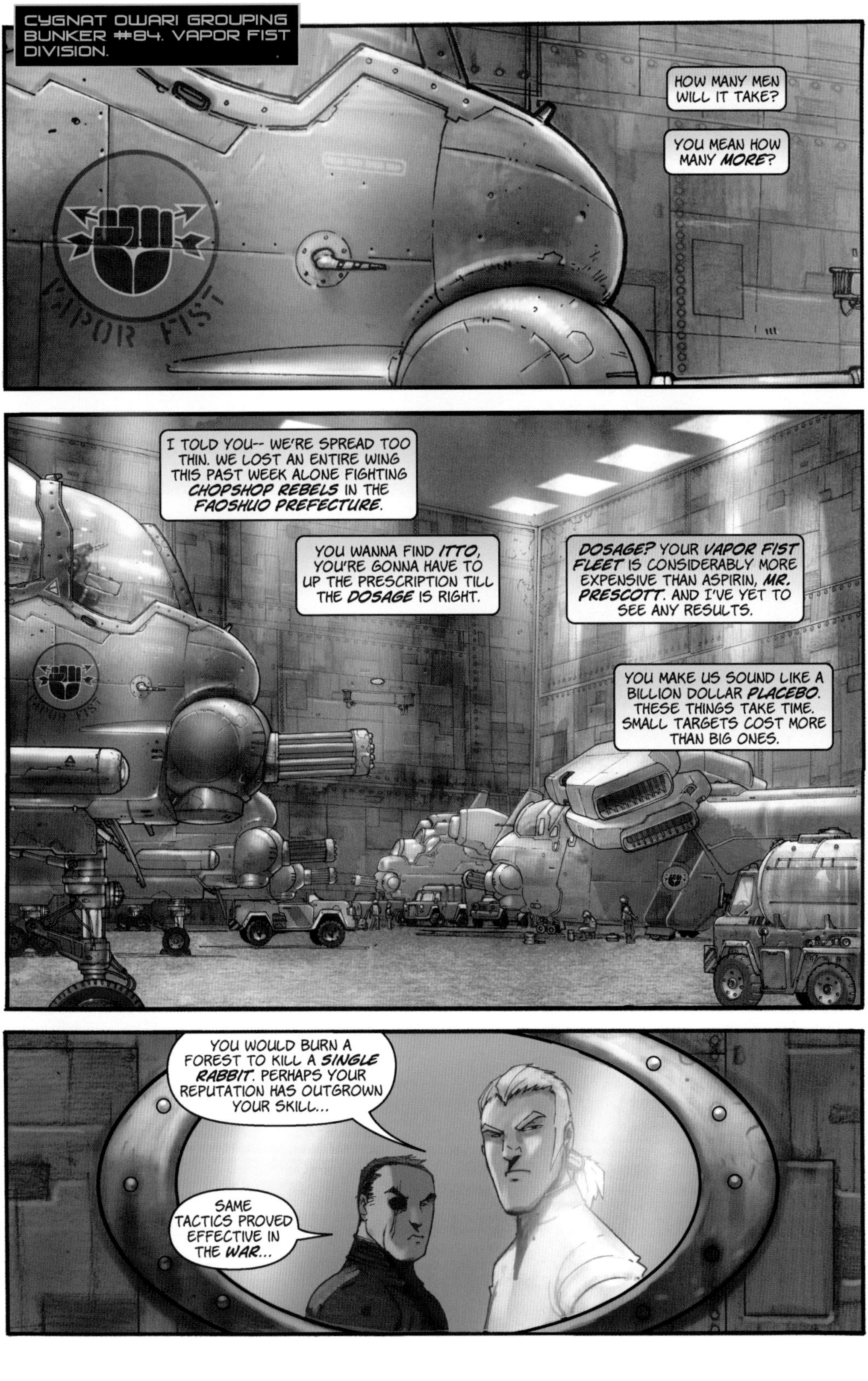
CYGNAT OWARI GROUPING BUNKER #84. VAPOR FIST DIVISION.
HOW MANY MEN WILL IT TAKE?
YOU MEAN HOW MANY MORE?
VAPOR FIST
I TOLD YOU-- WE'RE SPREAD TOO THIN. WE LOST AN ENTIRE WING THIS PAST WEEK ALONE FIGHTING CHOPSHOP REBELS IN THE FAOSHUO PREFECTURE.
YOU WANNA FIND ITTO, YOU'RE GONNA HAVE TO UP THE PRESCRIPTION TILL THE DOSAGE IS RIGHT.
DOSAGE? YOUR VAPOR FIST FLEET IS CONSIDERABLY MORE EXPENSIVE THAN ASPIRIN, MR. PRESCOTT. AND I'VE YET TO SEE ANY RESULTS.
YOU MAKE US SOUND LIKE A BILLION DOLLAR PLACEBO. THESE THINGS TAKE TIME. SMALL TARGETS COST MORE THAN BIG ONES.
YOU WOULD BURN A FOREST TO KILL A SINGLE RABBIT. PERHAPS YOUR REPUTATION HAS OUTGROWN YOUR SKILL...
SAME TACTICS PROVED EFFECTIVE IN THE WAR...

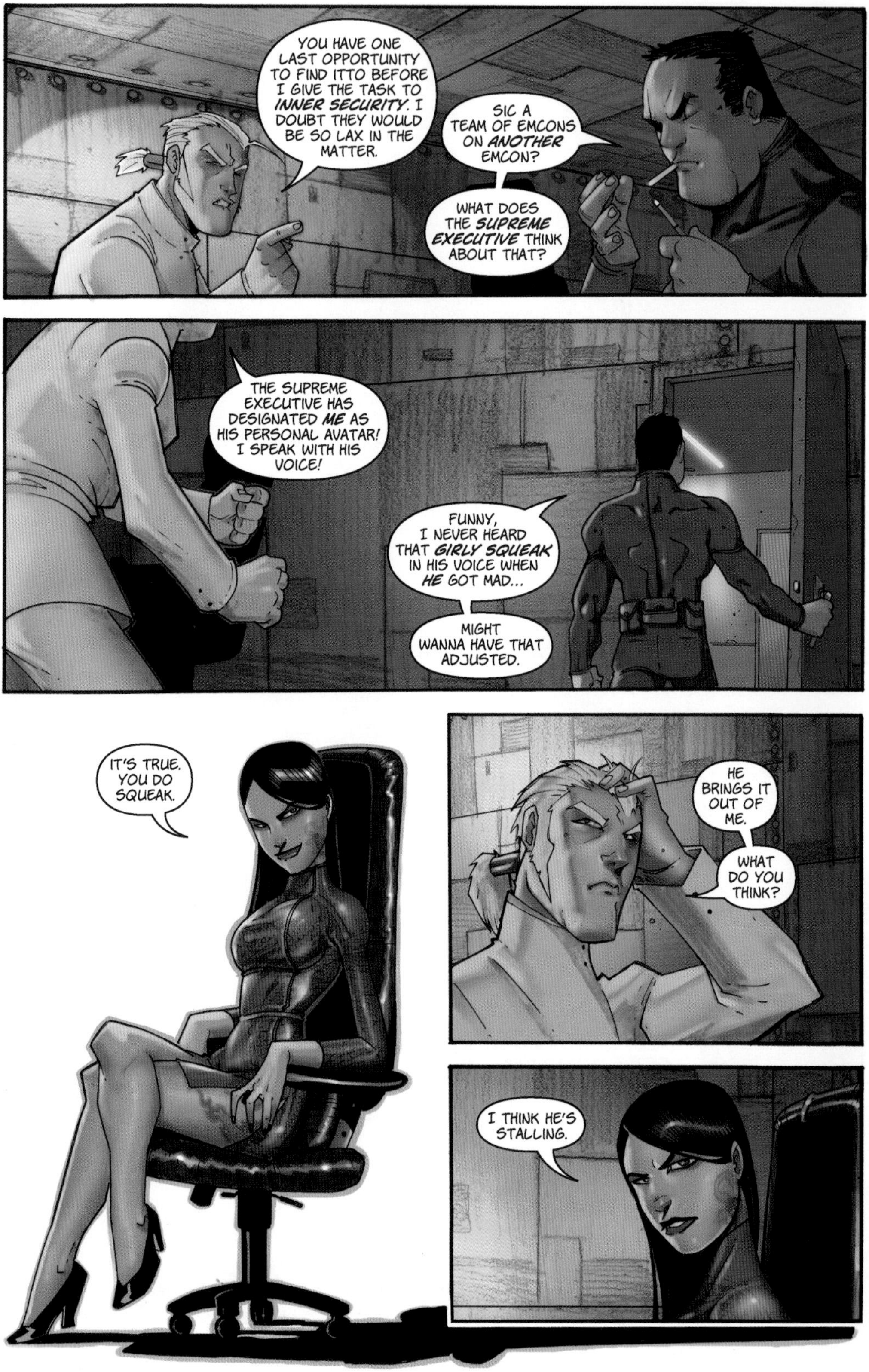
YOU HAVE ONE LAST OPPORTUNITY TO FIND ITTO BEFORE I GIVE THE TASK TO INNER SECURITY. I DOUBT THEY WOULD BE SO LAX IN THE MATTER.
SIC A TEAM OF EMCONS ON ANOTHER EMCON?
WHAT DOES THE SUPREME EXECUTIVE THINK ABOUT THAT?
THE SUPREME EXECUTIVE HAS DESIGNATED ME AS HIS PERSONAL AVATAR! I SPEAK WITH HIS VOICE!
FUNNY, I NEVER HEARD THAT GIRLY SQUEAK IN HIS VOICE WHEN HE GOT MAD...
MIGHT WANNA HAVE THAT ADJUSTED.
IT'S TRUE. YOU DO SQUEAK.
HE BRINGS IT OUT OF ME.
WHAT DO YOU THINK?
I THINK HE'S STALLING.

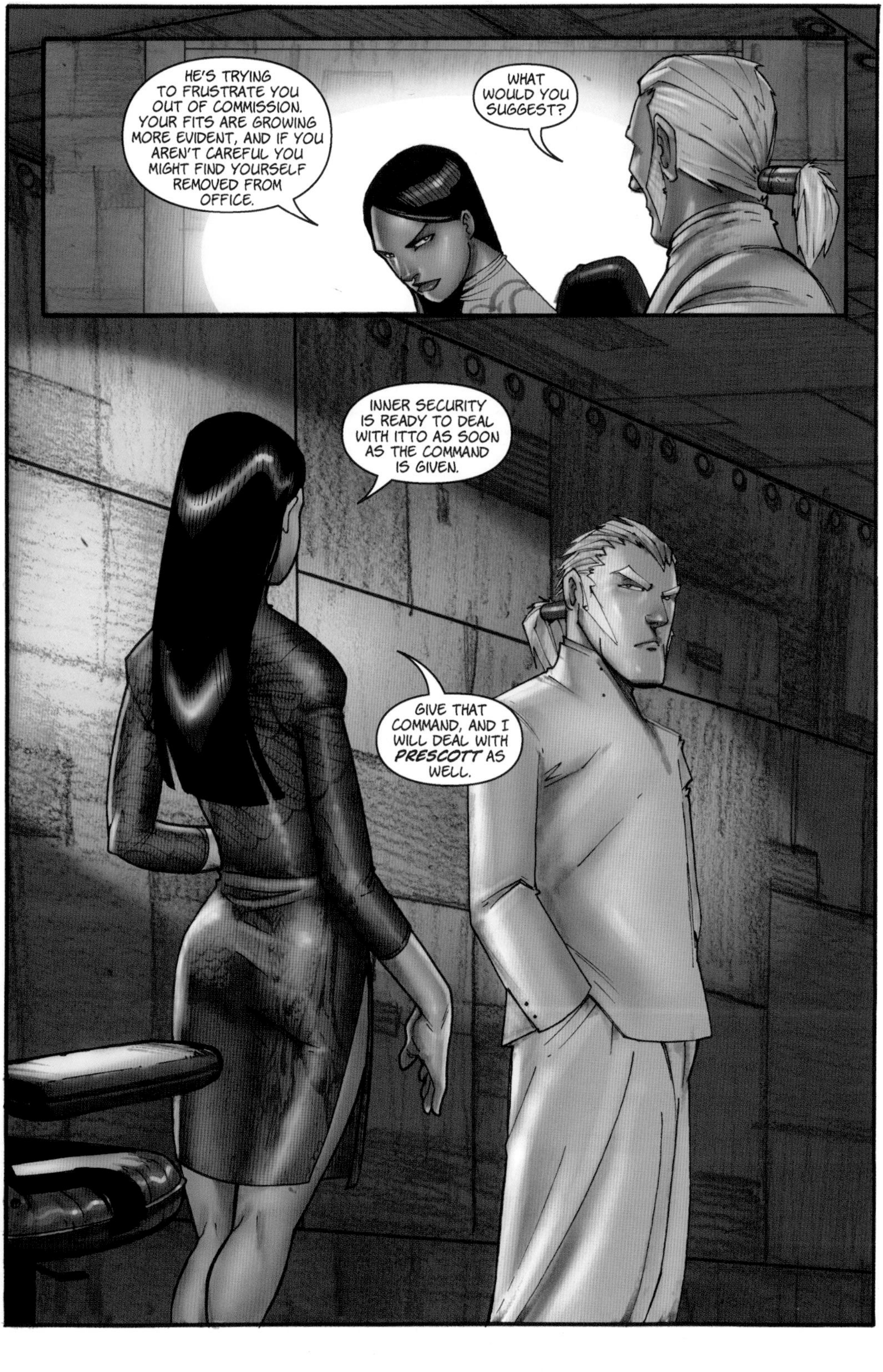
HE'S TRYING TO FRUSTRATE YOU OUT OF COMMISSION. YOUR FITS ARE GROWING MORE EVIDENT, AND IF YOU AREN'T CAREFUL YOU MIGHT FIND YOURSELF REMOVED FROM OFFICE.
WHAT WOULD YOU SUGGEST?
INNER SECURITY IS READY TO DEAL WITH ITTO AS SOON AS THE COMMAND IS GIVEN.
GIVE THAT COMMAND, AND I WILL DEAL WITH PRESCOTT AS WELL.

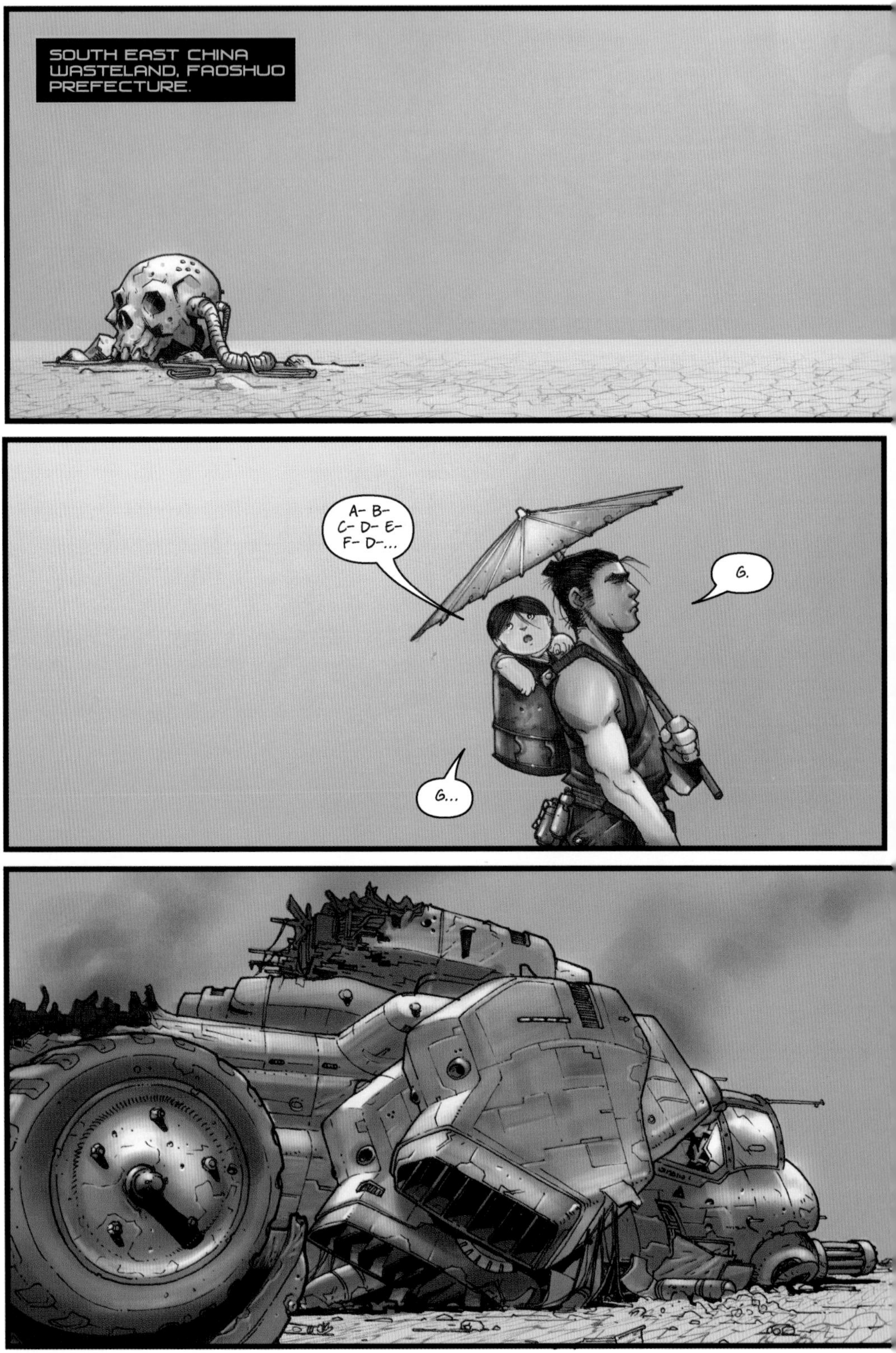
SOUTH EAST CHINA WASTELAND, FAOSHUO PREFECTURE.
A- B- C- D- E- F- D-...
G.
G...

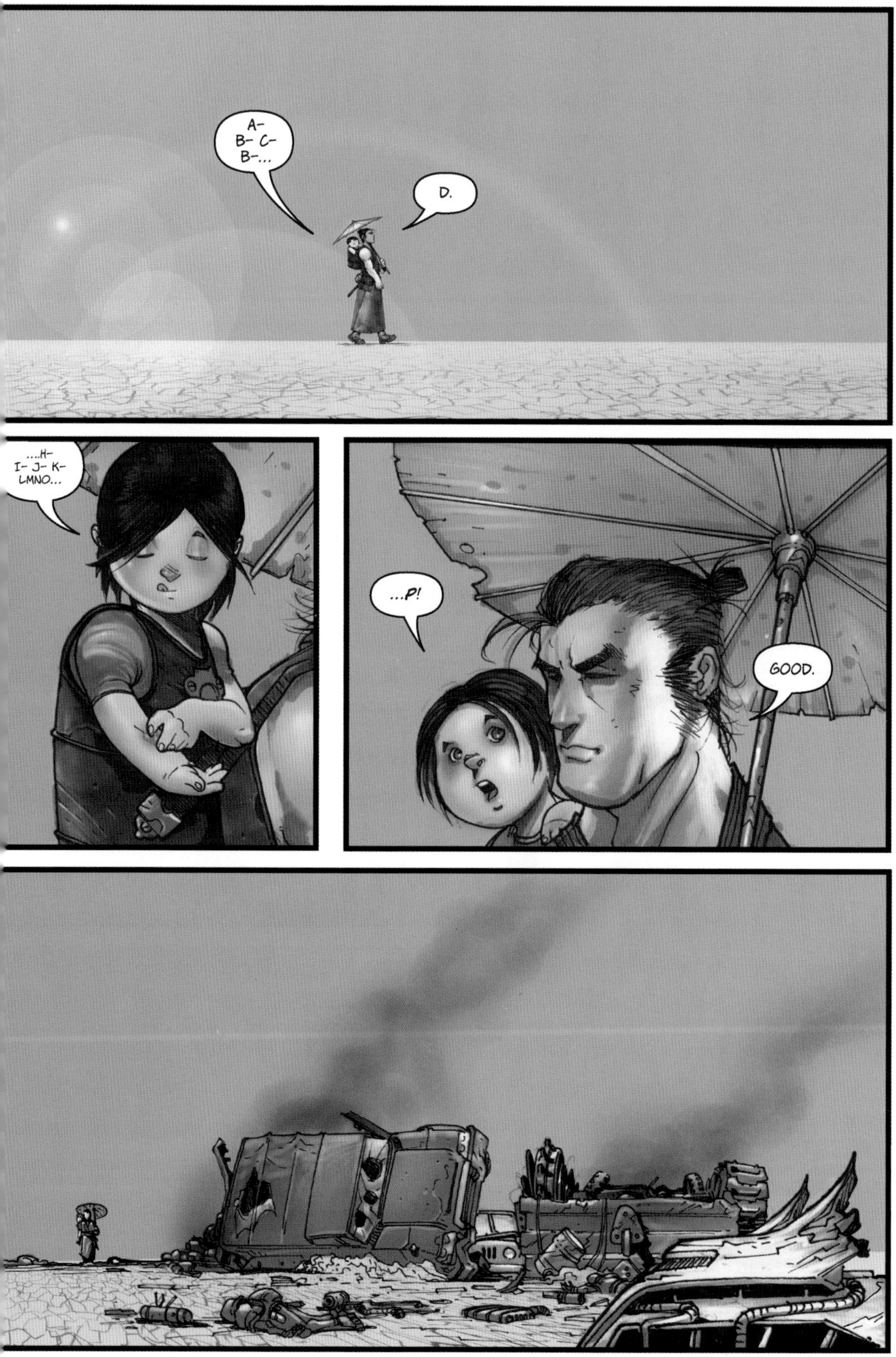
A- B- C- B-...
D.
...H- I- J- K- LMNO...
...P!
GOOD.

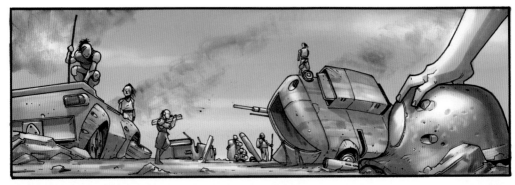

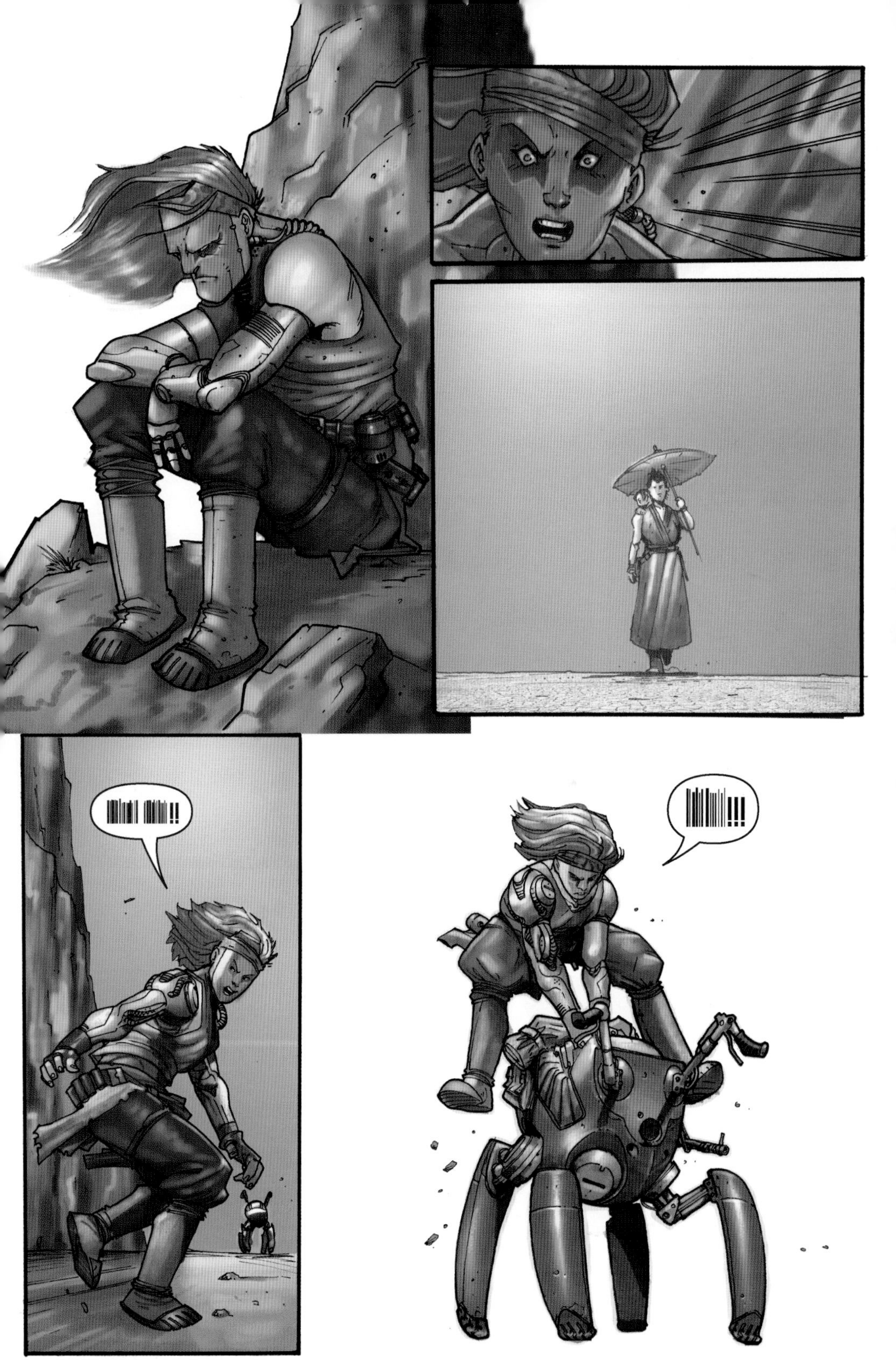

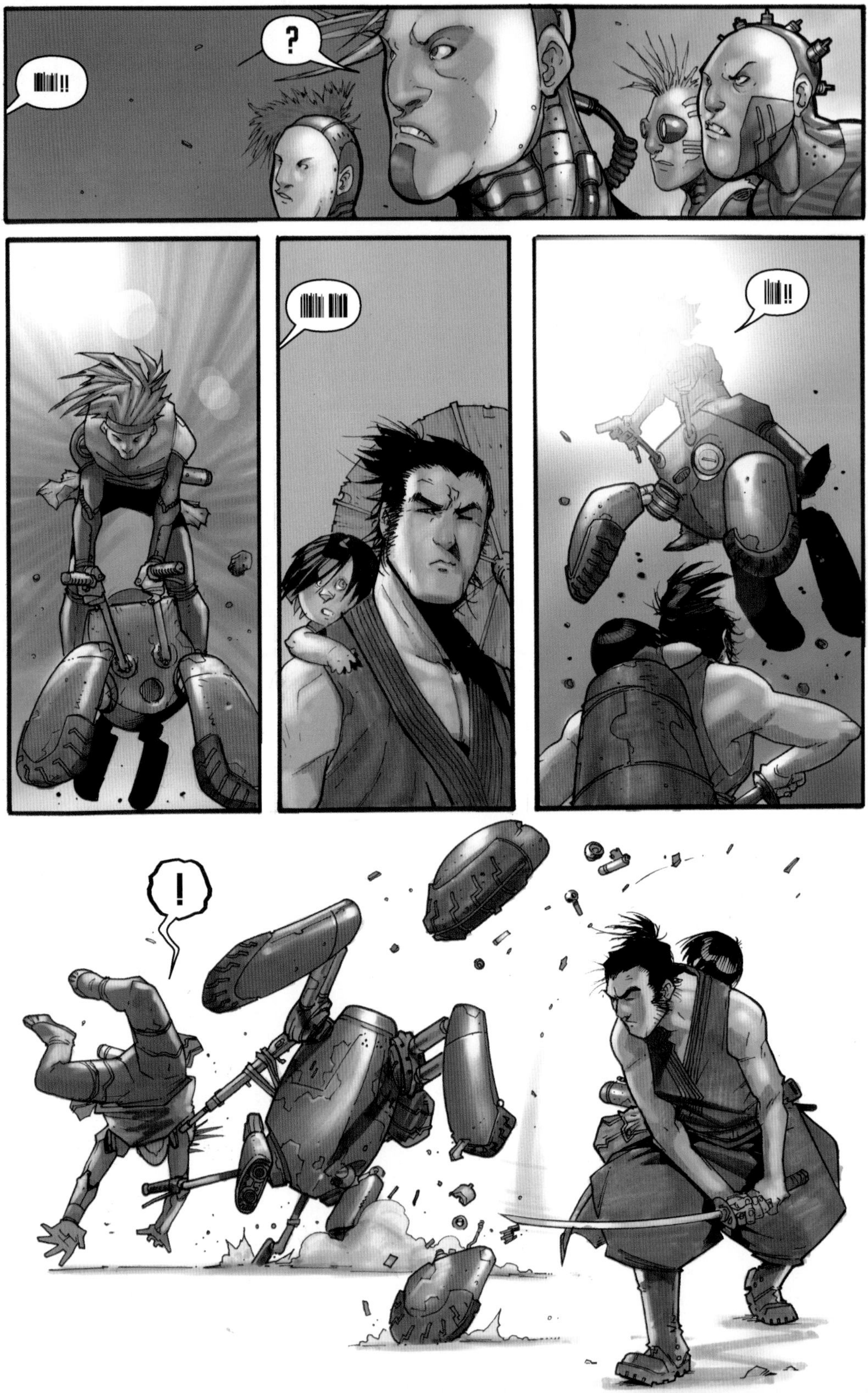
?
!

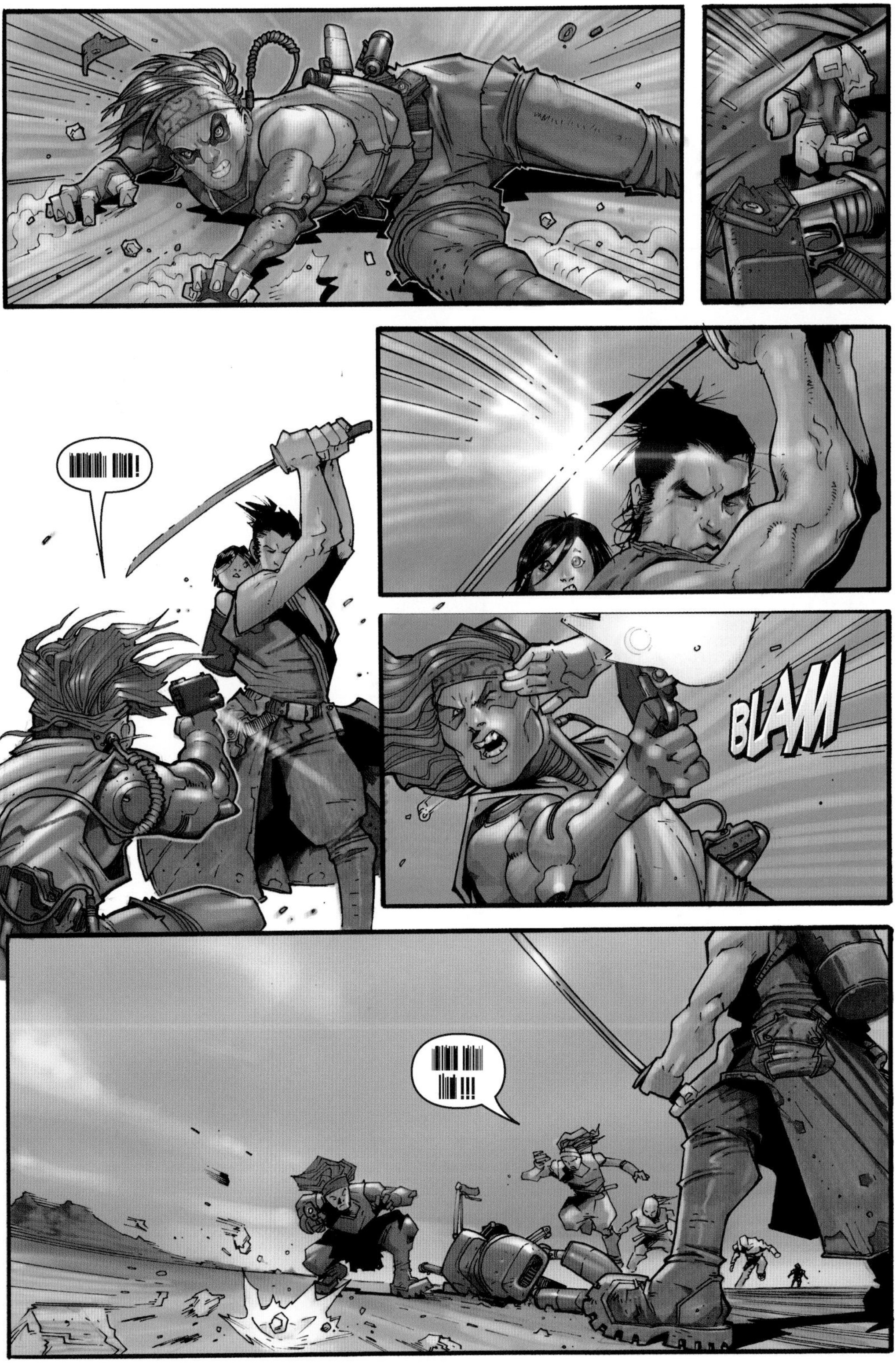
BLAM

NIHON-GO ▮▮▮▮!

▮▮▮ - CAN UNDERSTAND. IS THAT BETTER?

YES.

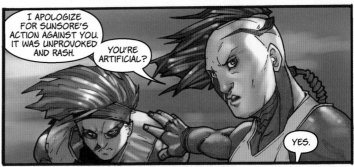

I APOLOGIZE FOR SUNSORE'S ACTION AGAINST YOU. IT WAS UNPROVOKED AND RASH.

YOU'RE ARTIFICIAL?

YES.

THEN WE'RE BROTHERS TO A DEGREE. FELLOW OUTCASTS, SHUNNED BY HUMANITY.

ARE YOU RUNNING *TO* SOMETHING, OR *AWAY?*

BOTH.

THEN YOU'RE WELCOME IN OUR CAMP. WE HAVE FLUID AND SHELTER NEARBY IF YOU REQUIRE THEM.

...

THANK YOU. THAT WOULD BE HELPFUL.

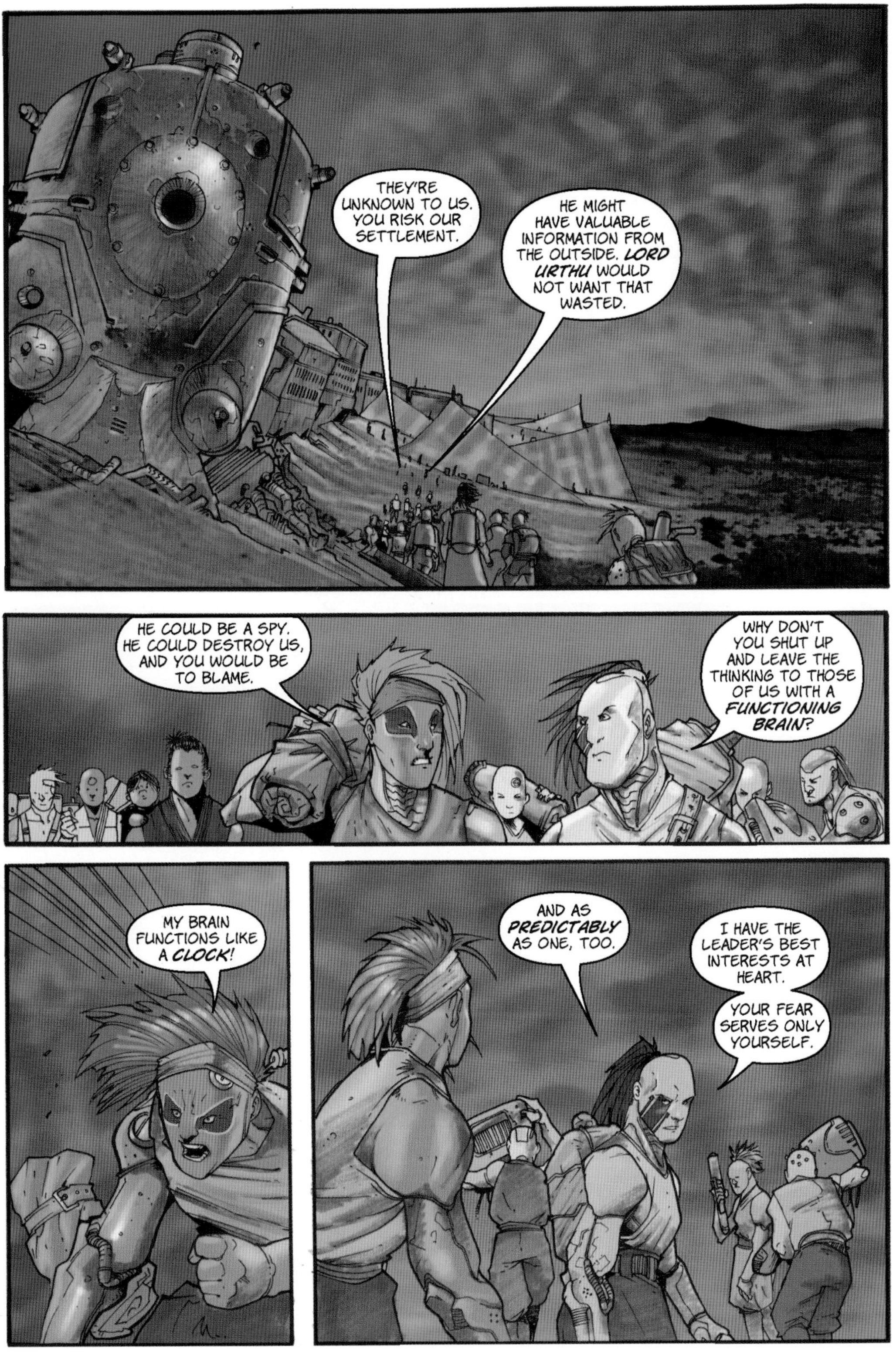
THEY'RE UNKNOWN TO US. YOU RISK OUR SETTLEMENT.
HE MIGHT HAVE VALUABLE INFORMATION FROM THE OUTSIDE. LORD URTHU WOULD NOT WANT THAT WASTED.
HE COULD BE A SPY. HE COULD DESTROY US, AND YOU WOULD BE TO BLAME.
WHY DON'T YOU SHUT UP AND LEAVE THE THINKING TO THOSE OF US WITH A FUNCTIONING BRAIN?
MY BRAIN FUNCTIONS LIKE A CLOCK!
AND AS PREDICTABLY AS ONE, TOO.
I HAVE THE LEADER'S BEST INTERESTS AT HEART.
YOUR FEAR SERVES ONLY YOURSELF.

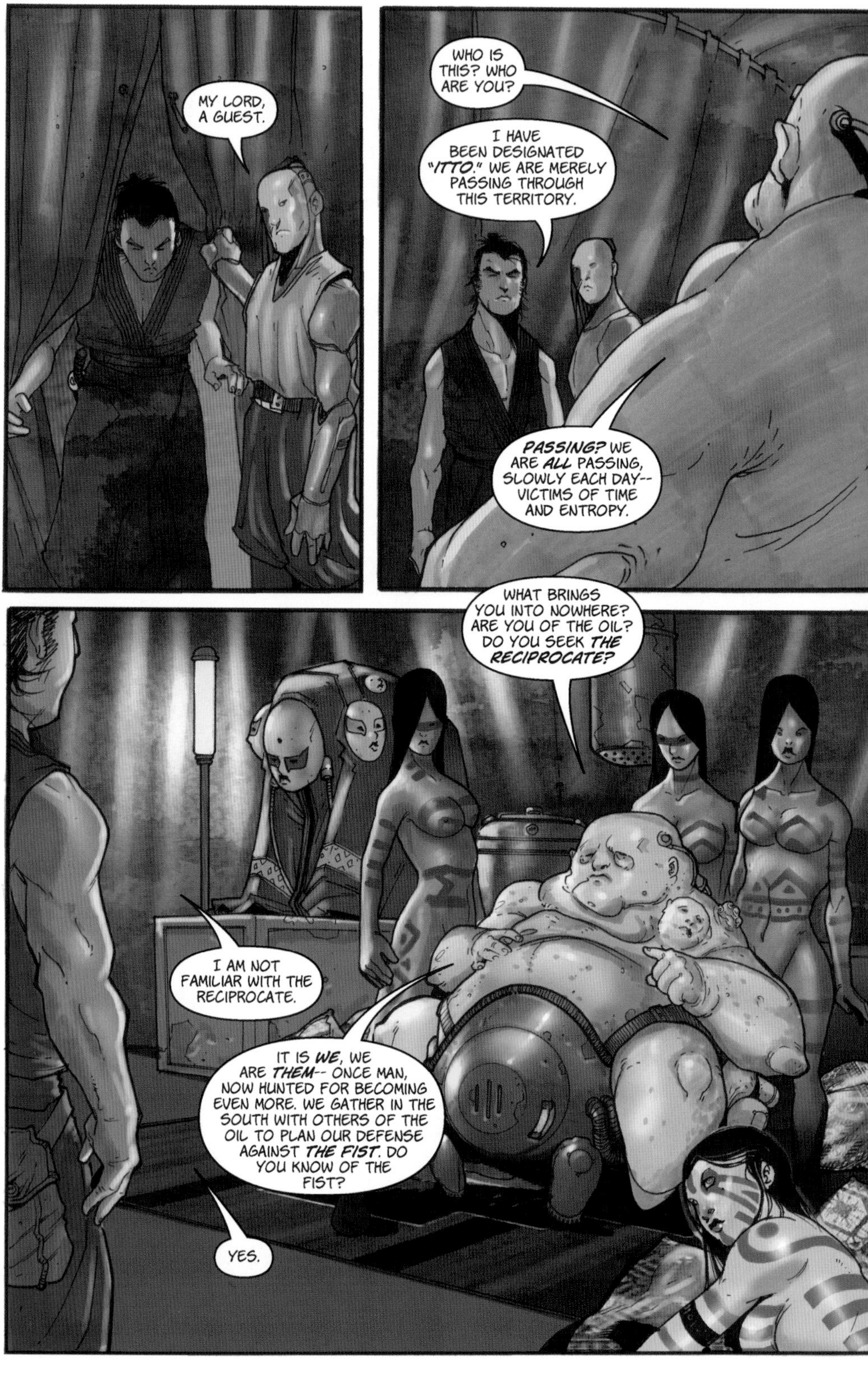
MY LORD, A GUEST.
WHO IS THIS? WHO ARE YOU?
I HAVE BEEN DESIGNATED "ITTO." WE ARE MERELY PASSING THROUGH THIS TERRITORY.
PASSING? WE ARE ALL PASSING, SLOWLY EACH DAY-- VICTIMS OF TIME AND ENTROPY.
WHAT BRINGS YOU INTO NOWHERE? ARE YOU OF THE OIL? DO YOU SEEK THE RECIPROCATE?
I AM NOT FAMILIAR WITH THE RECIPROCATE.
IT IS WE, WE ARE THEM-- ONCE MAN, NOW HUNTED FOR BECOMING EVEN MORE. WE GATHER IN THE SOUTH WITH OTHERS OF THE OIL TO PLAN OUR DEFENSE AGAINST THE FIST. DO YOU KNOW OF THE FIST?
YES.

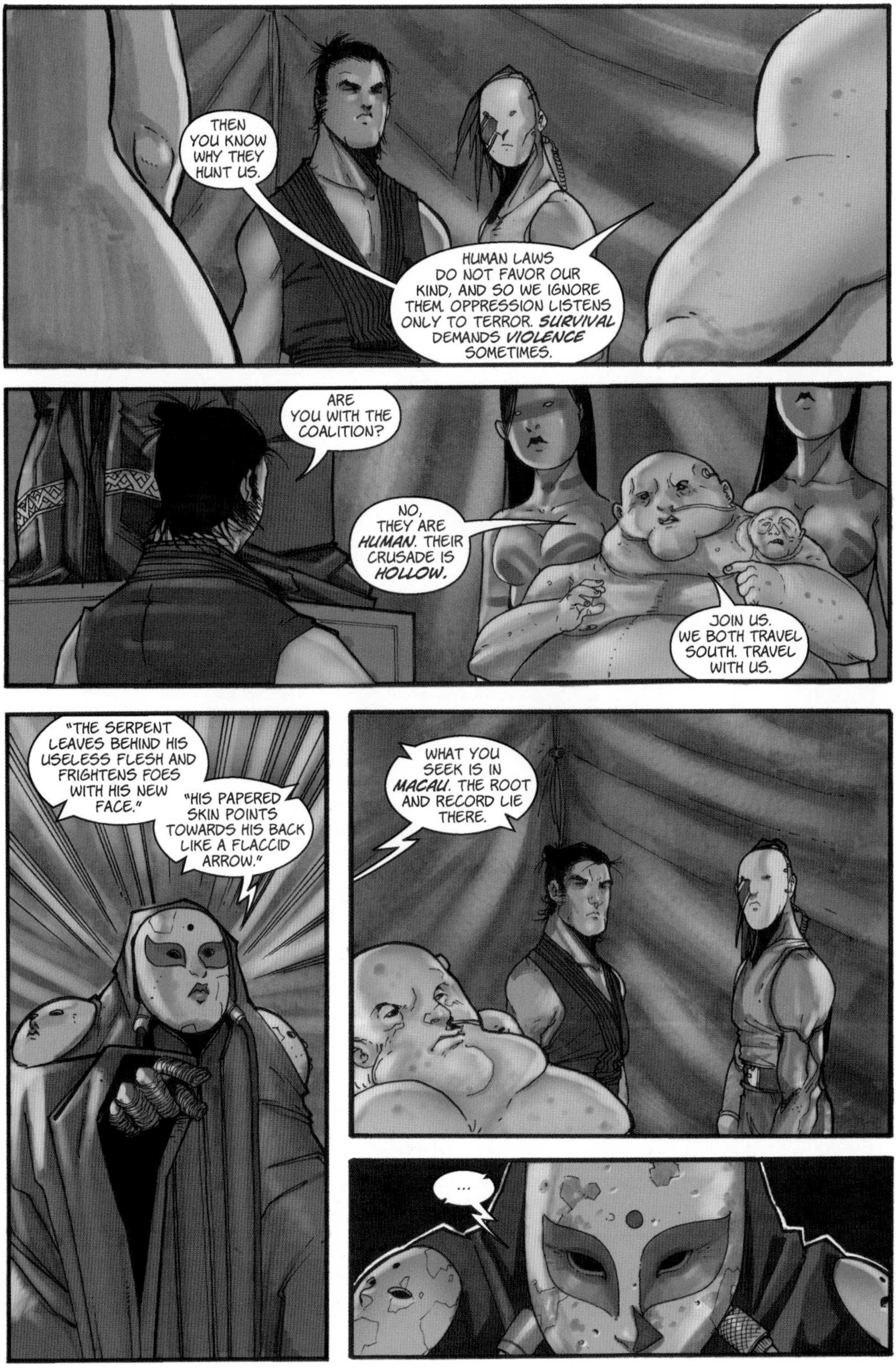
THEN YOU KNOW WHY THEY HUNT US.
HUMAN LAWS DO NOT FAVOR OUR KIND, AND SO WE IGNORE THEM. OPPRESSION LISTENS ONLY TO TERROR. SURVIVAL DEMANDS VIOLENCE SOMETIMES.
ARE YOU WITH THE COALITION?
NO, THEY ARE HUMAN. THEIR CRUSADE IS HOLLOW.
JOIN US. WE BOTH TRAVEL SOUTH. TRAVEL WITH US.
"THE SERPENT LEAVES BEHIND HIS USELESS FLESH AND FRIGHTENS FOES WITH HIS NEW FACE."
"HIS PAPERED SKIN POINTS TOWARDS HIS BACK LIKE A FLACCID ARROW."
WHAT YOU SEEK IS IN MACAU. THE ROOT AND RECORD LIE THERE.
...

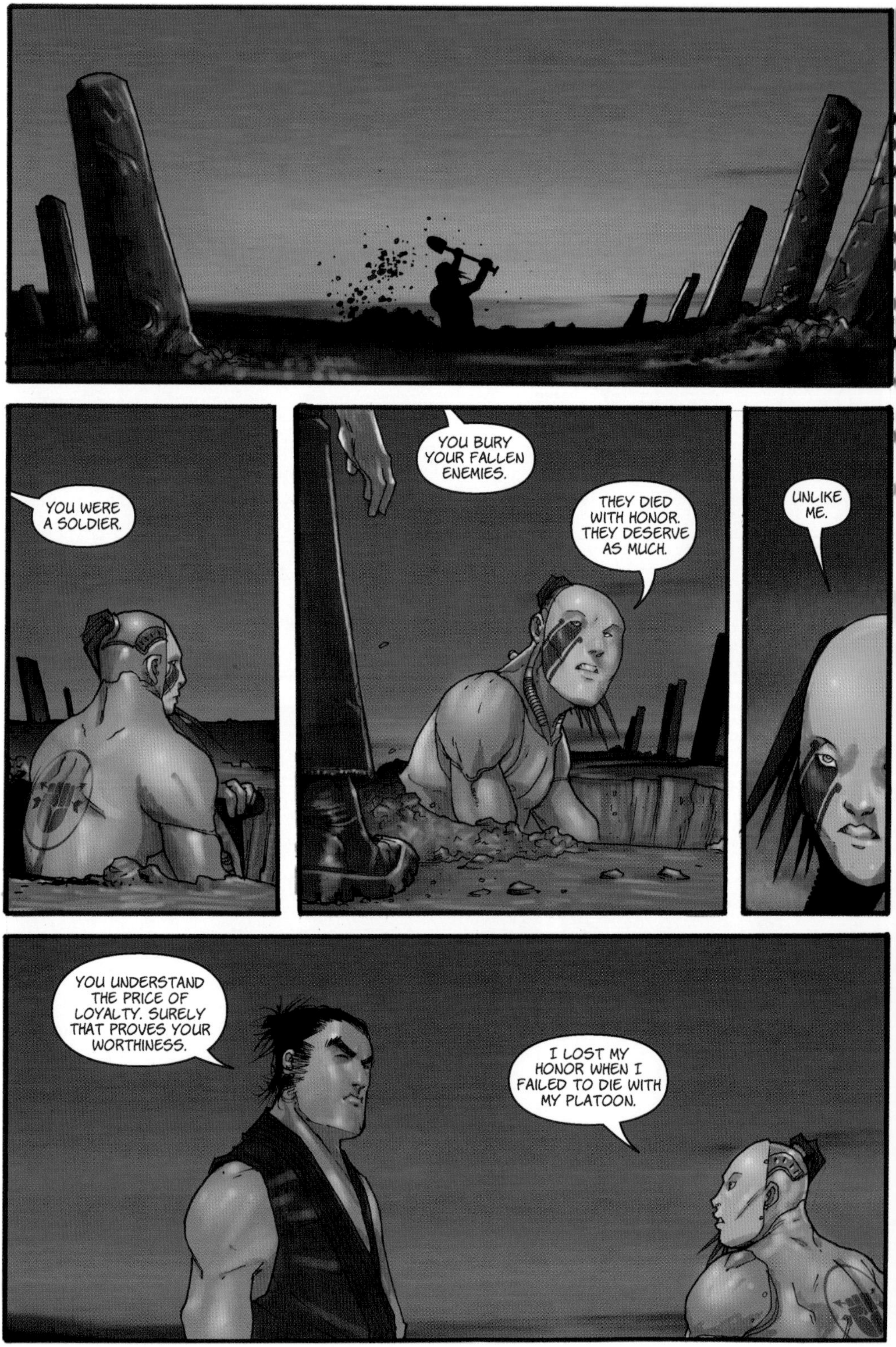

YOU WERE A SOLDIER.
YOU BURY YOUR FALLEN ENEMIES.
THEY DIED WITH HONOR. THEY DESERVE AS MUCH.
UNLIKE ME.
YOU UNDERSTAND THE PRICE OF LOYALTY. SURELY THAT PROVES YOUR WORTHINESS.
I LOST MY HONOR WHEN I FAILED TO DIE WITH MY PLATOON.

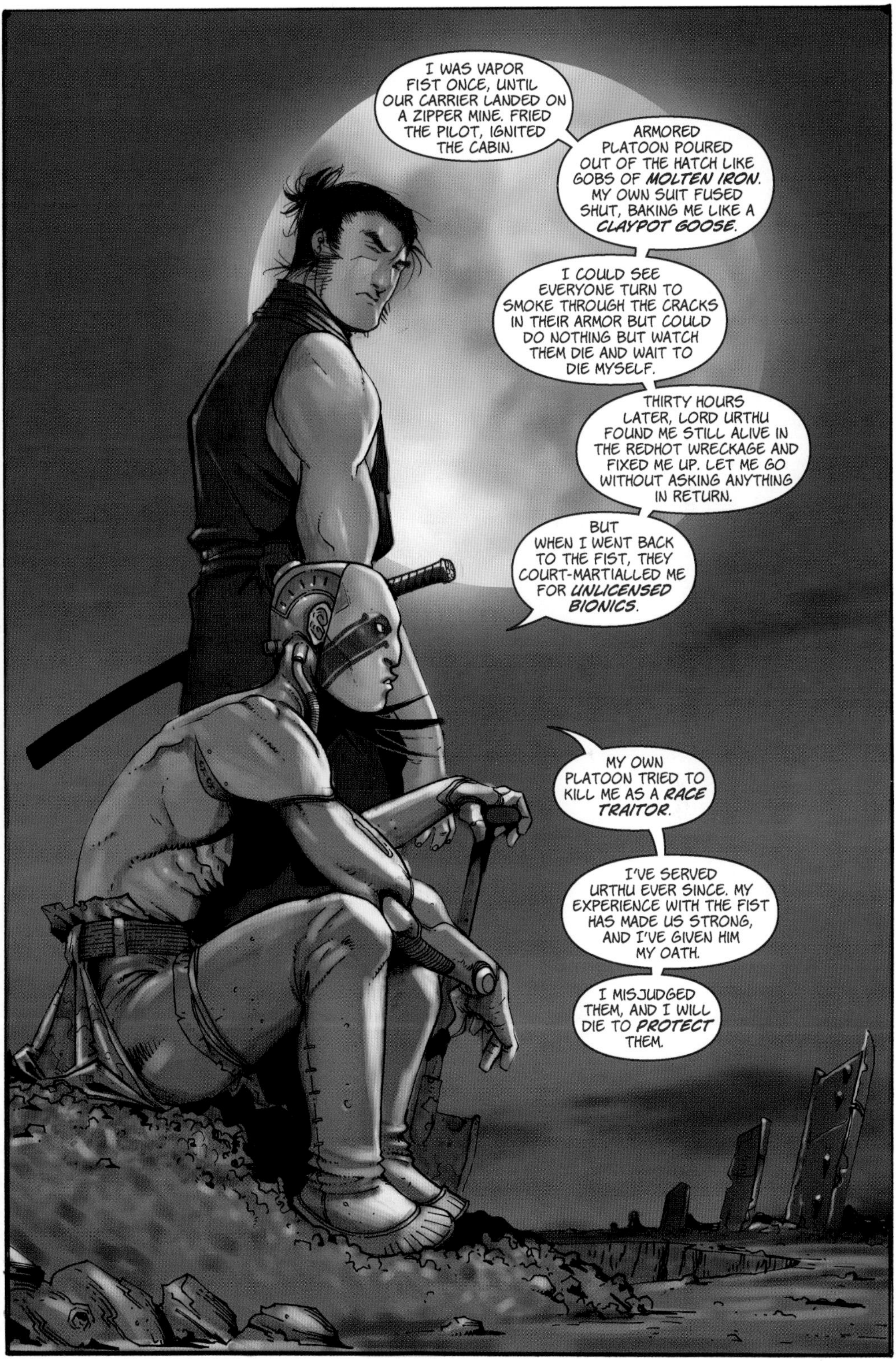
I WAS VAPOR FIST ONCE, UNTIL OUR CARRIER LANDED ON A ZIPPER MINE. FRIED THE PILOT, IGNITED THE CABIN.
ARMORED PLATOON POURED OUT OF THE HATCH LIKE GOBS OF MOLTEN IRON. MY OWN SUIT FUSED SHUT, BAKING ME LIKE A CLAYPOT GOOSE.
I COULD SEE EVERYONE TURN TO SMOKE THROUGH THE CRACKS IN THEIR ARMOR BUT COULD DO NOTHING BUT WATCH THEM DIE AND WAIT TO DIE MYSELF.
THIRTY HOURS LATER, LORD URTHU FOUND ME STILL ALIVE IN THE REDHOT WRECKAGE AND FIXED ME UP. LET ME GO WITHOUT ASKING ANYTHING IN RETURN.
BUT WHEN I WENT BACK TO THE FIST, THEY COURT-MARTIALLED ME FOR UNLICENSED BIONICS.
MY OWN PLATOON TRIED TO KILL ME AS A RACE TRAITOR.
I'VE SERVED URTHU EVER SINCE. MY EXPERIENCE WITH THE FIST HAS MADE US STRONG, AND I'VE GIVEN HIM MY OATH.
I MISJUDGED THEM, AND I WILL DIE TO PROTECT THEM.

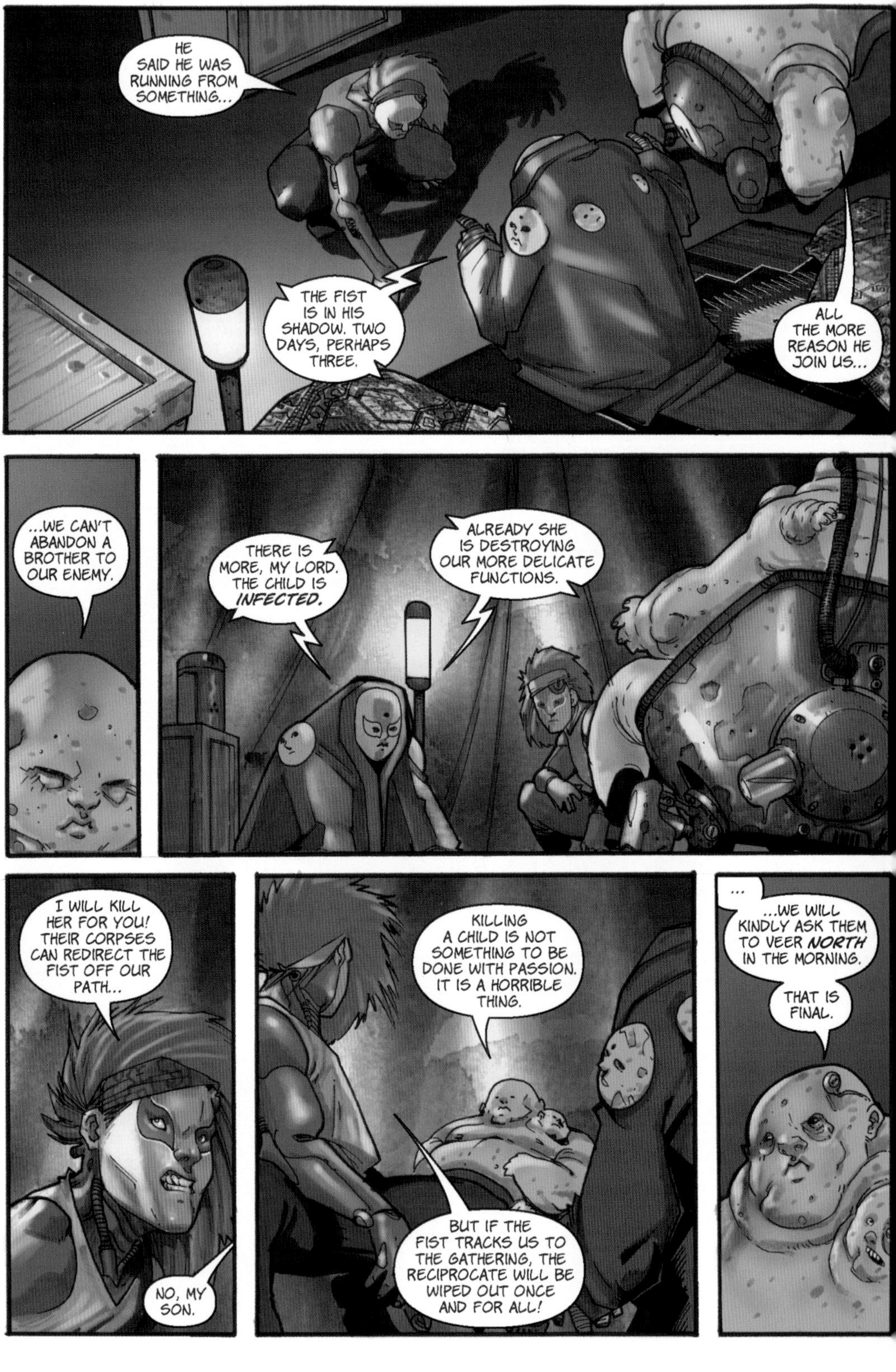

HE SAID HE WAS RUNNING FROM SOMETHING...
THE FIST IS IN HIS SHADOW. TWO DAYS, PERHAPS THREE.
ALL THE MORE REASON HE JOIN US...
...WE CAN'T ABANDON A BROTHER TO OUR ENEMY.
THERE IS MORE, MY LORD. THE CHILD IS INFECTED.
ALREADY SHE IS DESTROYING OUR MORE DELICATE FUNCTIONS.
I WILL KILL HER FOR YOU! THEIR CORPSES CAN REDIRECT THE FIST OFF OUR PATH...
NO, MY SON.
KILLING A CHILD IS NOT SOMETHING TO BE DONE WITH PASSION. IT IS A HORRIBLE THING.
BUT IF THE FIST TRACKS US TO THE GATHERING, THE RECIPROCATE WILL BE WIPED OUT ONCE AND FOR ALL!
...
...WE WILL KINDLY ASK THEM TO VEER NORTH IN THE MORNING.
THAT IS FINAL.

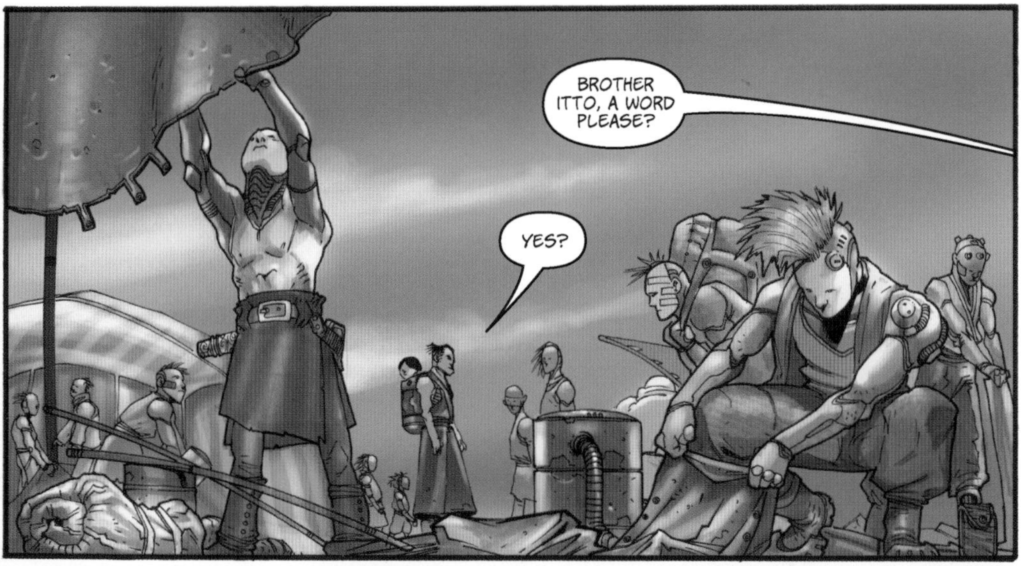
BROTHER ITTO, A WORD PLEASE?
YES?

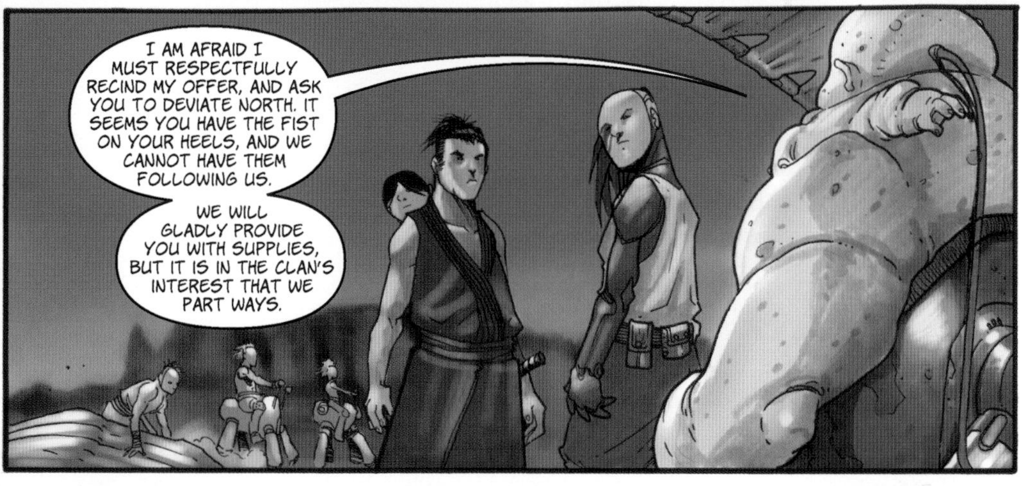
I AM AFRAID I MUST RESPECTFULLY RECIND MY OFFER, AND ASK YOU TO DEVIATE NORTH. IT SEEMS YOU HAVE THE FIST ON YOUR HEELS, AND WE CANNOT HAVE THEM FOLLOWING US.
WE WILL GLADLY PROVIDE YOU WITH SUPPLIES, BUT IT IS IN THE CLAN'S INTEREST THAT WE PART WAYS.

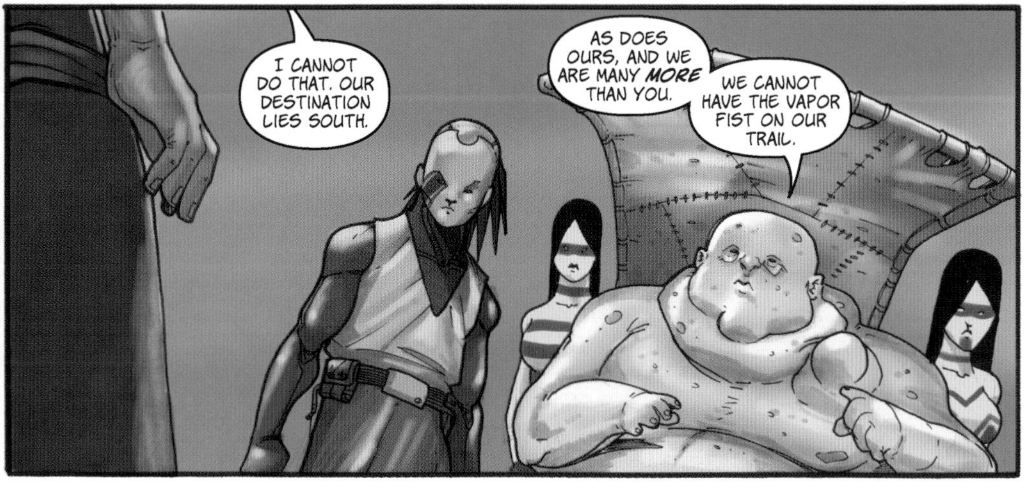
I CANNOT DO THAT. OUR DESTINATION LIES SOUTH.
AS DOES OURS, AND WE ARE MANY ***MORE*** THAN YOU.
WE CANNOT HAVE THE VAPOR FIST ON OUR TRAIL.

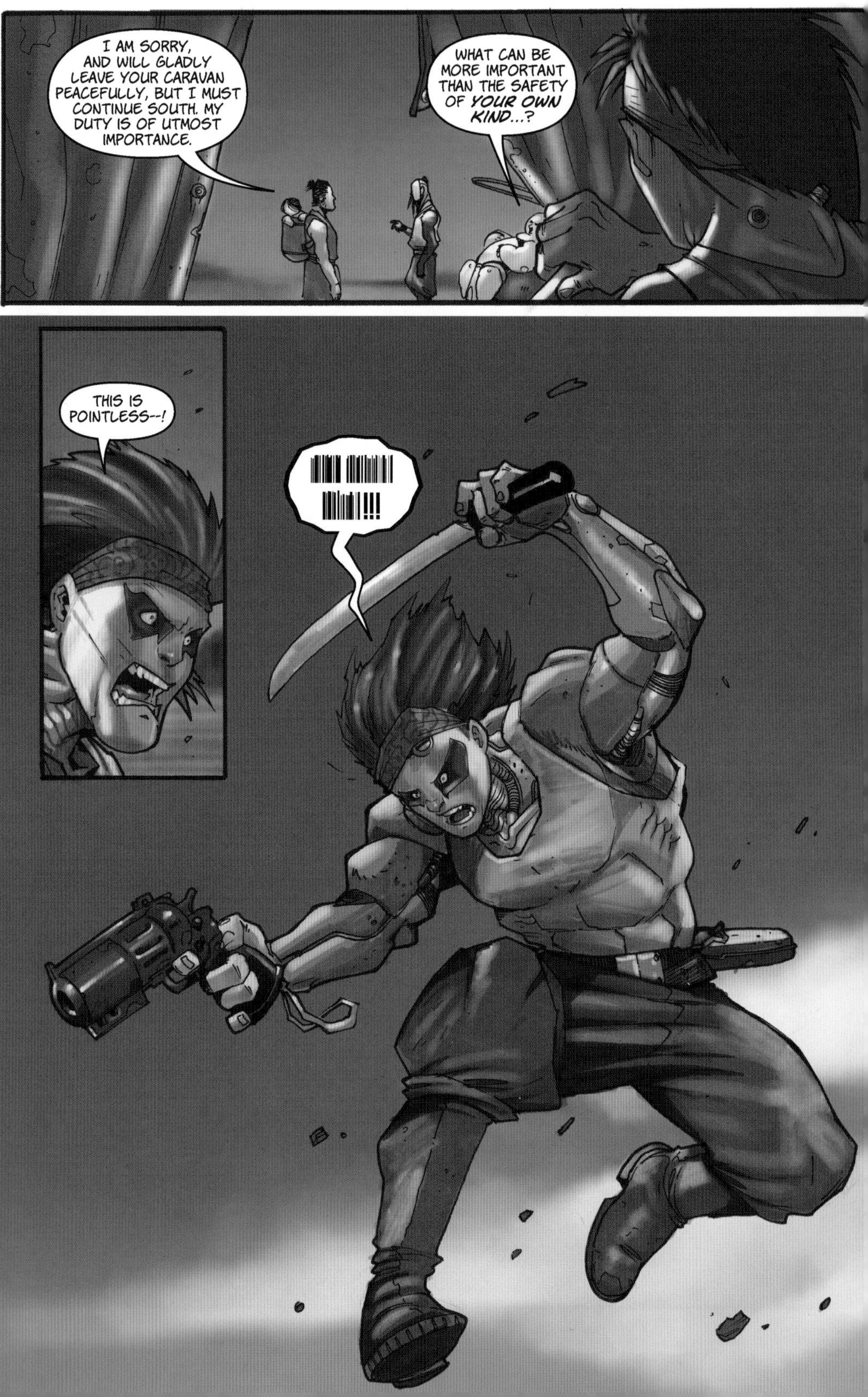
I AM SORRY, AND WILL GLADLY LEAVE YOUR CARAVAN PEACEFULLY, BUT I MUST CONTINUE SOUTH. MY DUTY IS OF UTMOST IMPORTANCE.
WHAT CAN BE MORE IMPORTANT THAN THE SAFETY OF *YOUR OWN KIND*...?
THIS IS POINTLESS--!

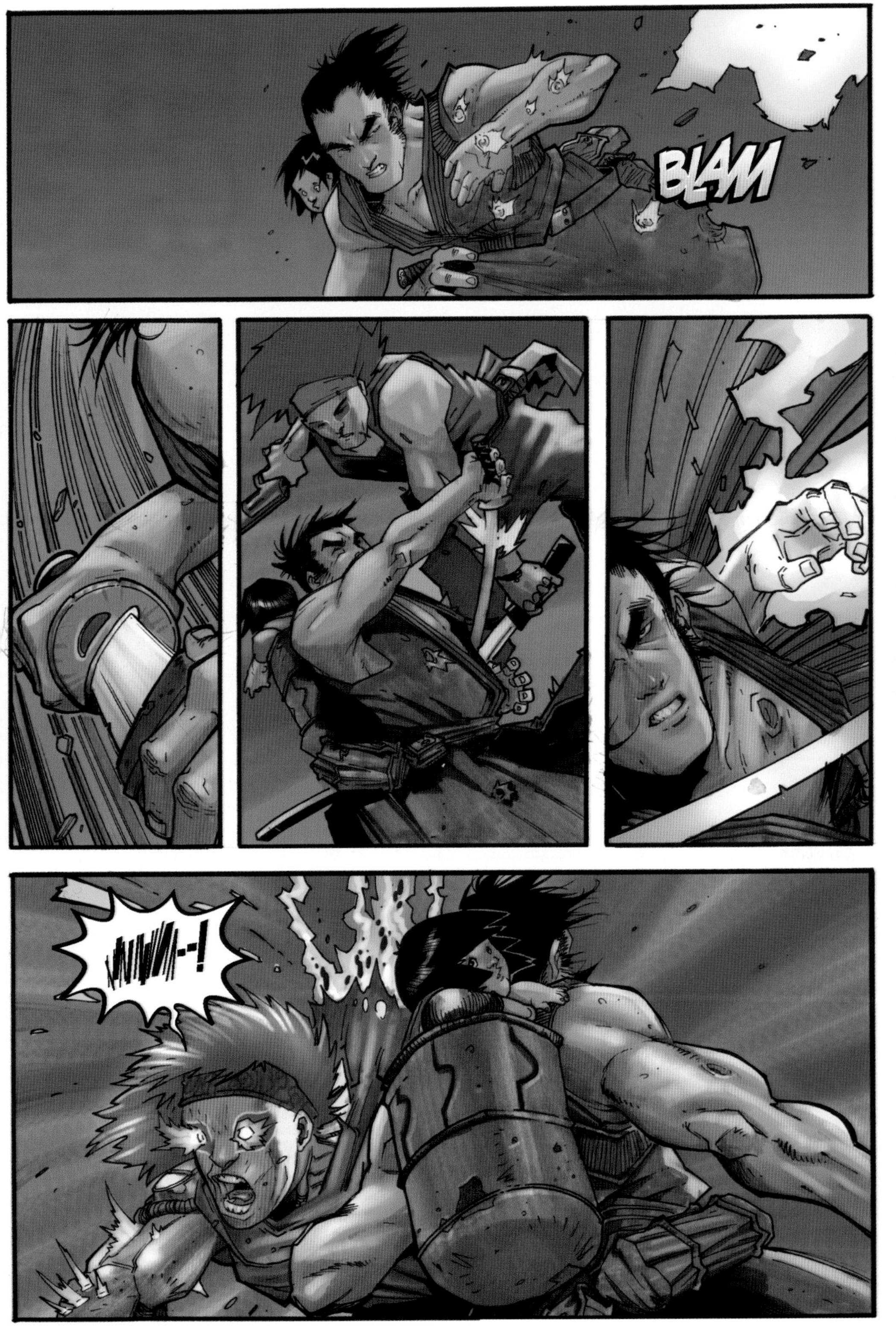
BLAM
WNNN--!

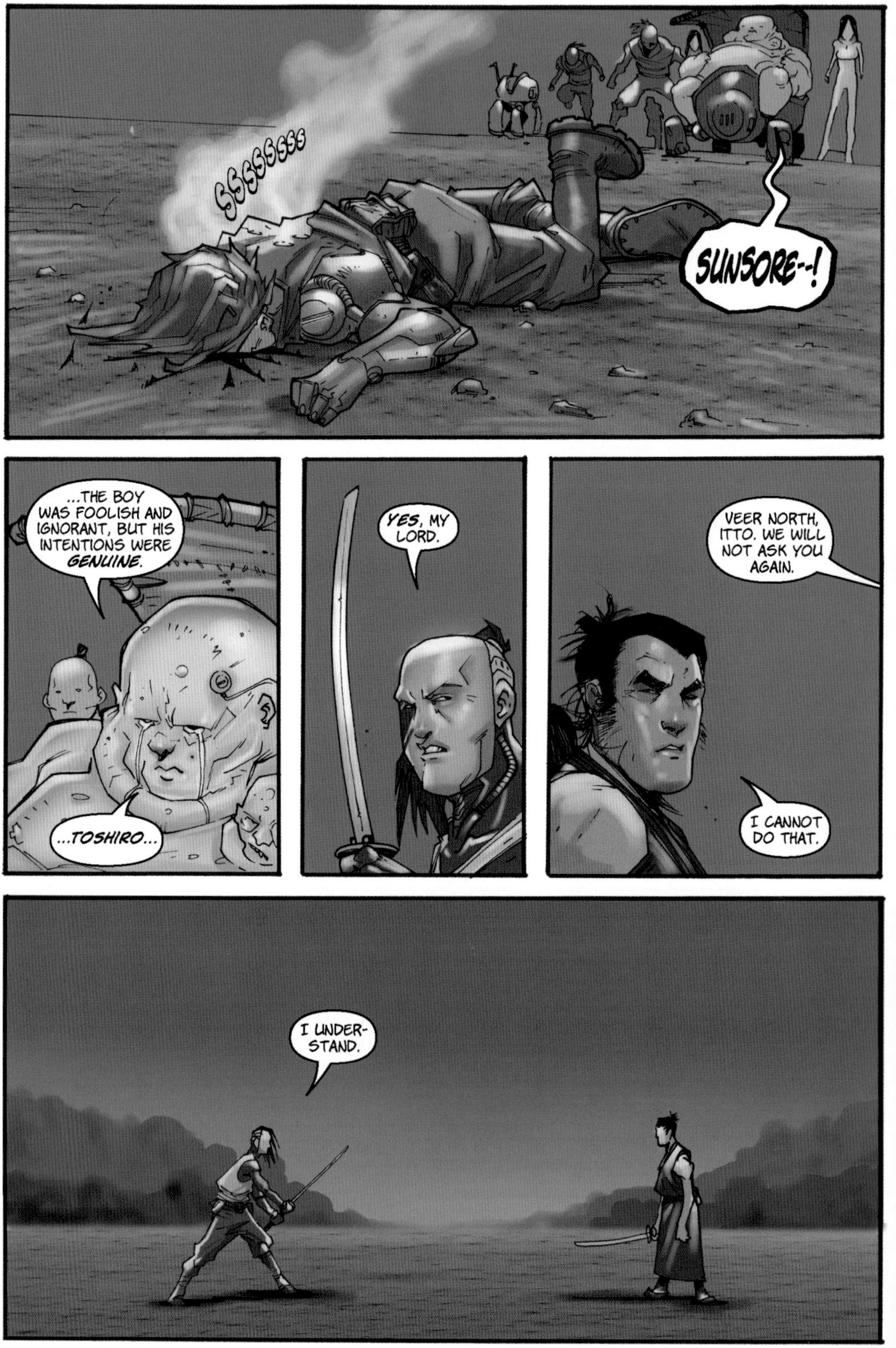
SSSSSSSS
SUNSORE--!
...THE BOY WAS FOOLISH AND IGNORANT, BUT HIS INTENTIONS WERE GENUINE.
...TOSHIRO...
YES, MY LORD.
VEER NORTH, ITTO. WE WILL NOT ASK YOU AGAIN.
I CANNOT DO THAT.
I UNDER-STAND.

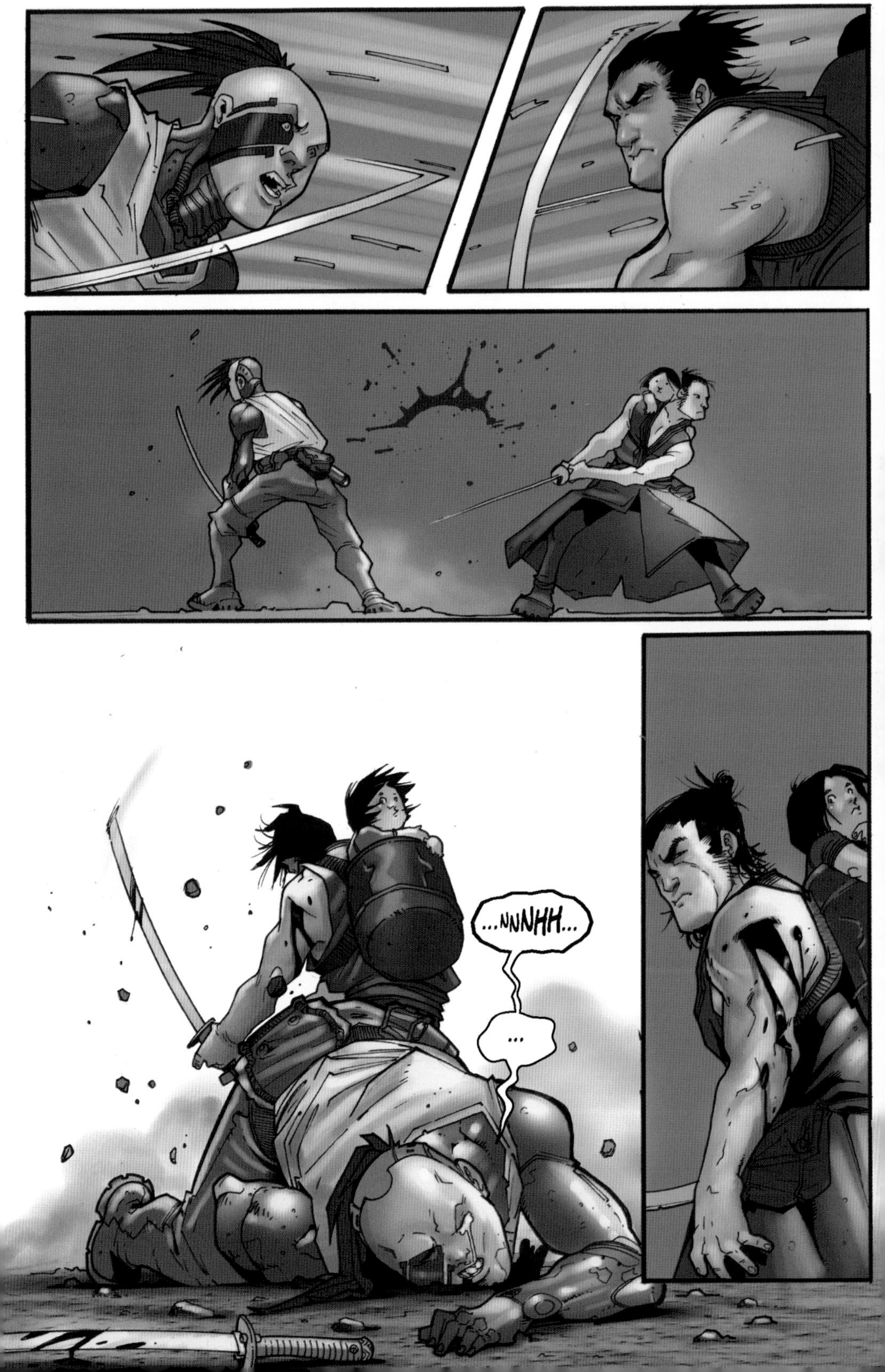
...NNNHH...
...

YOU'VE KILLED US *ALL*, YOU KNOW THAT, DON'T YOU? TOSHIRO WAS OUR KEY TO BEATING THE FIST!

WITHOUT HIS GUIDANCE, WE ARE *HELPLESS!*

WHEN THEY FIND US IN YOUR SHADOW, THEY WILL DESTROY US WITHOUT PAUSE OR PITY!

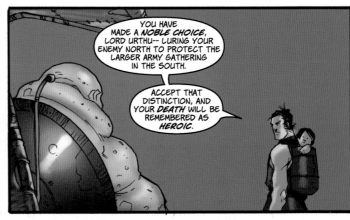

YOU HAVE MADE A *NOBLE CHOICE*, LORD URTHU-- LURING YOUR ENEMY NORTH TO PROTECT THE LARGER ARMY GATHERING IN THE SOUTH.

ACCEPT THAT DISTINCTION, AND YOUR *DEATH* WILL BE REMEMBERED AS *HEROIC.*

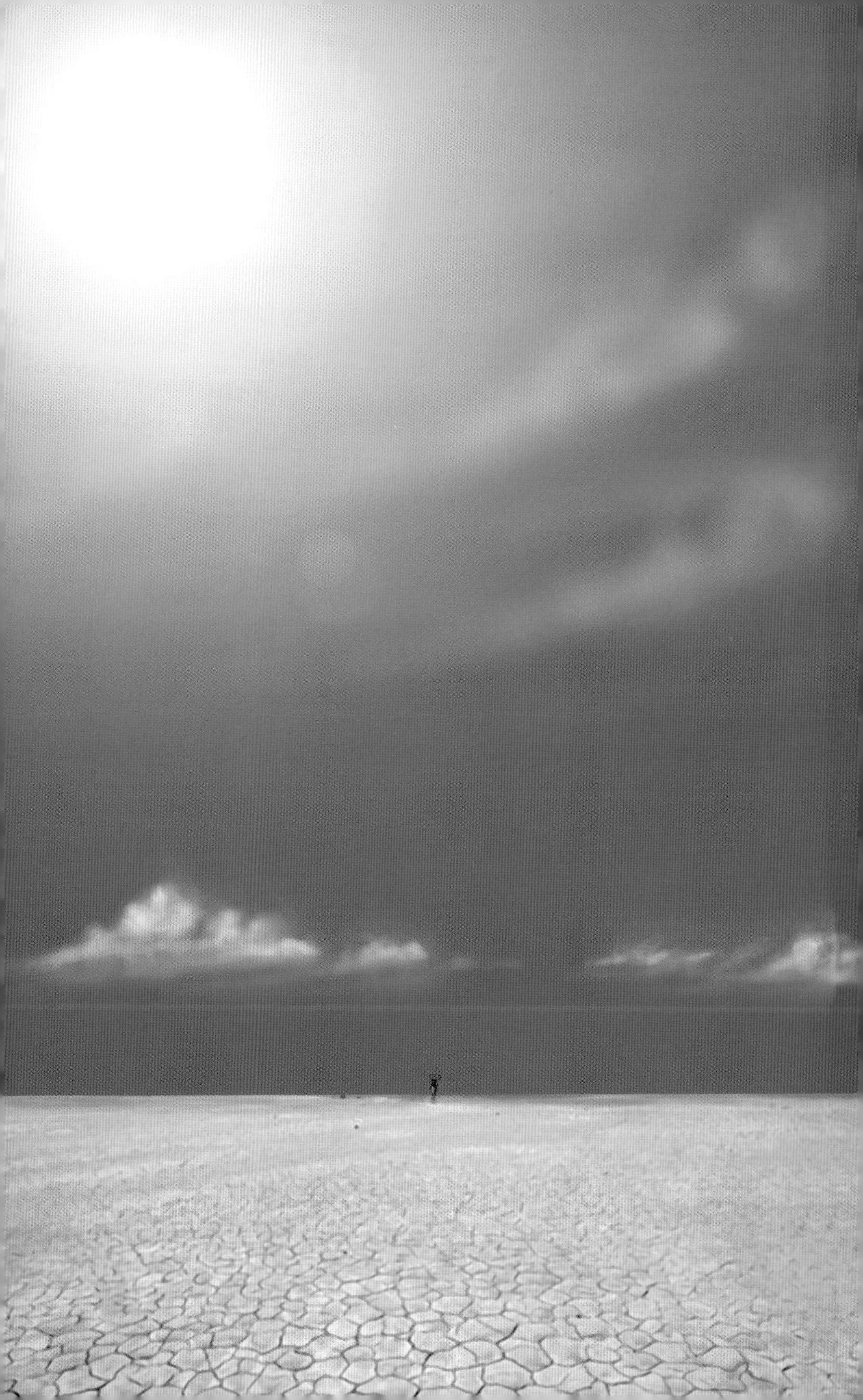

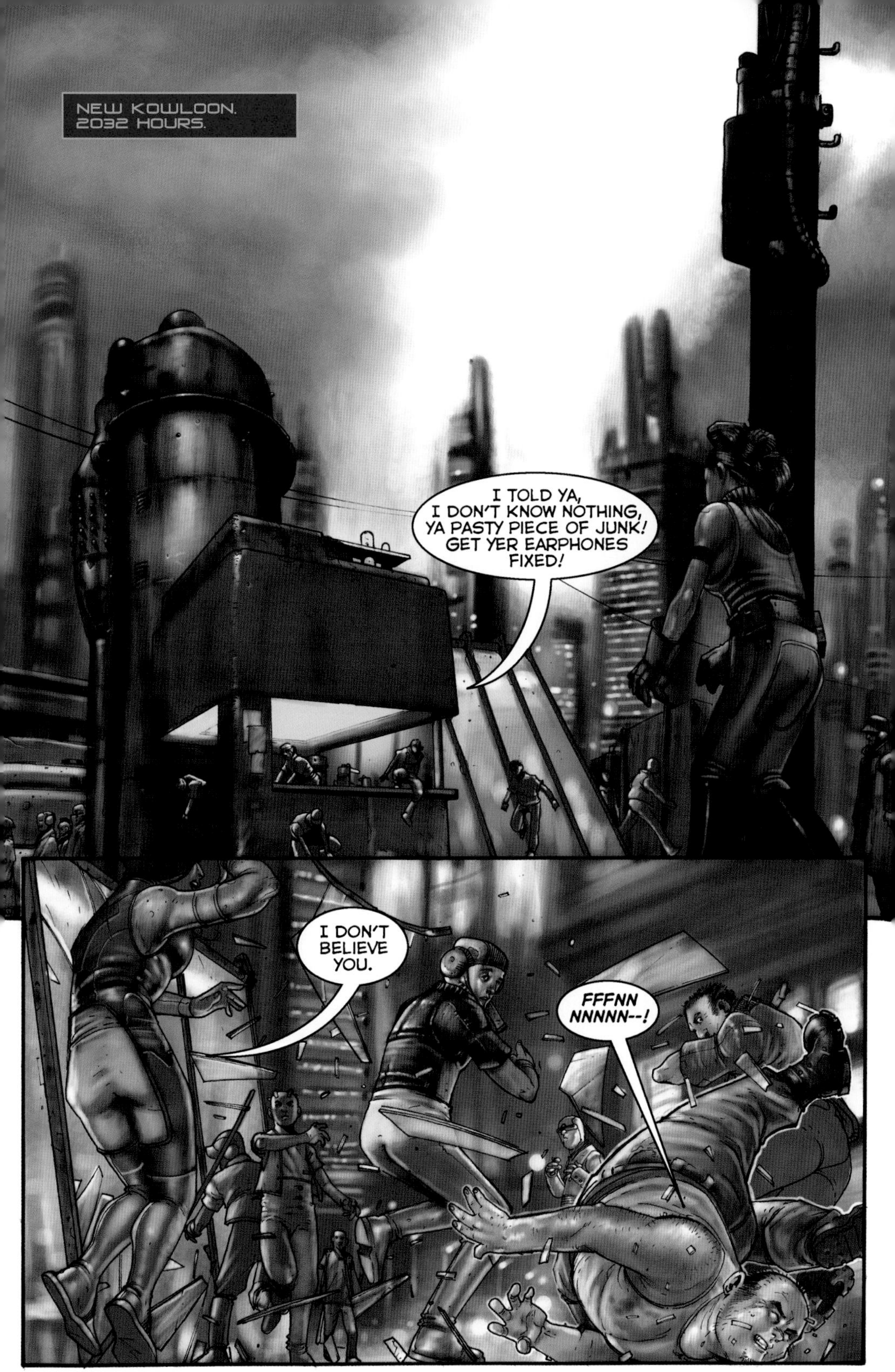
NEW KOWLOON.
2032 HOURS.
I TOLD YA, I DON'T KNOW NOTHING, YA PASTY PIECE OF JUNK! GET YER EARPHONES FIXED!
I DON'T BELIEVE YOU.
FFFNN NNNNN--!

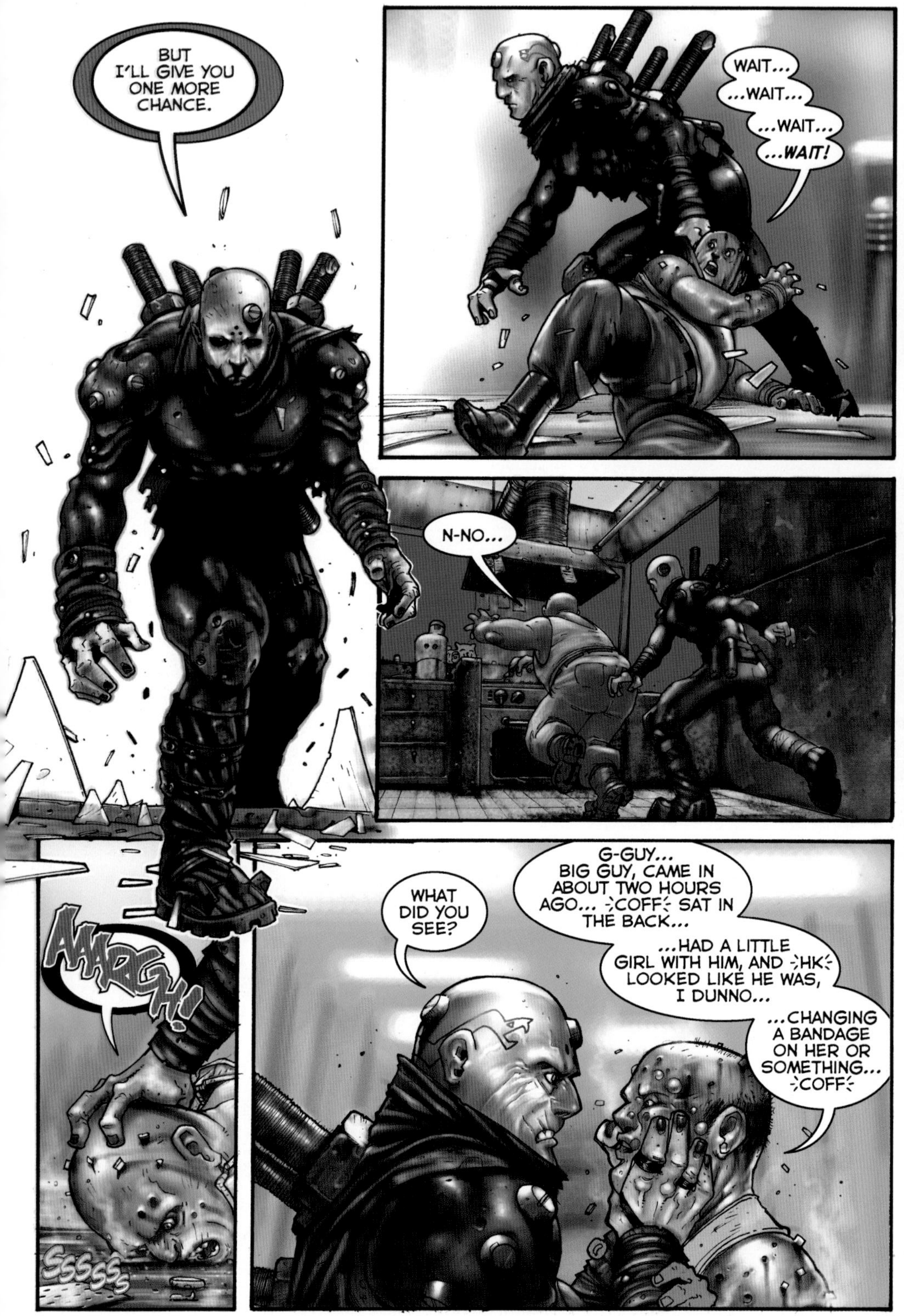
BUT I'LL GIVE YOU ONE MORE CHANCE.
WAIT...
...WAIT...
...WAIT...
...WAIT!
N-NO...
AAARGH!
SSSSSS
WHAT DID YOU SEE?
G-GUY... BIG GUY, CAME IN ABOUT TWO HOURS AGO... COFF SAT IN THE BACK...
...HAD A LITTLE GIRL WITH HIM, AND HK LOOKED LIKE HE WAS, I DUNNO...
...CHANGING A BANDAGE ON HER OR SOMETHING... COFF

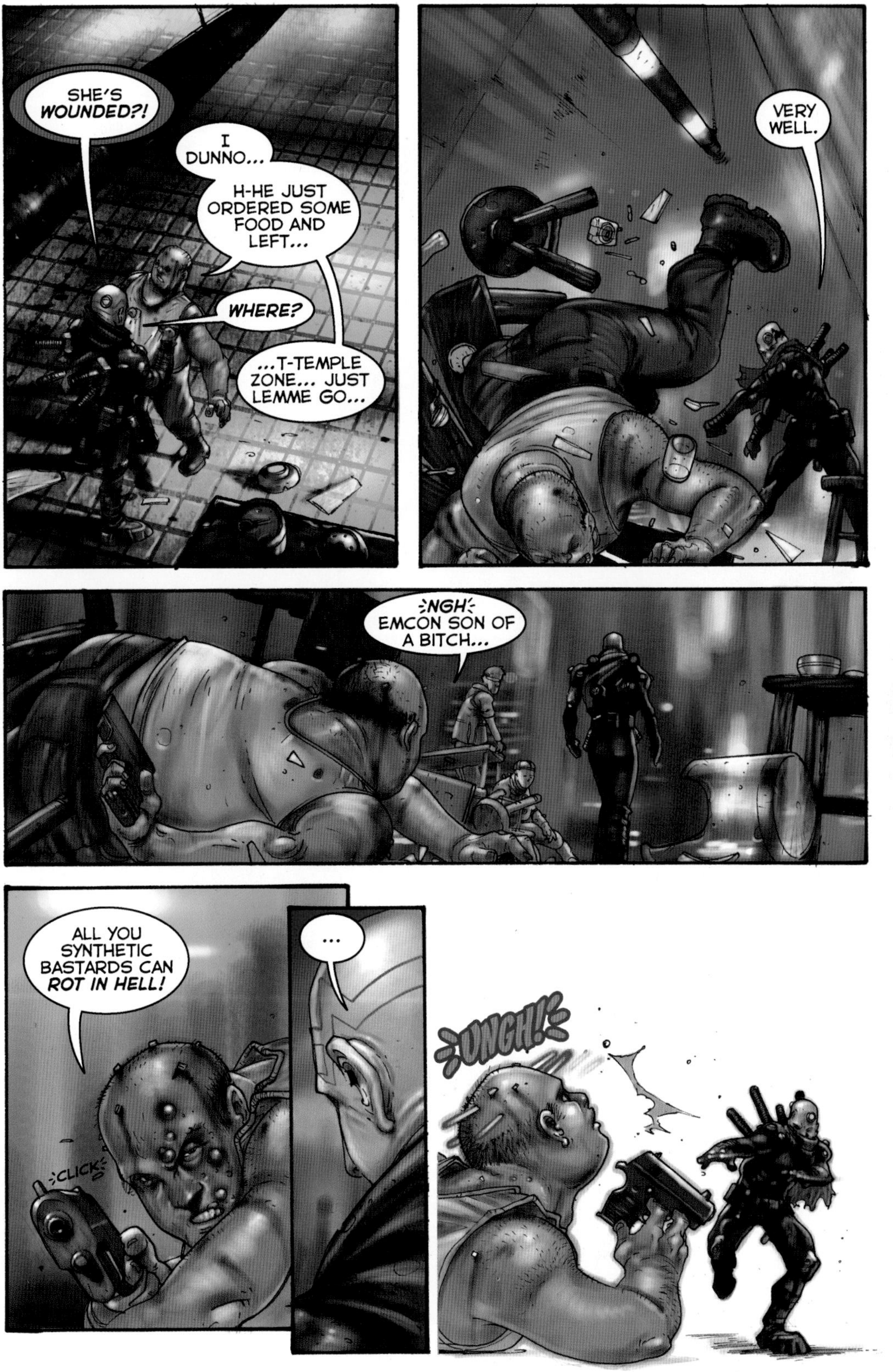
SHE'S *WOUNDED?!*
I DUNNO...
H-HE JUST ORDERED SOME FOOD AND LEFT...
WHERE?
...T-TEMPLE ZONE... JUST LEMME GO...
VERY WELL.
NGH
EMCON SON OF A BITCH...
ALL YOU SYNTHETIC BASTARDS CAN *ROT IN HELL!*
CLICK
...
UNGH!

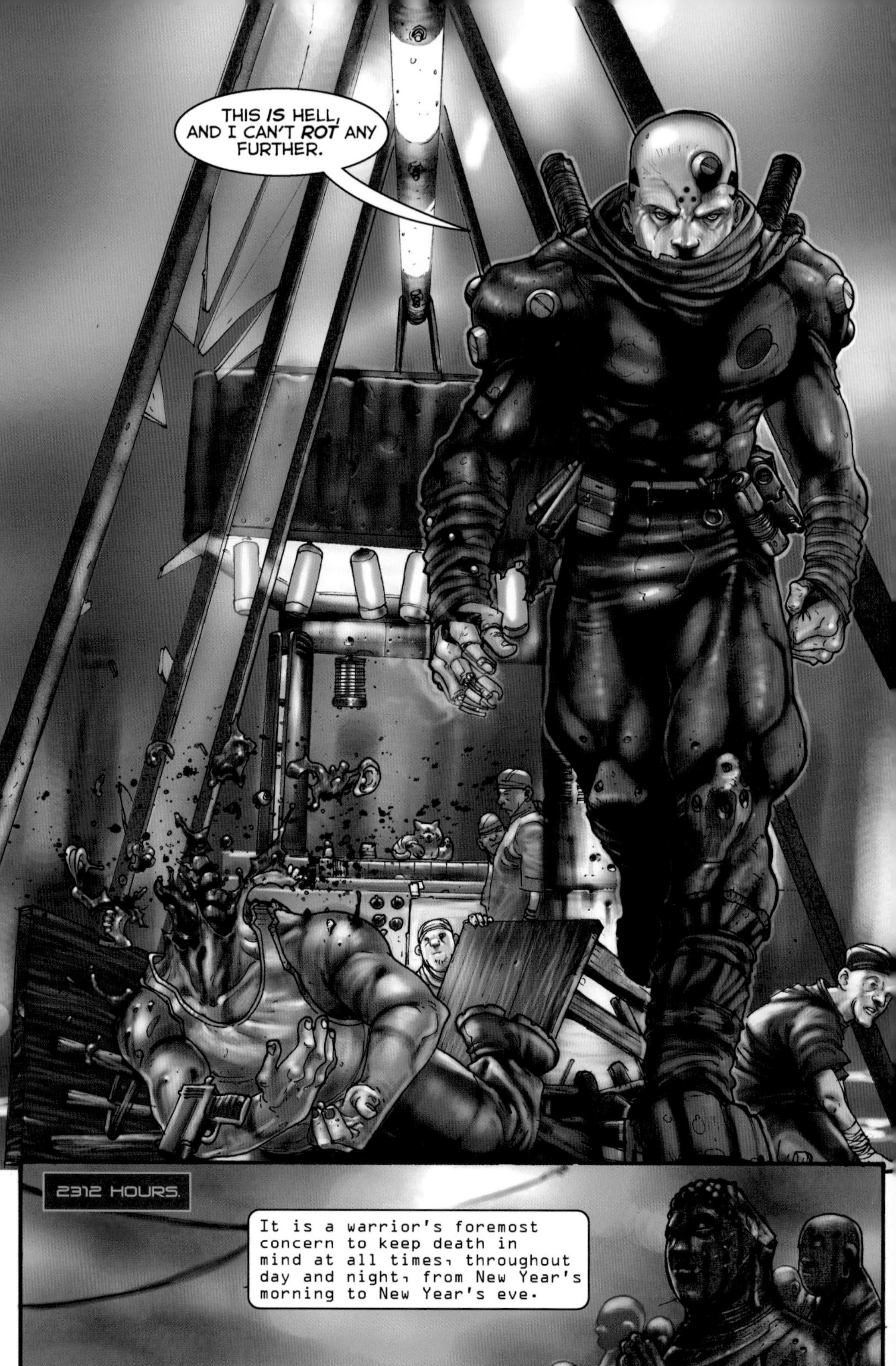
THIS IS HELL, AND I CAN'T ROT ANY FURTHER.
2312 HOURS.
It is a warrior's foremost concern to keep death in mind at all times, throughout day and night, from New Year's morning to New Year's eve.

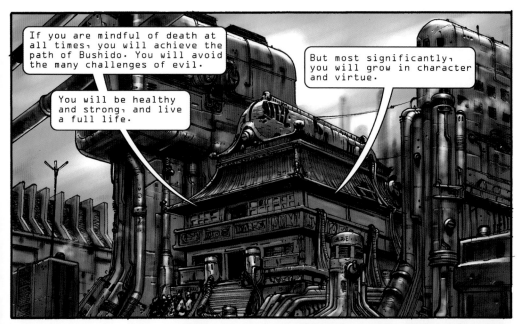

If you are mindful of death at all times, you will achieve the path of Bushido. You will avoid the many challenges of evil.

You will be healthy and strong, and live a full life.

But most significantly, you will grow in character and virtue.

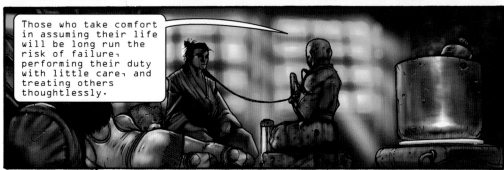

Those who take comfort in assuming their life will be long run the risk of failure, performing their duty with little care, and treating others thoughtlessly.

But to realize that life is uncertain, you will understand that each task you accept may be your last. Each moment spent with others may be the last.

Thus proven, being mindful of death fulfills the path of loyalty and familial duty.

Failure becomes unthinkable.

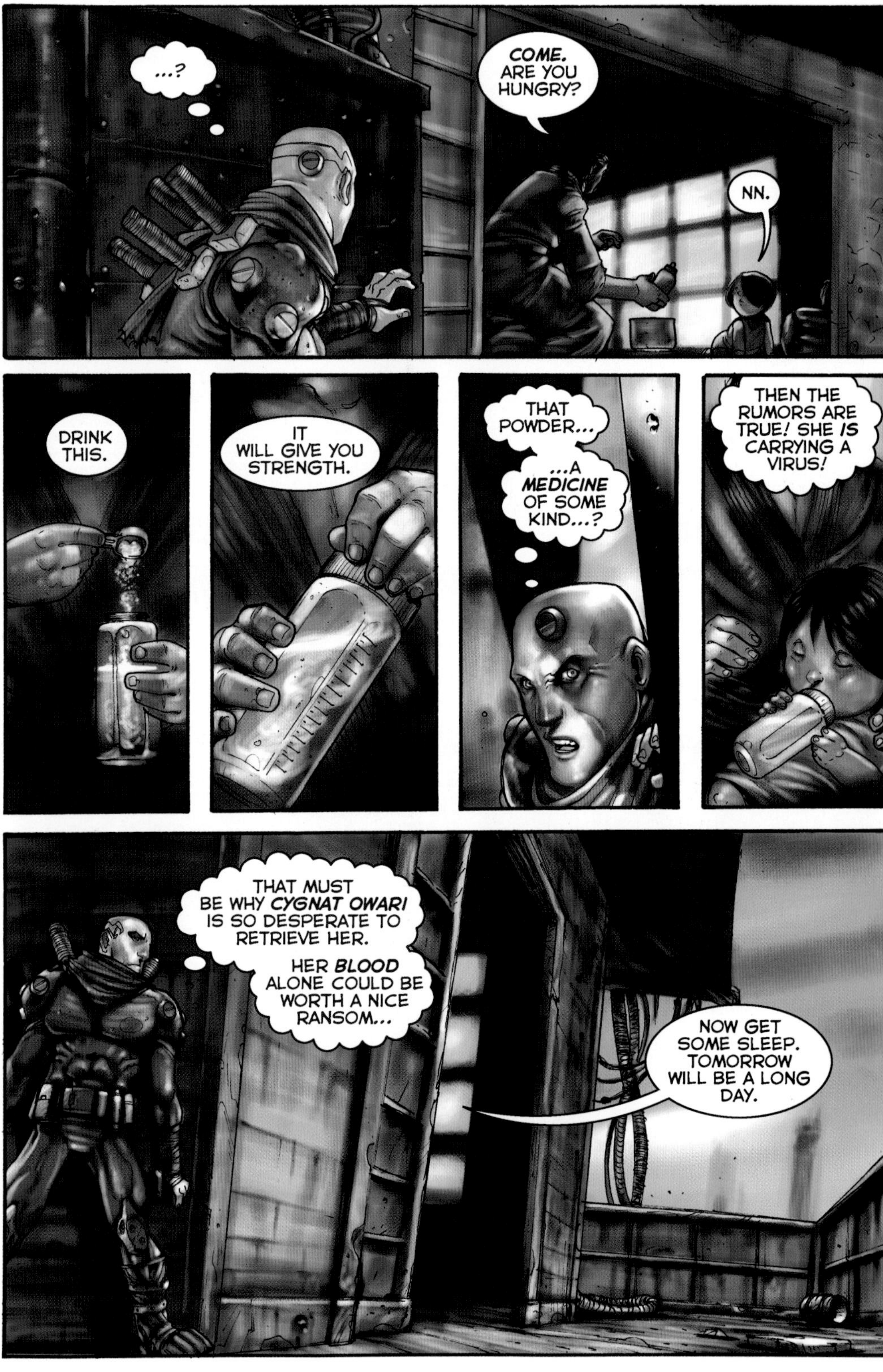
...?
COME. ARE YOU HUNGRY?
NN.
DRINK THIS.
IT WILL GIVE YOU STRENGTH.
THAT POWDER...
...A MEDICINE OF SOME KIND...?
THEN THE RUMORS ARE TRUE! SHE IS CARRYING A VIRUS!
THAT MUST BE WHY CYGNAT OWARI IS SO DESPERATE TO RETRIEVE HER.
HER BLOOD ALONE COULD BE WORTH A NICE RANSOM...
NOW GET SOME SLEEP. TOMORROW WILL BE A LONG DAY.

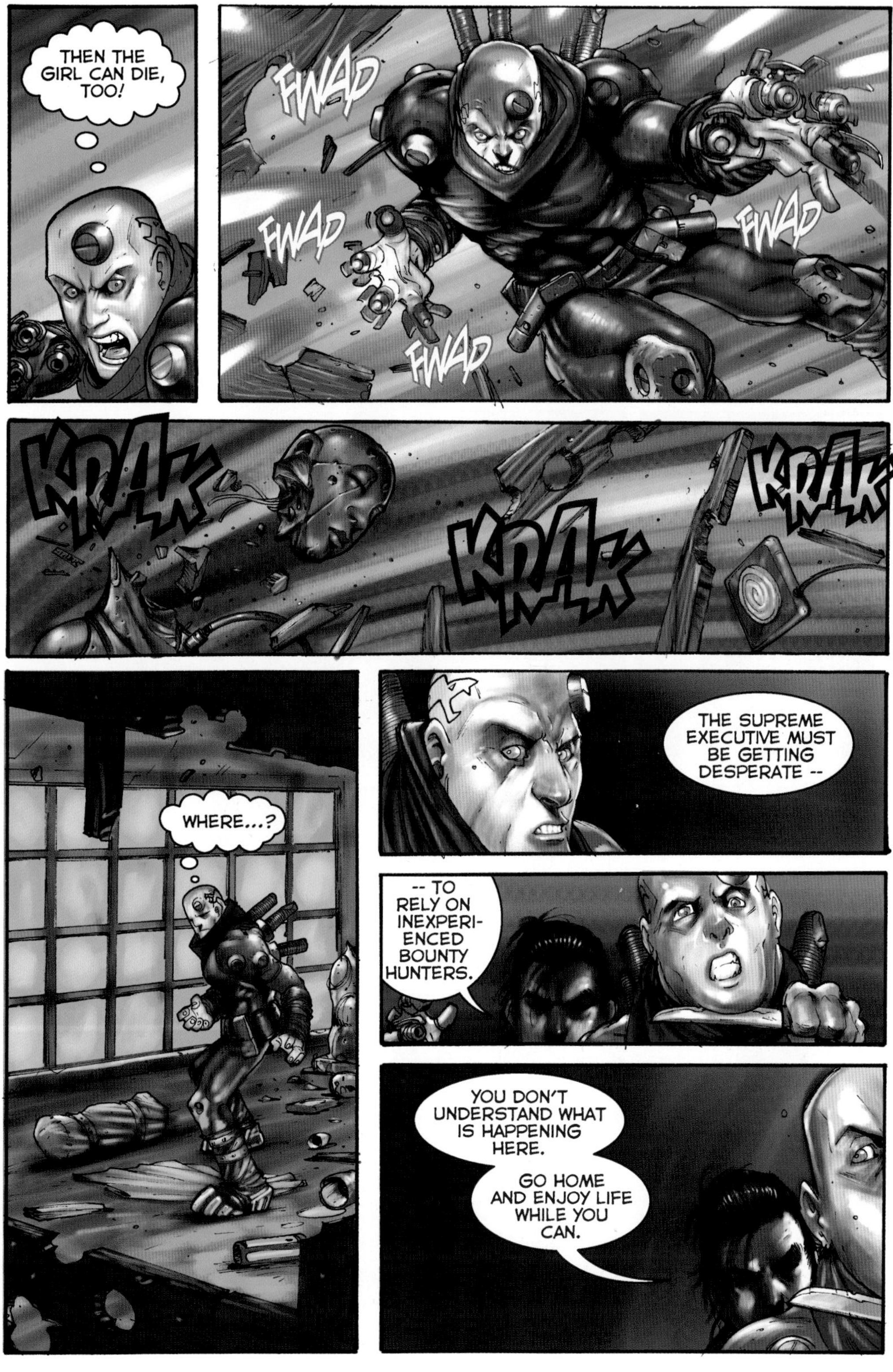
THEN THE GIRL CAN DIE, TOO!
FWAD
FWAD
FWAD
FWAD
KRAK
KRAK
KRAK
WHERE...?
THE SUPREME EXECUTIVE MUST BE GETTING DESPERATE --
-- TO RELY ON INEXPERIENCED BOUNTY HUNTERS.
YOU DON'T UNDERSTAND WHAT IS HAPPENING HERE.
GO HOME AND ENJOY LIFE WHILE YOU CAN.

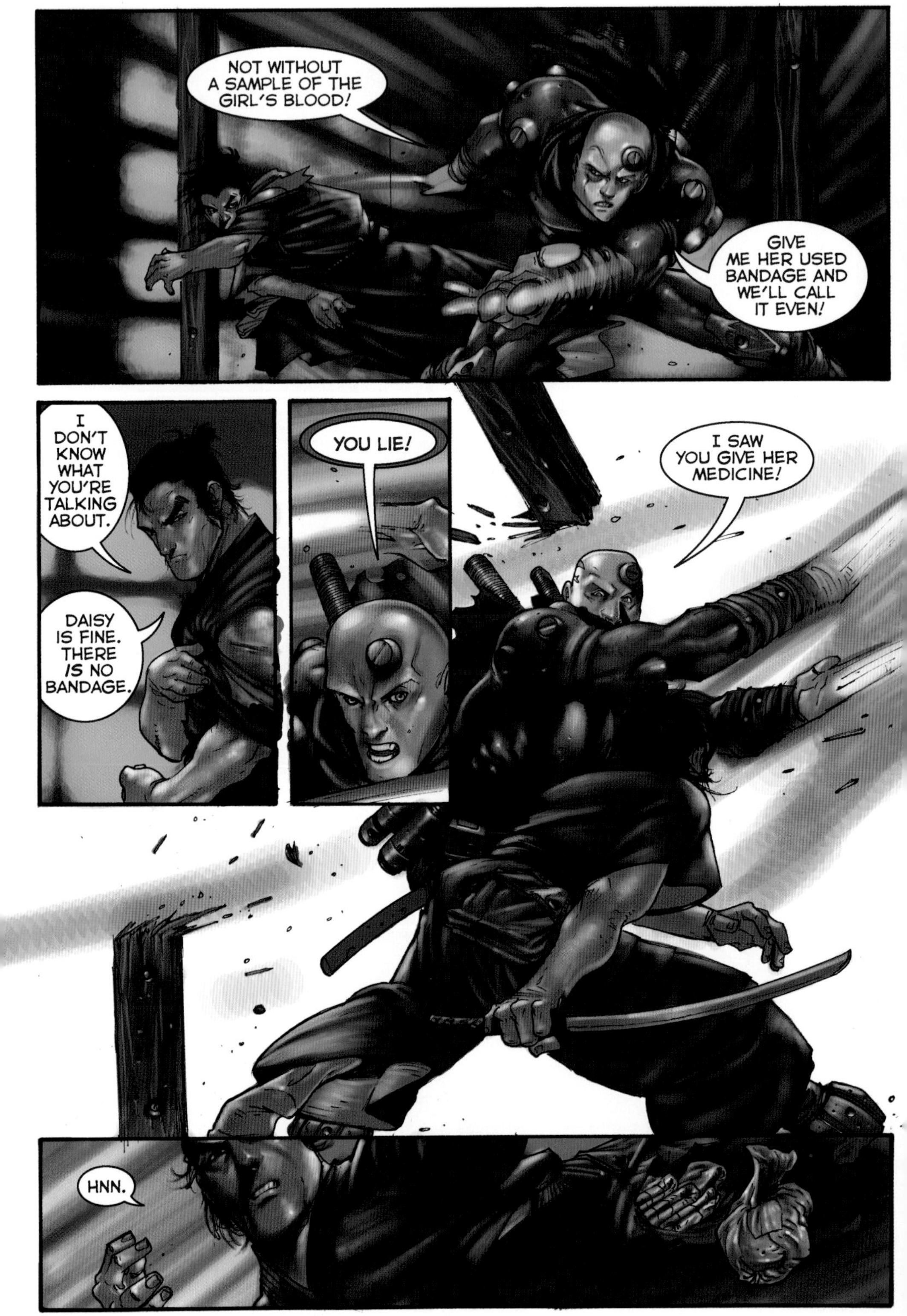
NOT WITHOUT A SAMPLE OF THE GIRL'S BLOOD!
GIVE ME HER USED BANDAGE AND WE'LL CALL IT EVEN!
I DON'T KNOW WHAT YOU'RE TALKING ABOUT.
DAISY IS FINE. THERE *IS* NO BANDAGE.
YOU LIE!
I SAW YOU GIVE HER MEDICINE!
HNN.

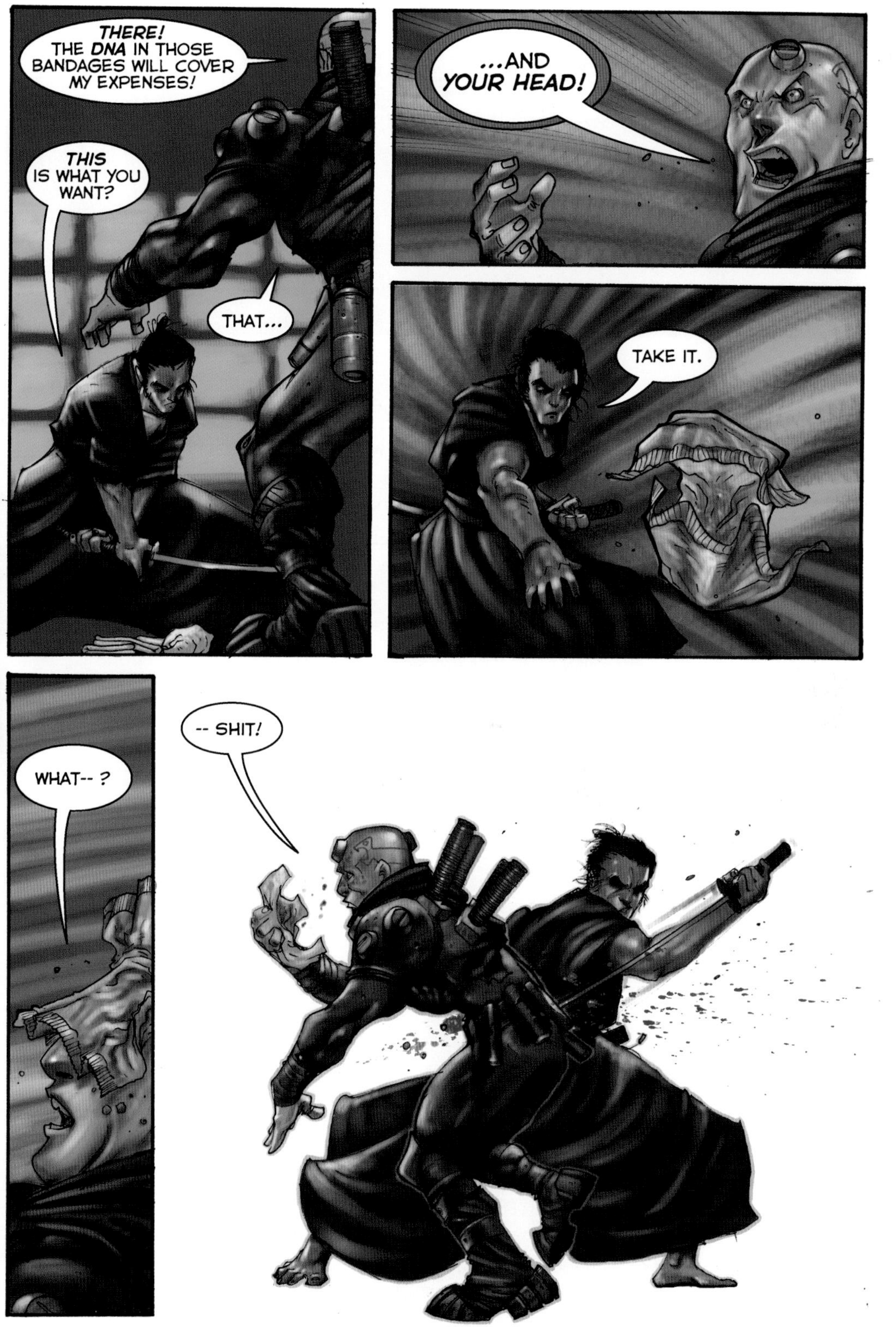
THERE! THE DNA IN THOSE BANDAGES WILL COVER MY EXPENSES!
THIS IS WHAT YOU WANT?
THAT...
...AND YOUR HEAD!
TAKE IT.
WHAT-- ?
-- SHIT!

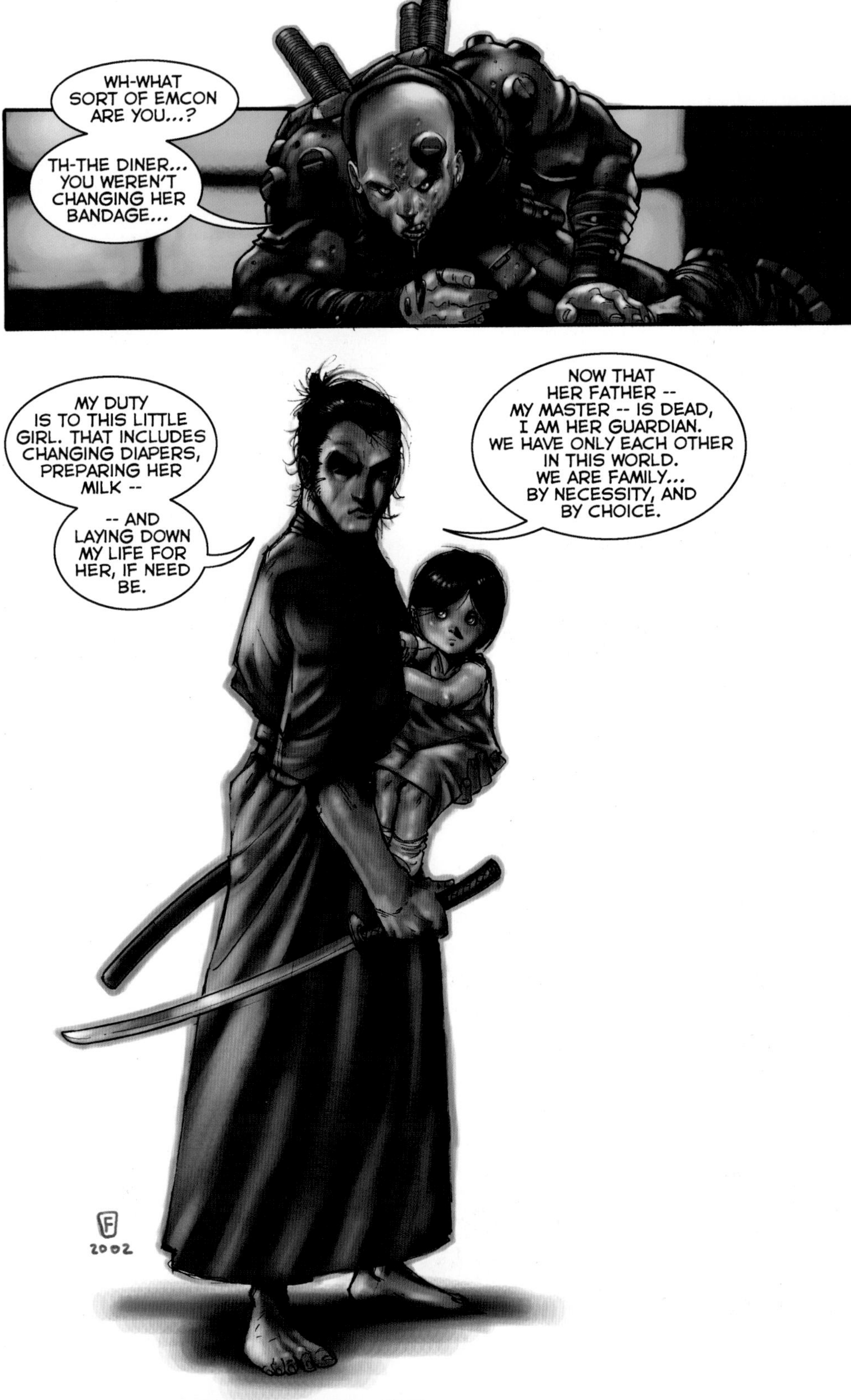
WH-WHAT SORT OF EMCON ARE YOU...?
TH-THE DINER... YOU WEREN'T CHANGING HER BANDAGE...
MY DUTY IS TO THIS LITTLE GIRL. THAT INCLUDES CHANGING DIAPERS, PREPARING HER MILK --
-- AND LAYING DOWN MY LIFE FOR HER, IF NEED BE.
NOW THAT HER FATHER -- MY MASTER -- IS DEAD, I AM HER GUARDIAN. WE HAVE ONLY EACH OTHER IN THIS WORLD. WE ARE FAMILY... BY NECESSITY, AND BY CHOICE.
F
2002

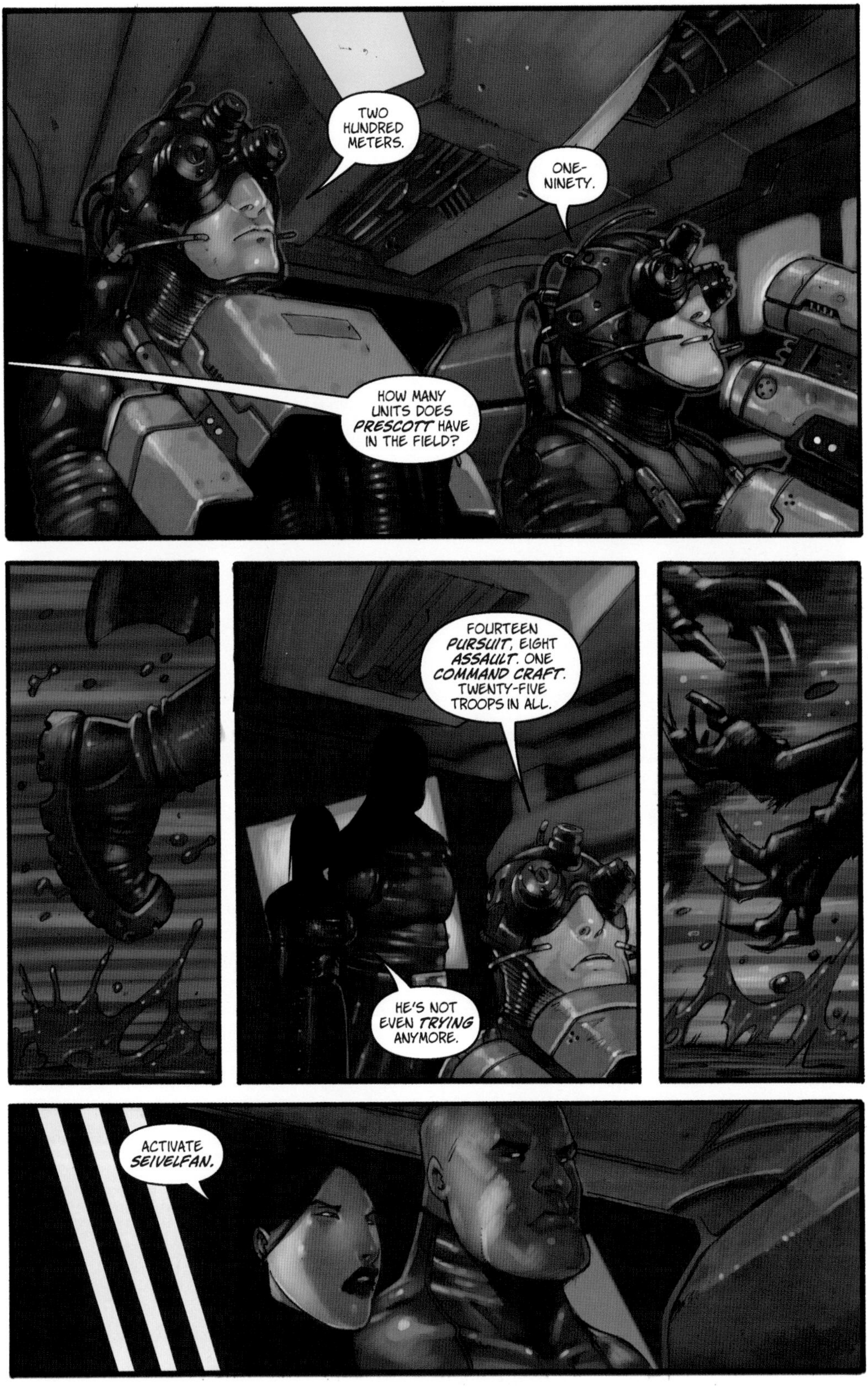
TWO HUNDRED METERS.
ONE-NINETY.
HOW MANY UNITS DOES PRESCOTT HAVE IN THE FIELD?
FOURTEEN PURSUIT, EIGHT ASSAULT. ONE COMMAND CRAFT. TWENTY-FIVE TROOPS IN ALL.
HE'S NOT EVEN TRYING ANYMORE.
ACTIVATE SEIVELFAN.

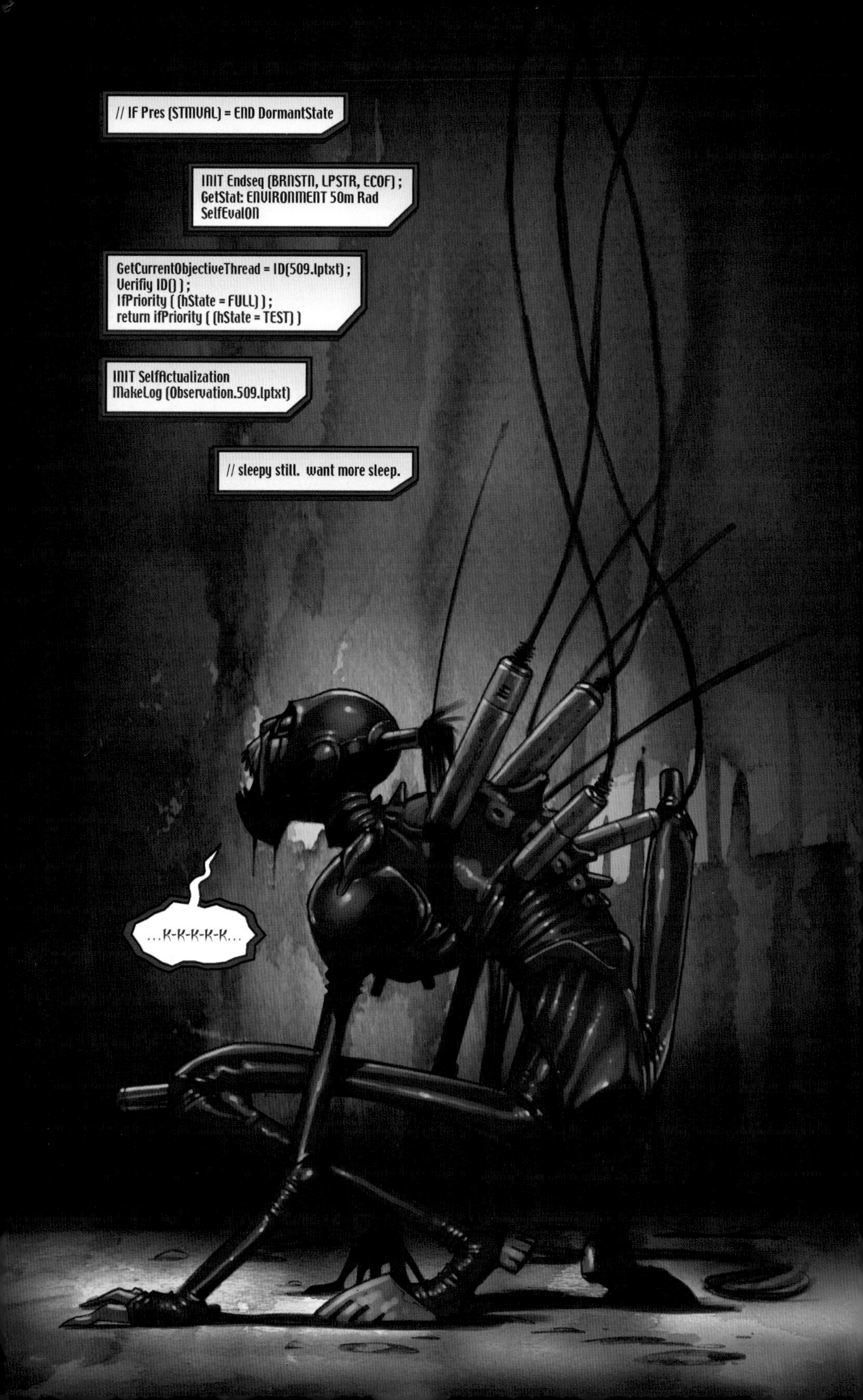

// IF Pres (STMVAL) = END DormantState
INIT Endseq (BRNSTN, LPSTR, ECOF) ; GetStat: ENVIRONMENT 50m Rad SelfEvalON
GetCurrentObjectiveThread = ID(509.lptxt) ; Verifiy ID() ; IfPriority ((hState = FULL)) ; return ifPriority ((hState = TEST))
INIT SelfActualization MakeLog (Observation.509.lptxt)
// sleepy still. want more sleep.
...K-K-K-K-K...

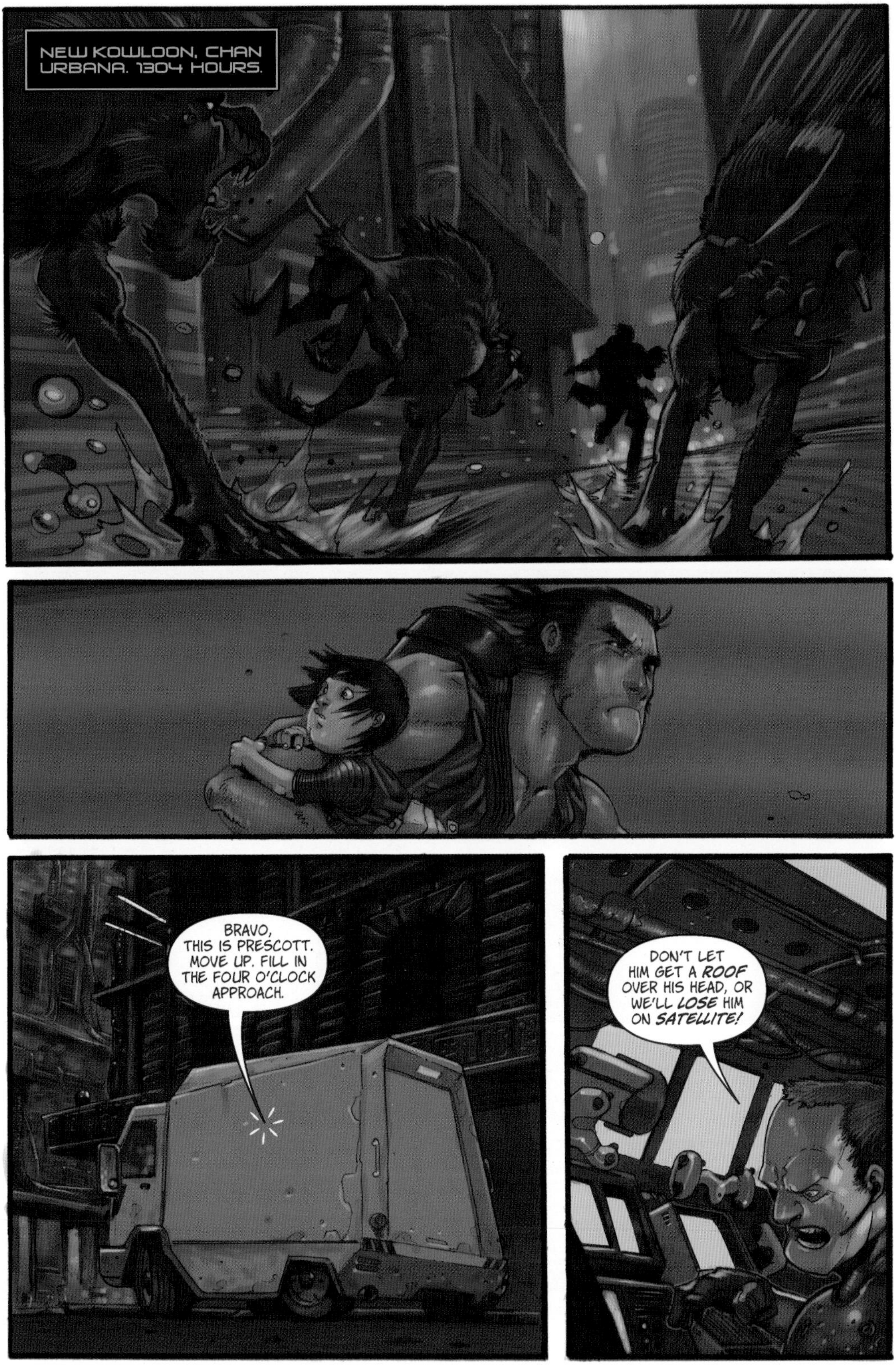
NEW KOWLOON, CHAN URBANA. 1304 HOURS.
BRAVO, THIS IS PRESCOTT. MOVE UP. FILL IN THE FOUR O'CLOCK APPROACH.
DON'T LET HIM GET A *ROOF* OVER HIS HEAD, OR WE'LL *LOSE* HIM ON *SATELLITE!*

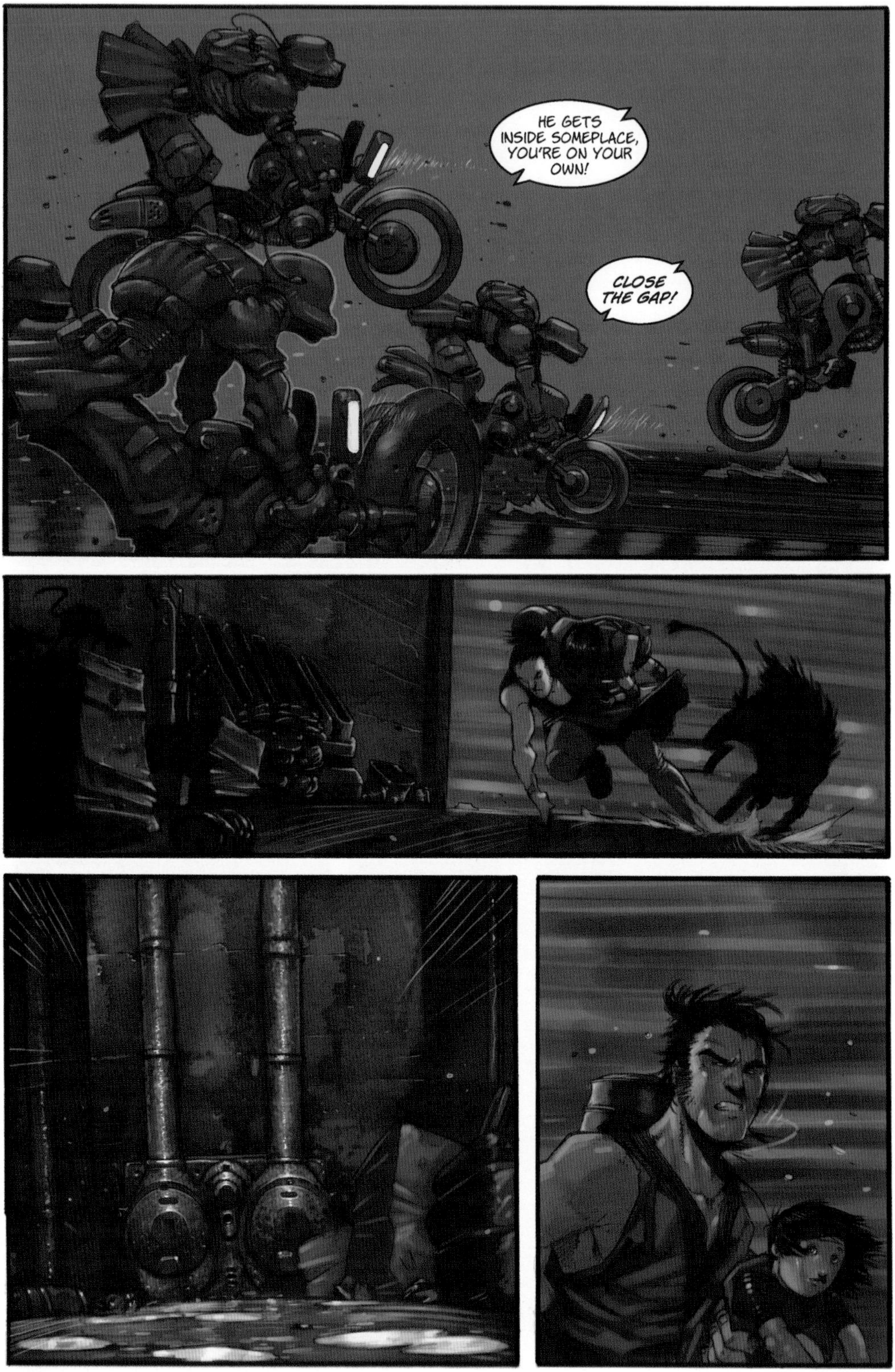
HE GETS INSIDE SOMEPLACE, YOU'RE ON YOUR OWN!
CLOSE THE GAP!

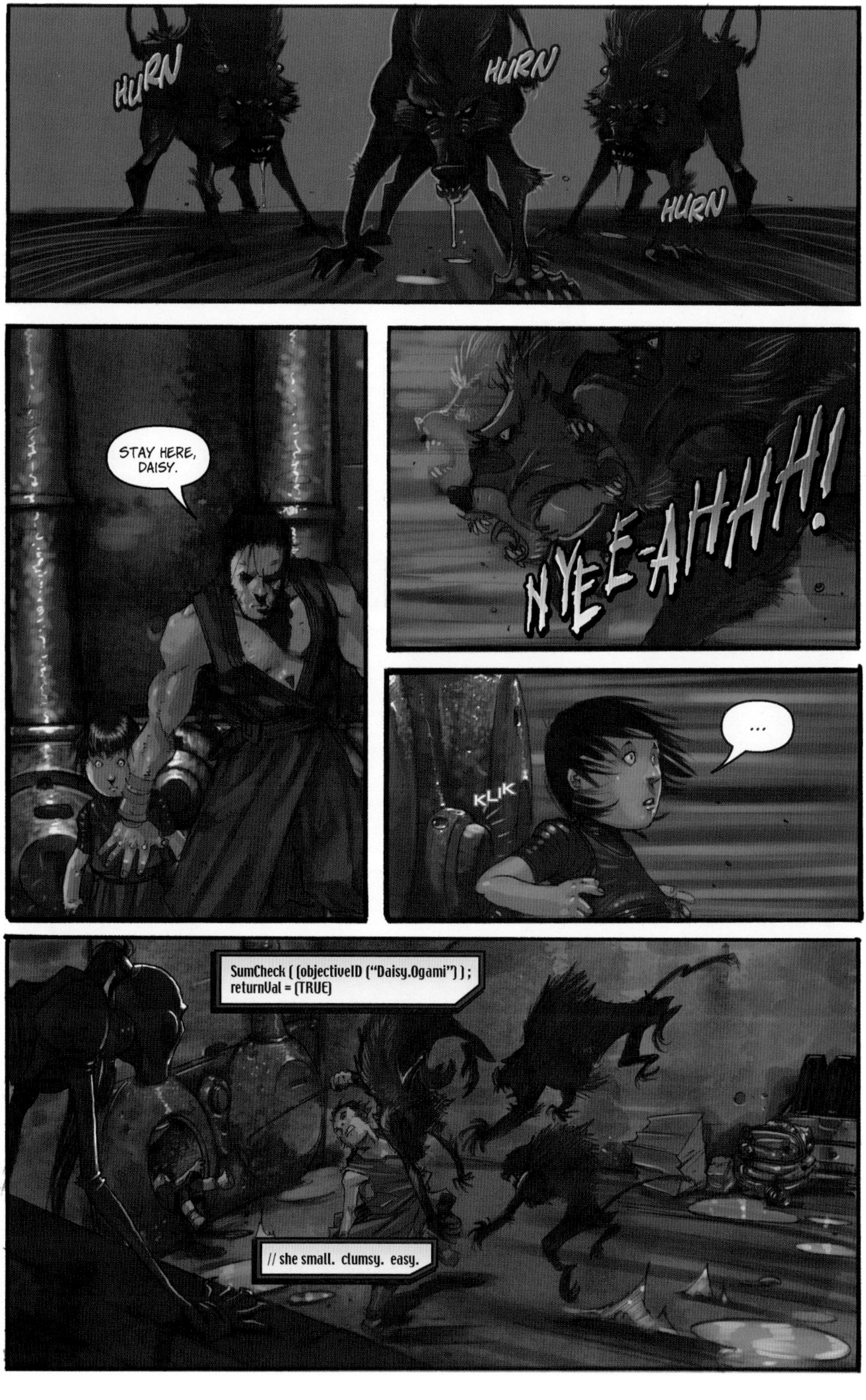
HURN
HURN
HURN
STAY HERE, DAISY.
NYEE-AHHHH!
KLIK
...
SumCheck ((objectiveID ("Daisy.Ogami")) ;
returnVal = (TRUE)
// she small. clumsy. easy.

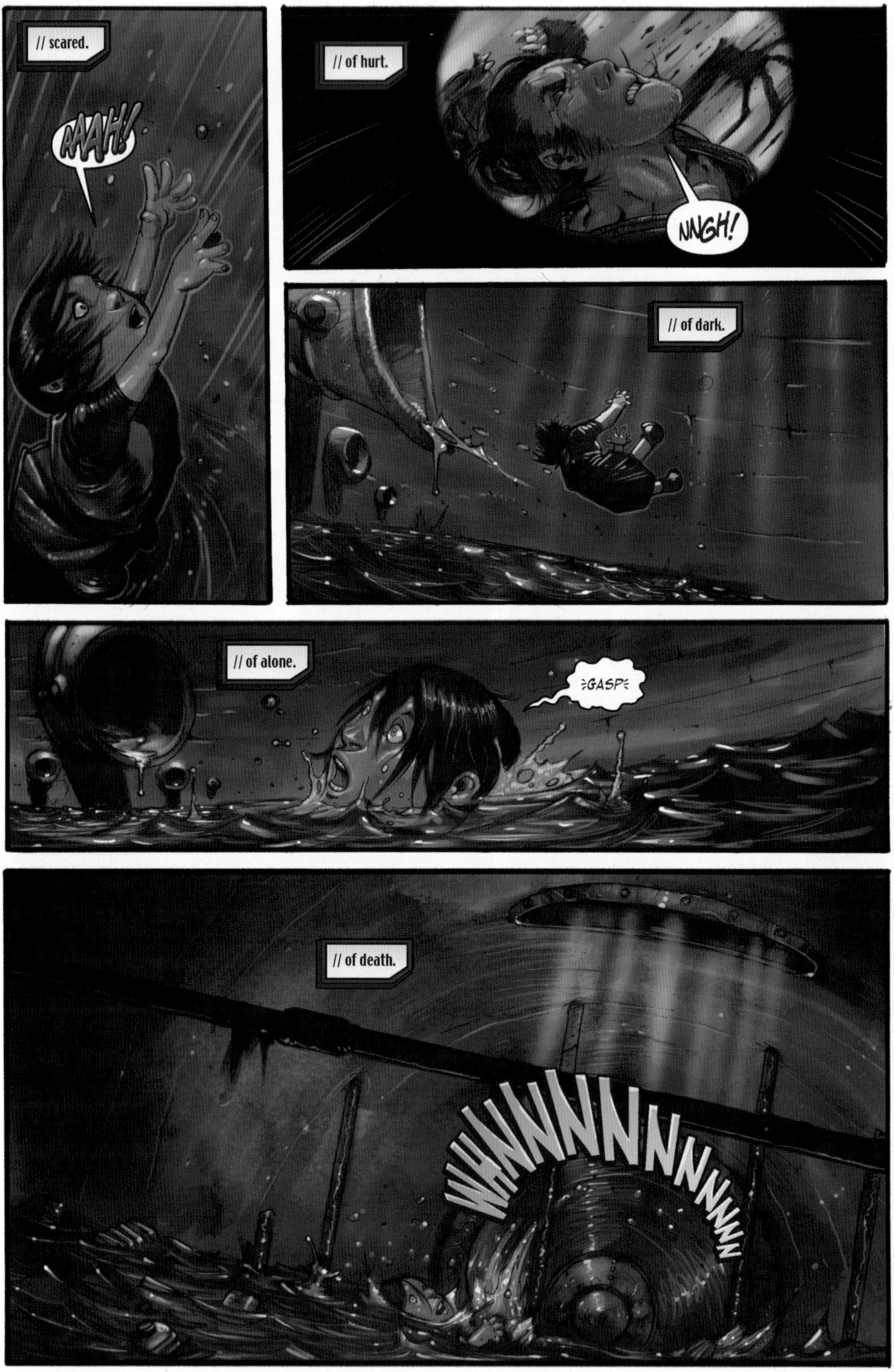
// scared.
RAAAH!
// of hurt.
NNGH!
// of dark.
// of alone.
GASP
// of death.
WHNNNNNNNNNN

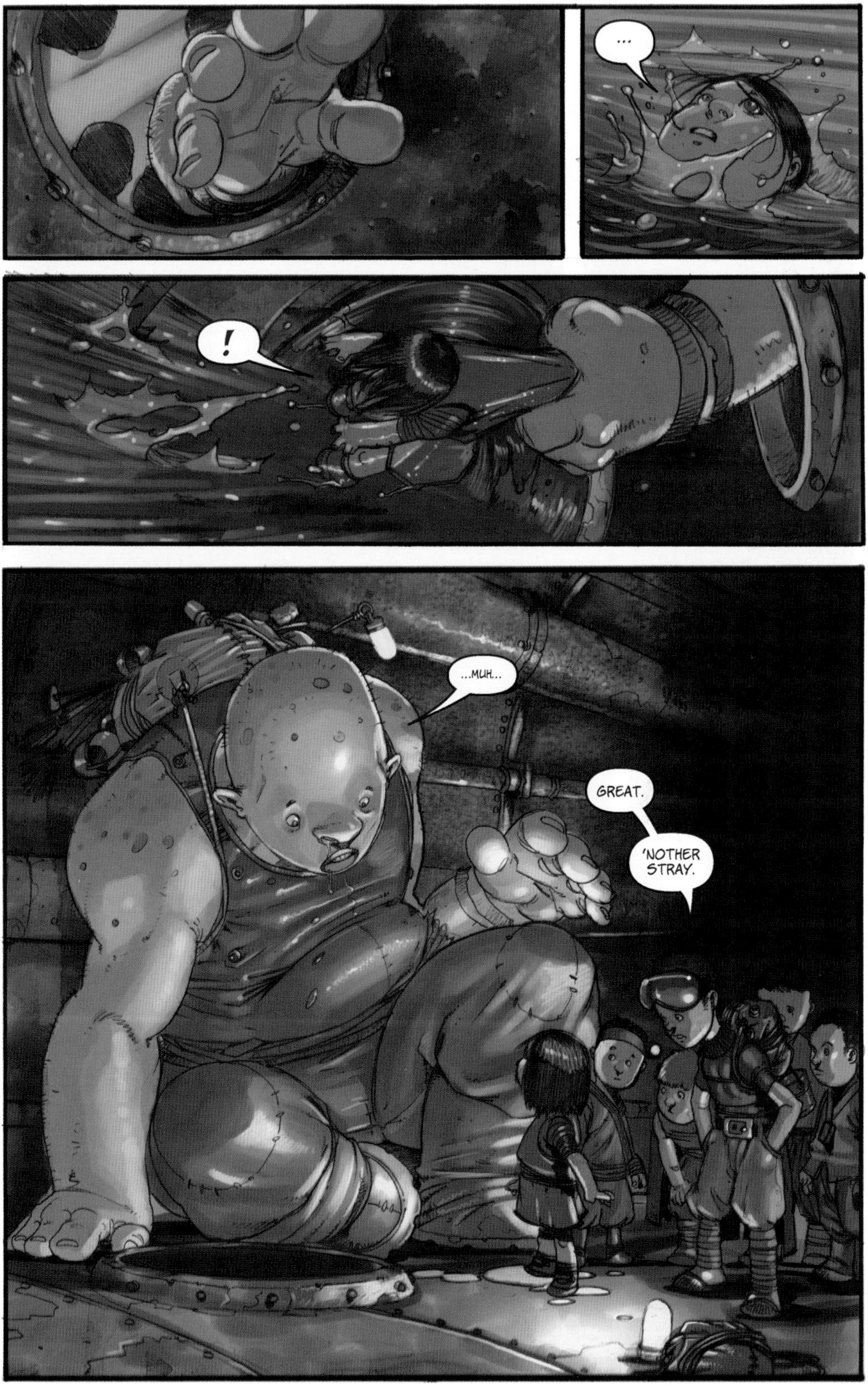
...
!
...MUH...
GREAT.
'NOTHER STRAY.

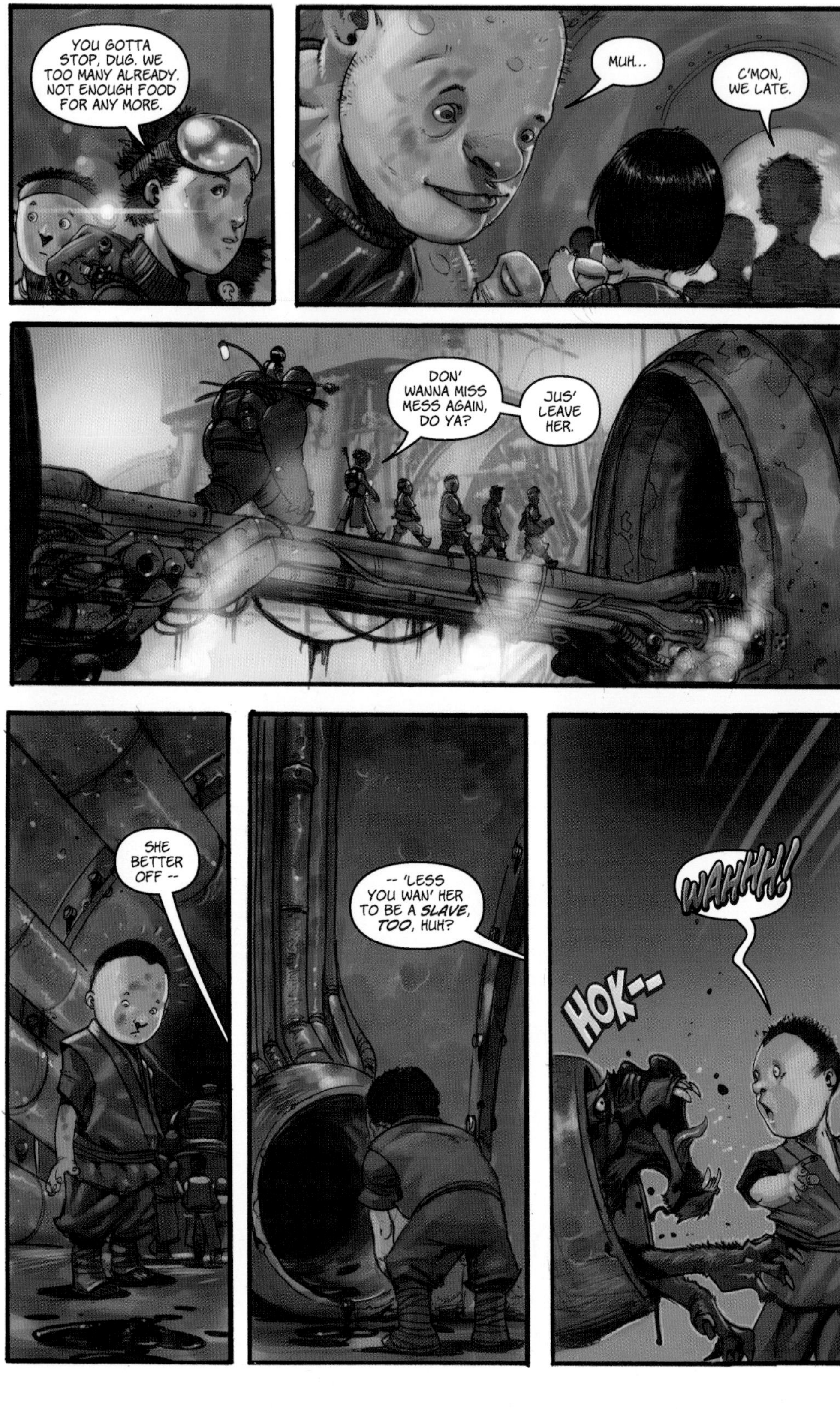
YOU GOTTA STOP, DUG. WE TOO MANY ALREADY. NOT ENOUGH FOOD FOR ANY MORE.
MUH...
C'MON, WE LATE.
DON' WANNA MISS MESS AGAIN, DO YA?
JUS' LEAVE HER.
SHE BETTER OFF --
-- 'LESS YOU WAN' HER TO BE A *SLAVE*, *TOO*, HUH?
WAHHH!
HOK--

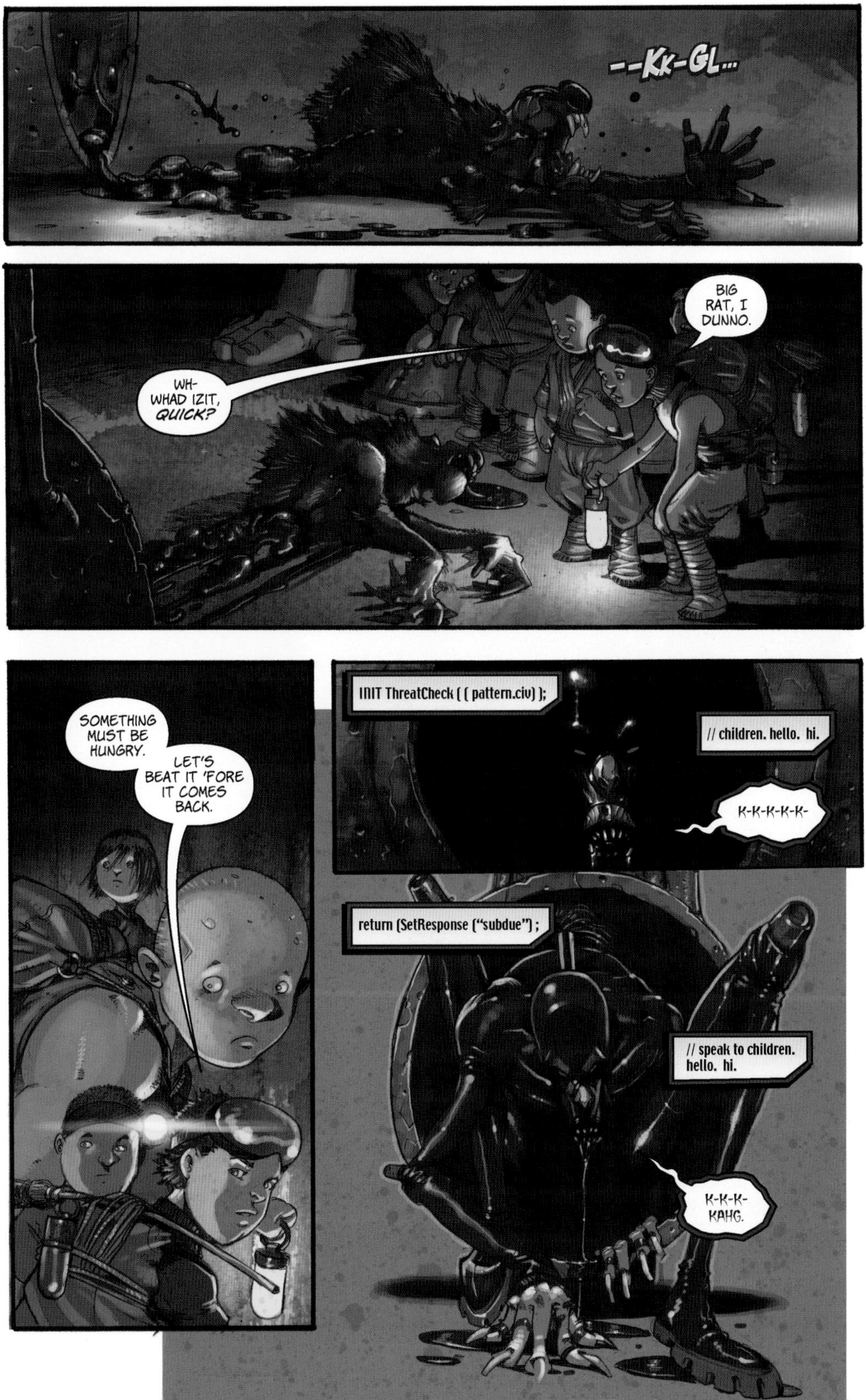
--KK-GL...
WH-WHAD IZIT, QUICK?
BIG RAT, I DUNNO.
SOMETHING MUST BE HUNGRY.
LET'S BEAT IT 'FORE IT COMES BACK.
INIT ThreatCheck ((pattern.civ));
// children. hello. hi.
K-K-K-K-K-
return (SetResponse ("subdue") ;
// speak to children. hello. hi.
K-K-K-KAHG.

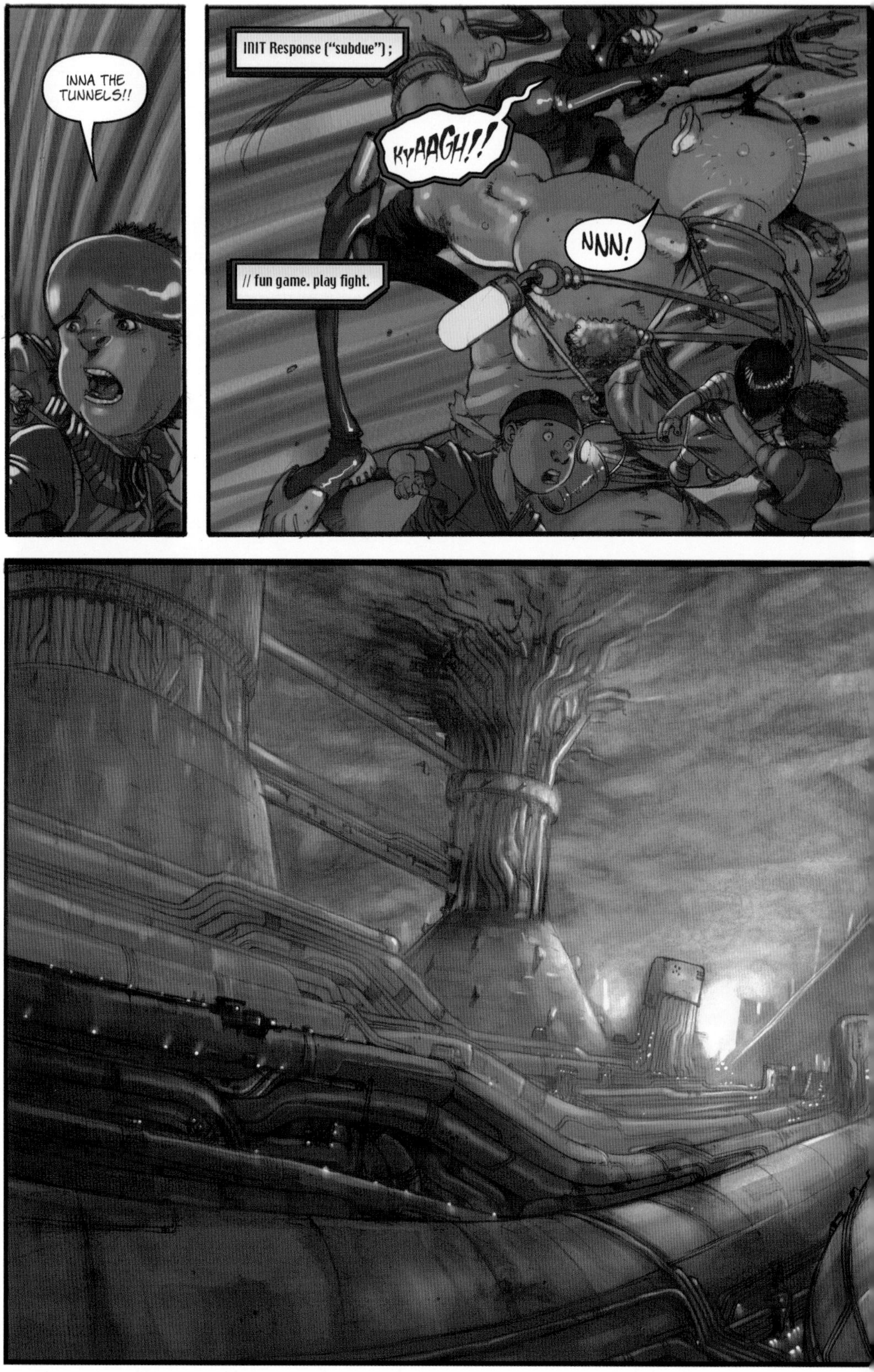
INNA THE TUNNELS!!
INIT Response ("subdue") ;
KYAAGH!!
NNN!
// fun game. play fight.

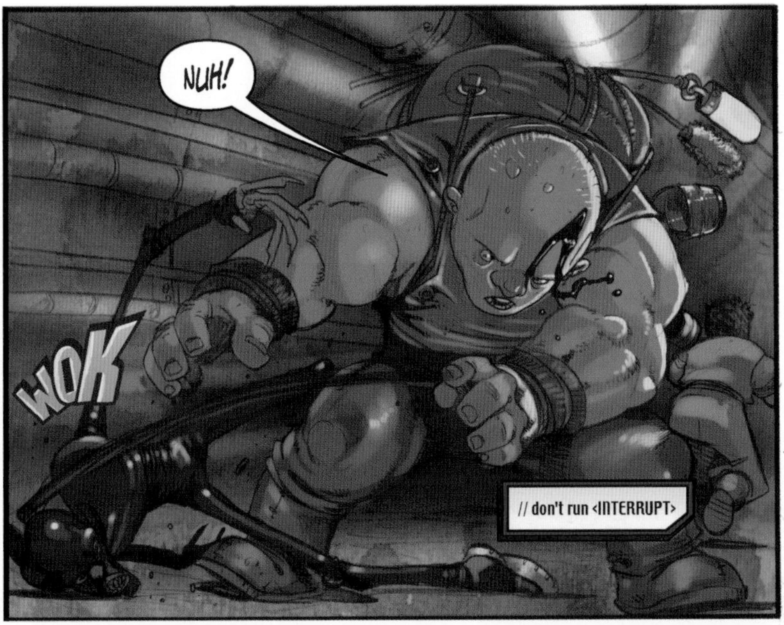
NUH!
WOK
// don't run <INTERRUPT>

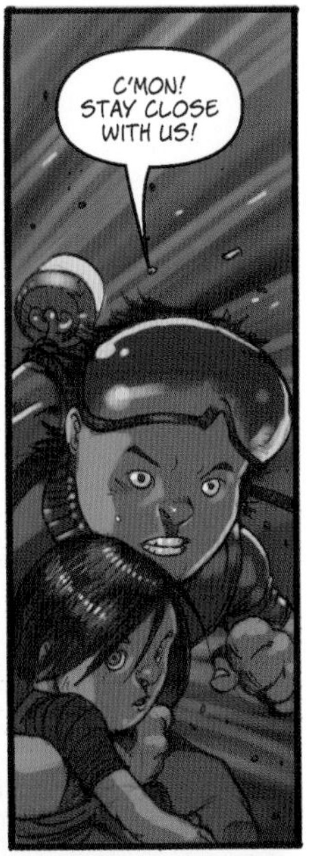
C'MON! STAY CLOSE WITH US!

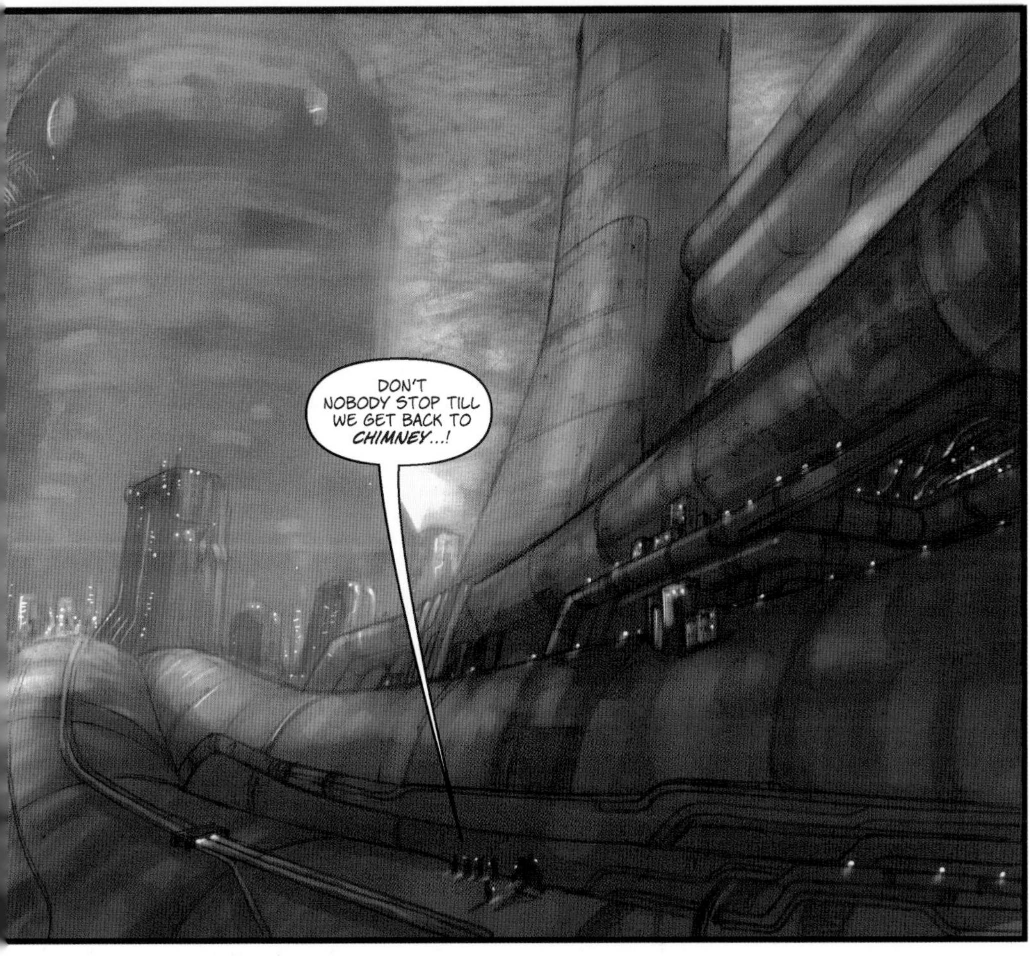
DON'T NOBODY STOP TILL WE GET BACK TO *CHIMNEY*...!

CHIMNEY, THERMO-ELECTRIC HUB.

WE GONNA TELL GALGO 'BOUT THE RAT?

HSSHH...

WHERE YOU BEEN?!?

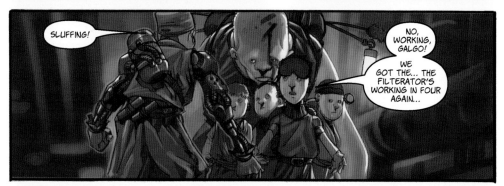

SLUFFING!

NO, WORKING, GALGO! WE GOT THE... THE FILTERATOR'S WORKING IN FOUR AGAIN...

ABOUT TIME! YOU TAKE TOO LONG!

HUH?

WHAT HAPPEN TO DUG?

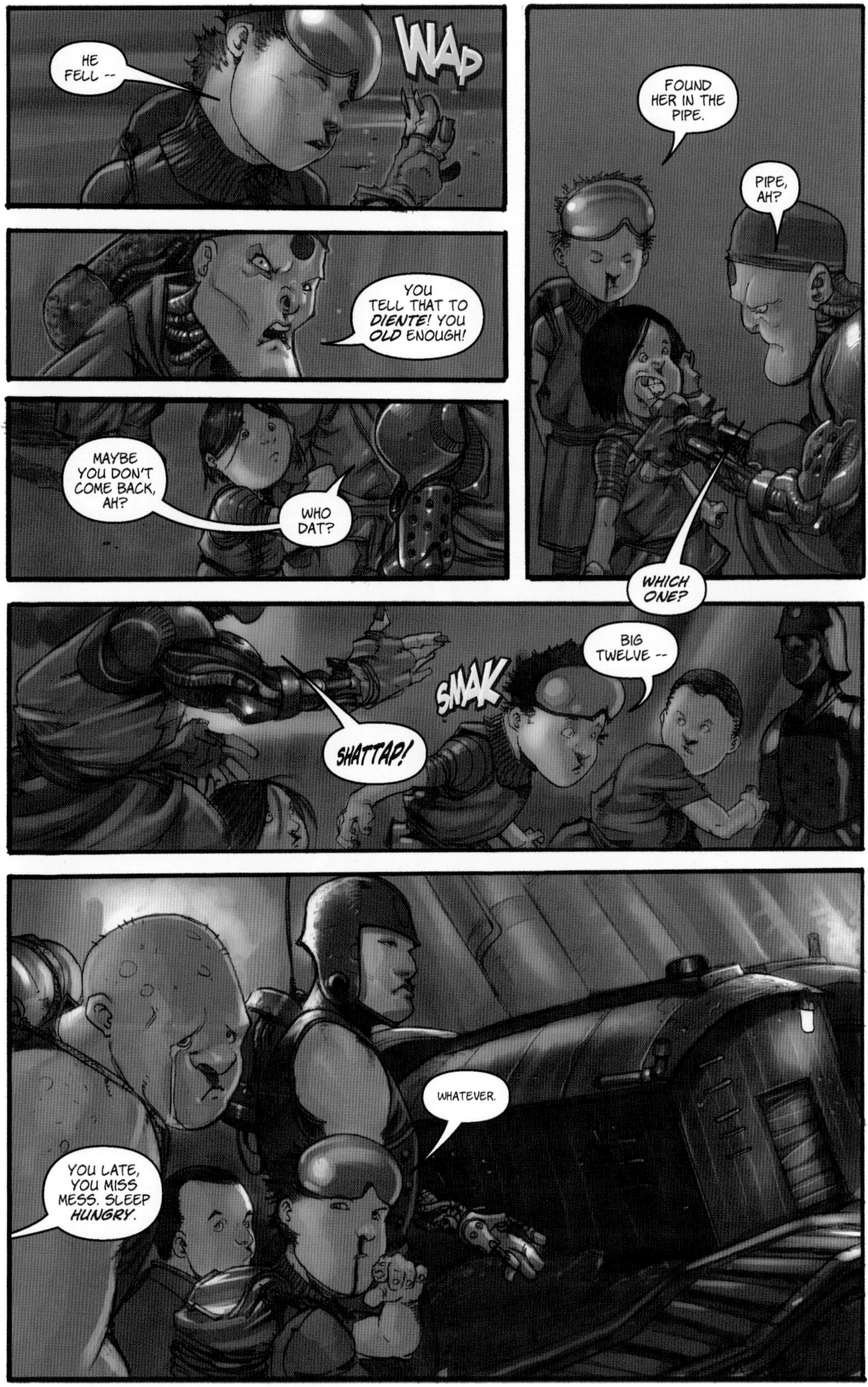
HE FELL --
WAP
YOU TELL THAT TO *DIENTE*! YOU *OLD* ENOUGH!
MAYBE YOU DON'T COME BACK, AH?
WHO DAT?
FOUND HER IN THE PIPE.
PIPE, AH?
WHICH ONE?
BIG TWELVE --
SMAK
SHATTAP!
WHATEVER.
YOU LATE, YOU MISS MESS. SLEEP *HUNGRY*.

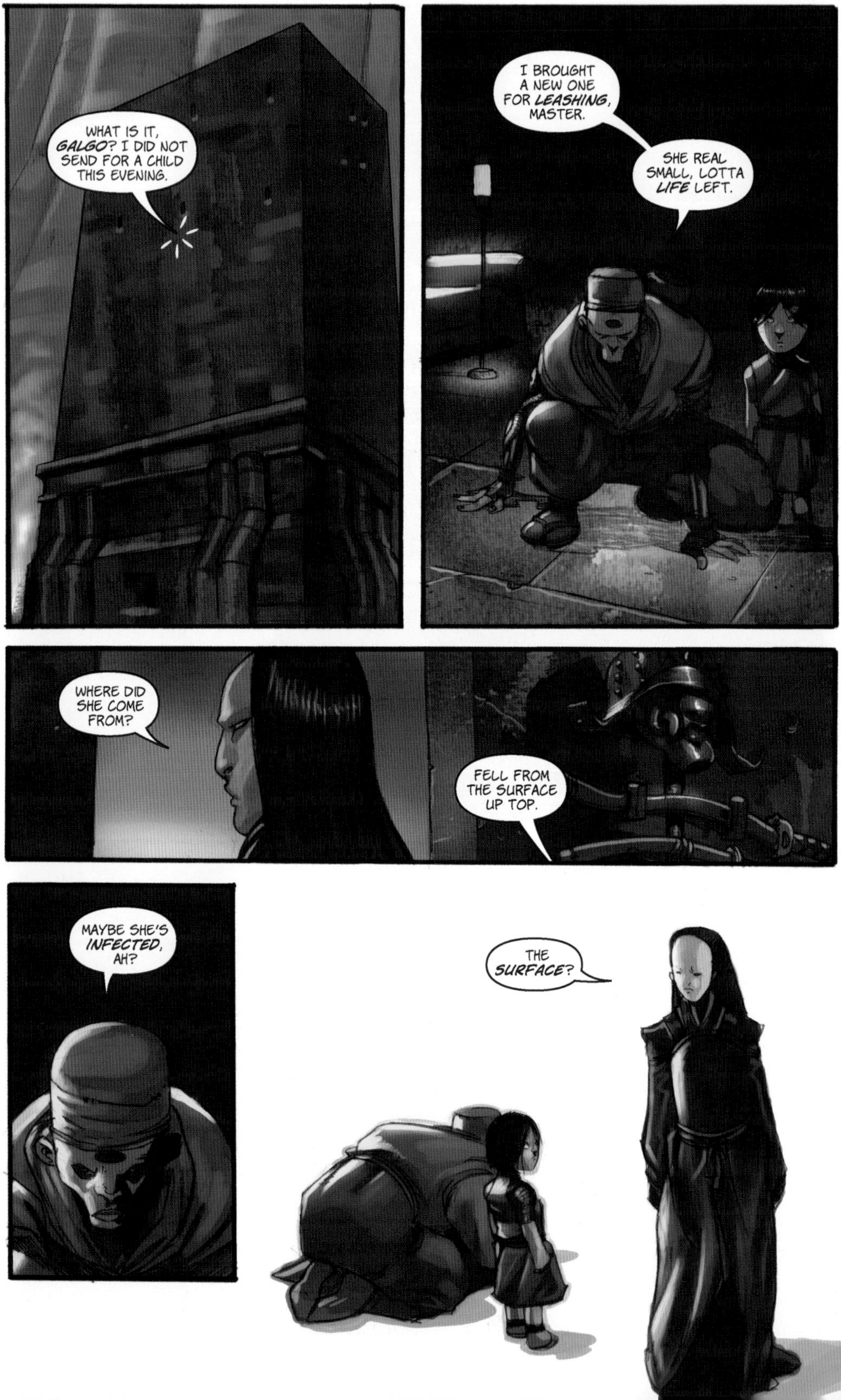
WHAT IS IT, GALGO? I DID NOT SEND FOR A CHILD THIS EVENING.
I BROUGHT A NEW ONE FOR LEASHING, MASTER.
SHE REAL SMALL, LOTTA LIFE LEFT.
WHERE DID SHE COME FROM?
FELL FROM THE SURFACE UP TOP.
MAYBE SHE'S INFECTED, AH?
THE SURFACE?

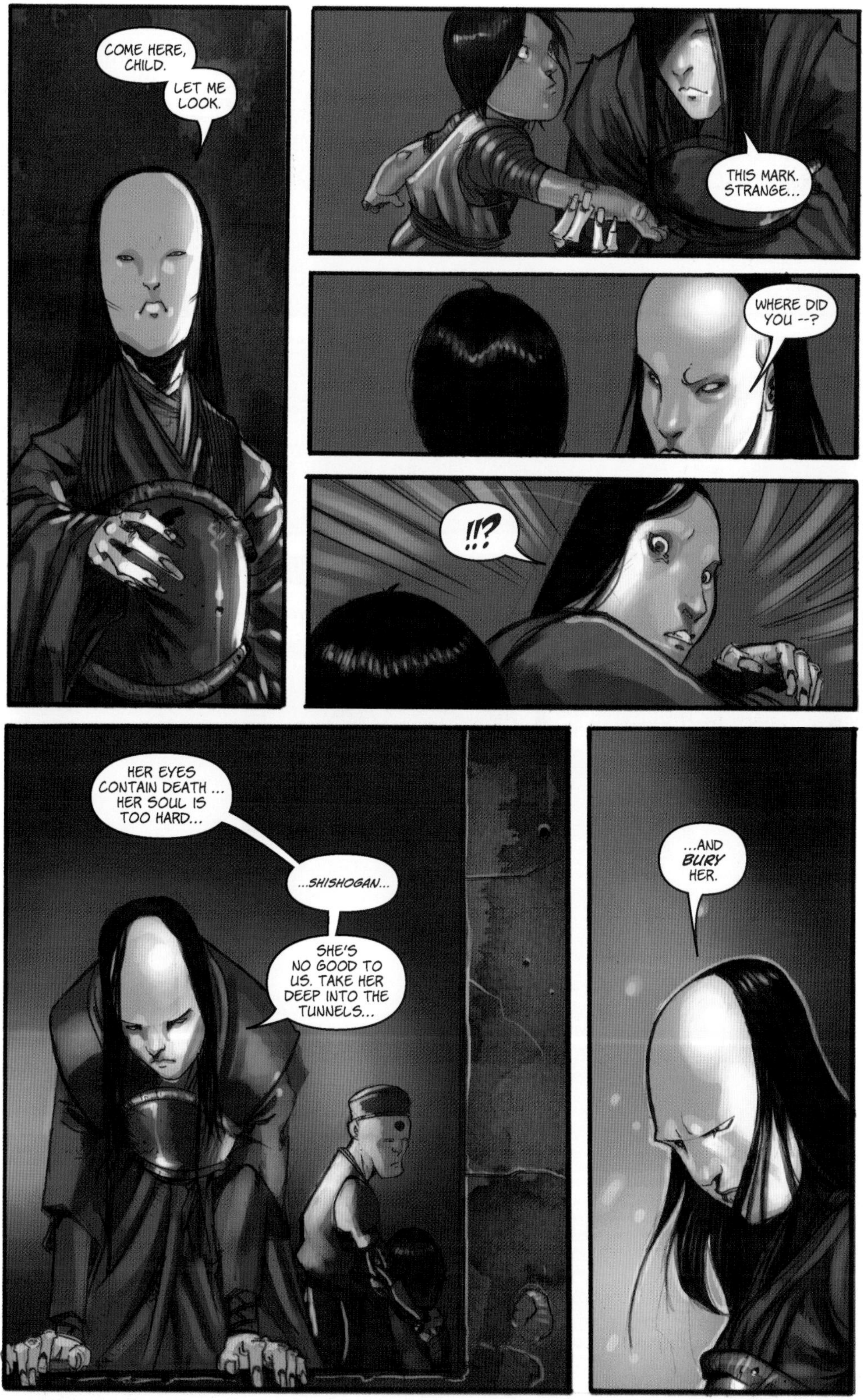
COME HERE, CHILD.
LET ME LOOK.
THIS MARK. STRANGE...
WHERE DID YOU --?
!!?
HER EYES CONTAIN DEATH ... HER SOUL IS TOO HARD...
...SHISHOGAN...
SHE'S NO GOOD TO US. TAKE HER DEEP INTO THE TUNNELS...
...AND BURY HER.

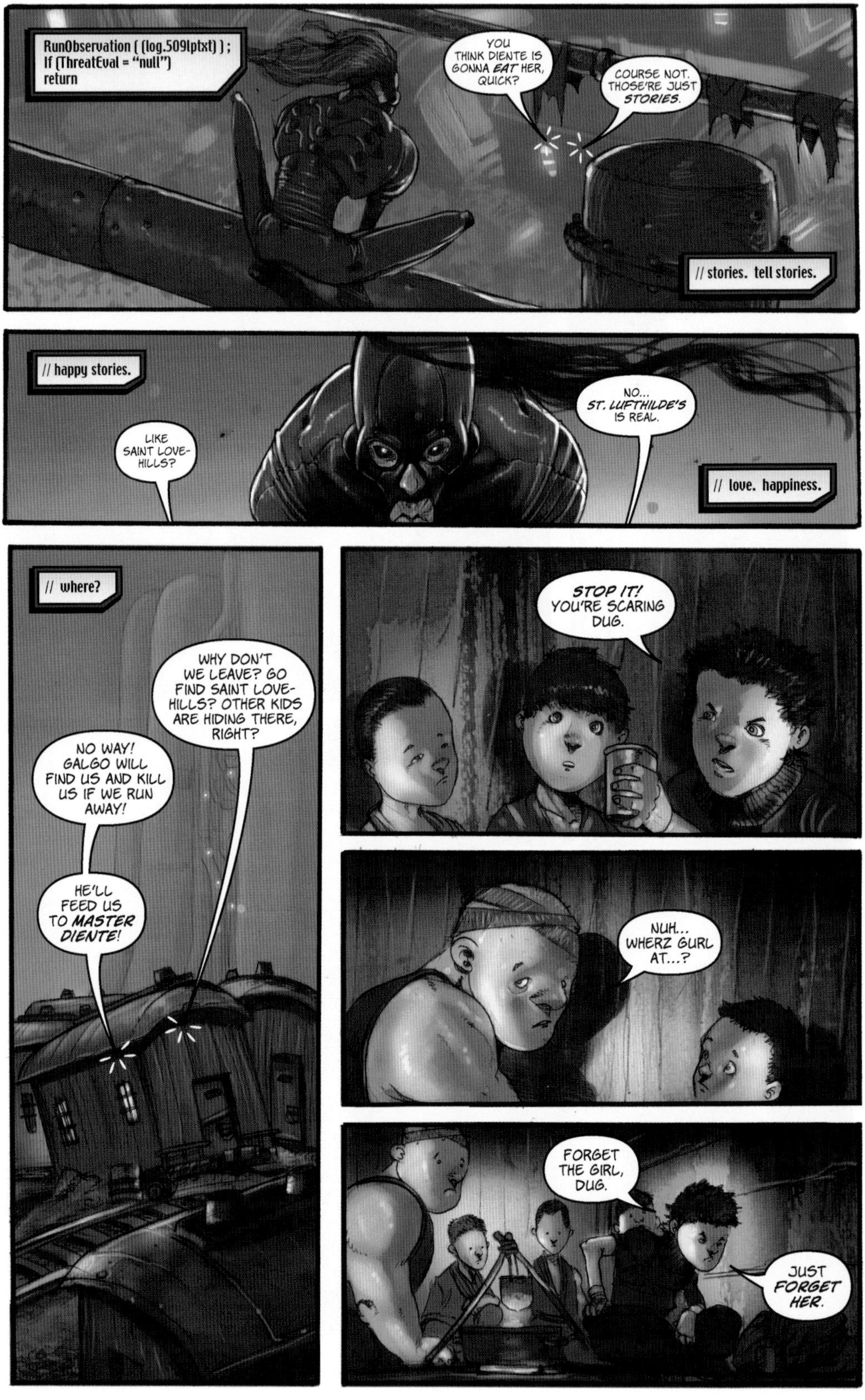
RunObservation ((log.509lptxt)) ;
If (ThreatEval = "null")
return
YOU THINK DIENTE IS GONNA EAT HER, QUICK?
COURSE NOT. THOSE'RE JUST STORIES.
// stories. tell stories.
// happy stories.
LIKE SAINT LOVE-HILLS?
NO... ST. LUFTHILDE'S IS REAL.
// love. happiness.
// where?
WHY DON'T WE LEAVE? GO FIND SAINT LOVE-HILLS? OTHER KIDS ARE HIDING THERE, RIGHT?
NO WAY! GALGO WILL FIND US AND KILL US IF WE RUN AWAY!
HE'LL FEED US TO MASTER DIENTE!
STOP IT! YOU'RE SCARING DUG.
NUH... WHERZ GURL AT...?
FORGET THE GIRL, DUG.
JUST FORGET HER.

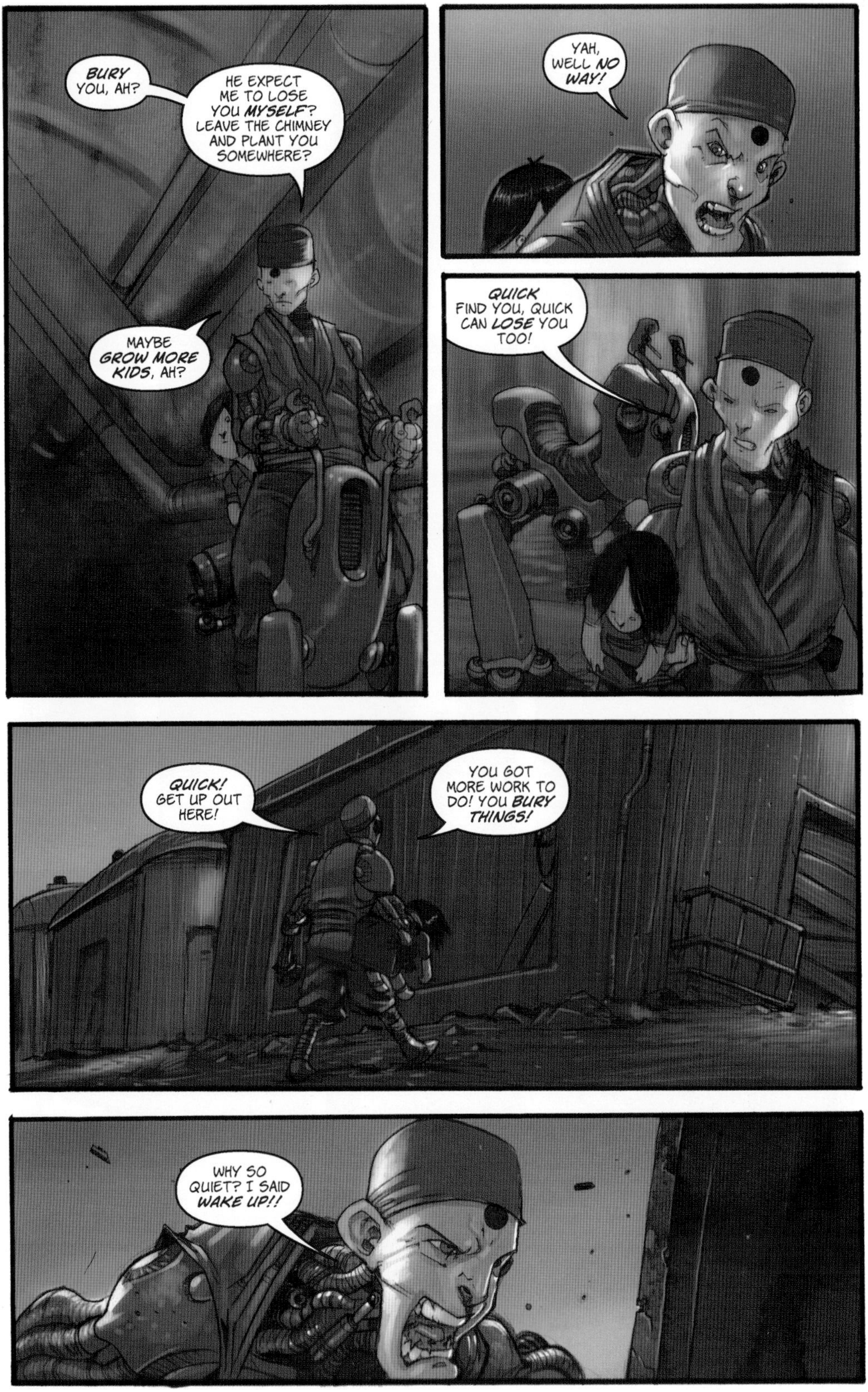
BURY YOU, AH?
HE EXPECT ME TO LOSE YOU MYSELF? LEAVE THE CHIMNEY AND PLANT YOU SOMEWHERE?
MAYBE GROW MORE KIDS, AH?
YAH, WELL NO WAY!
QUICK FIND YOU, QUICK CAN LOSE YOU TOO!
QUICK! GET UP OUT HERE!
YOU GOT MORE WORK TO DO! YOU BURY THINGS!
WHY SO QUIET? I SAID WAKE UP!!

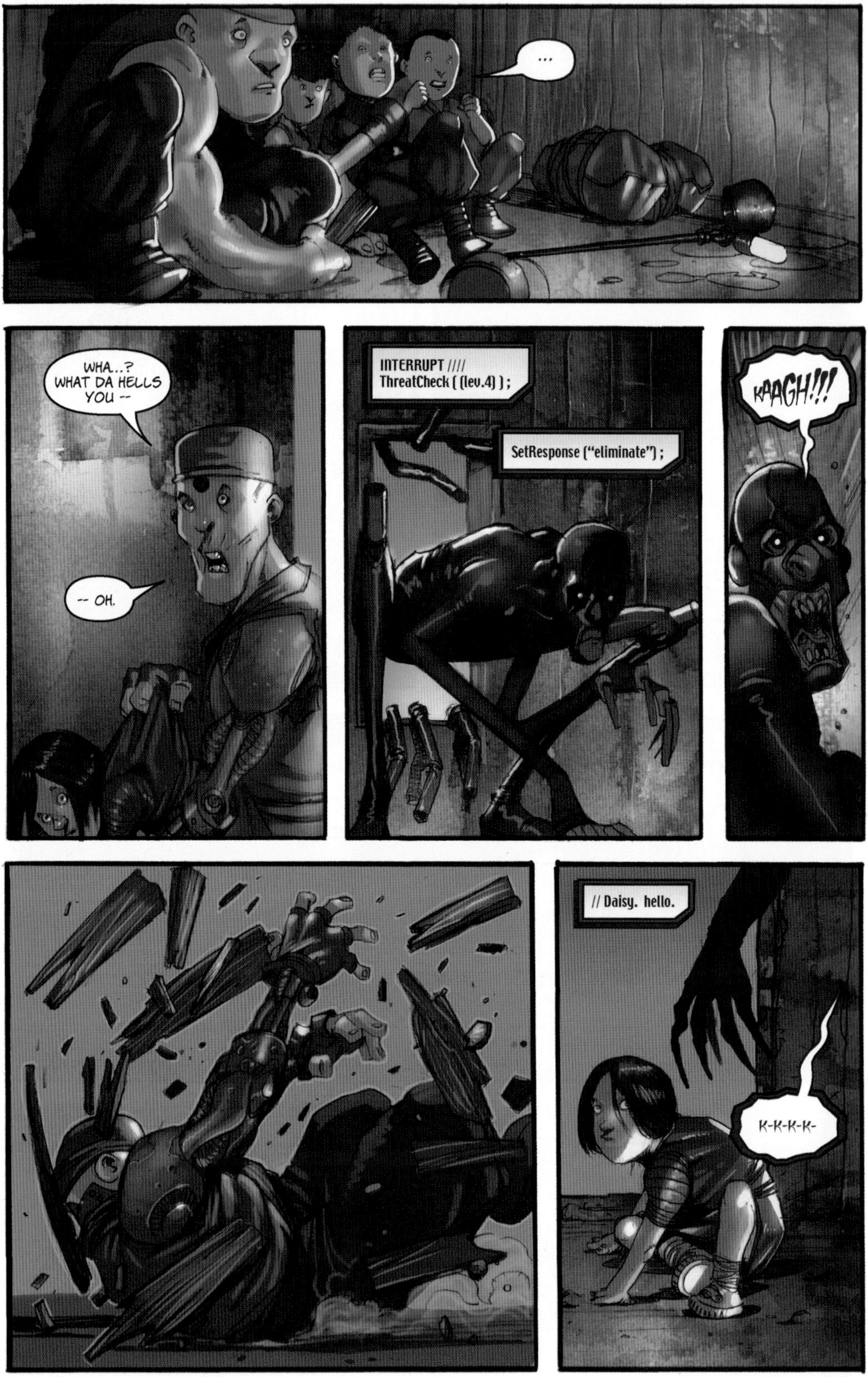
...
WHA...? WHAT DA HELLS YOU --
-- OH.
INTERRUPT ////
ThreatCheck ((lev.4)) ;
SetResponse ("eliminate") ;
KAAGH!!!
// Daisy. hello.
K-K-K-K-

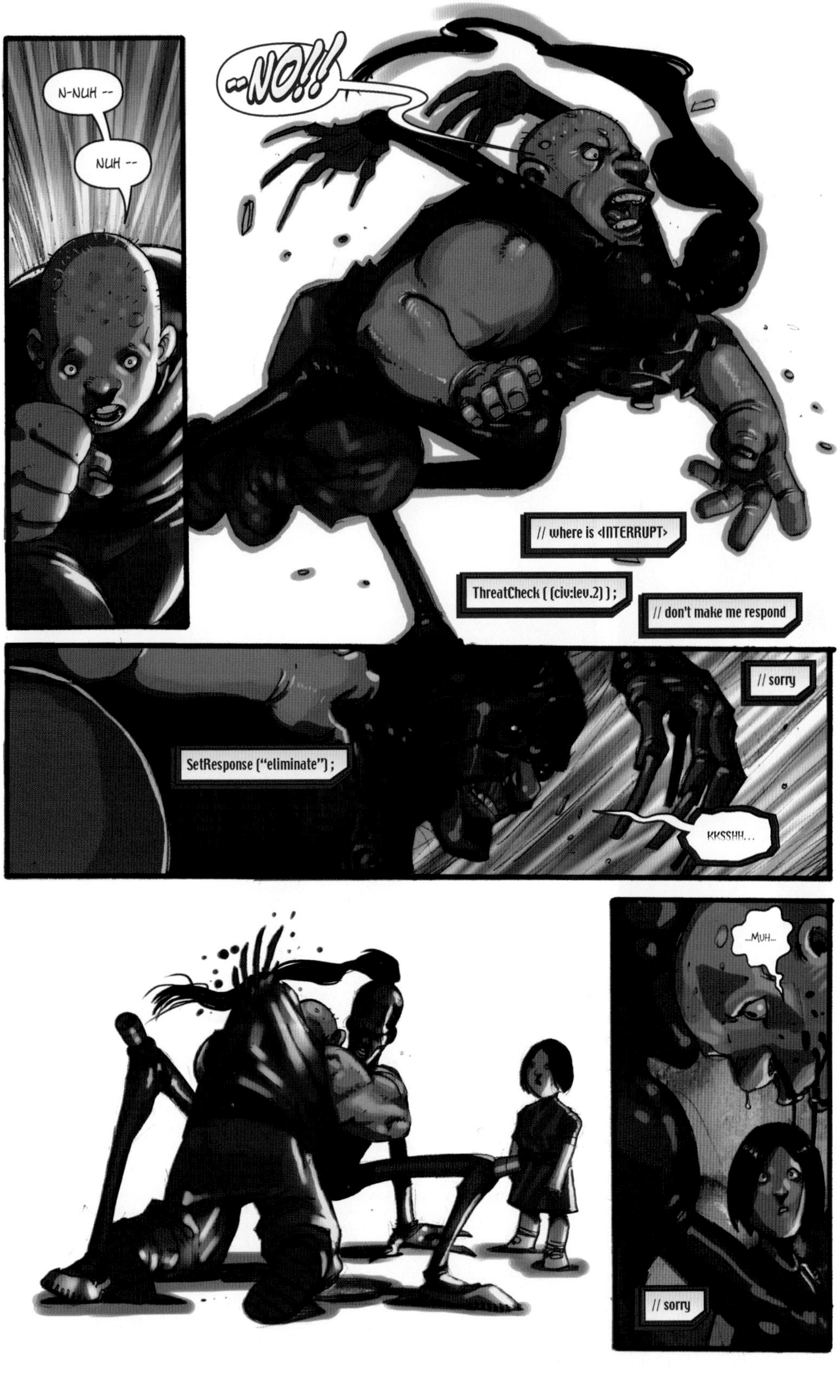

N-NUH --
NUH --
--NO!!
// where is <INTERRUPT>
ThreatCheck ((civ:lev.2)) ;
// don't make me respond
// sorry
SetResponse ("eliminate") ;
KKSSHH...
...MUH...
// sorry

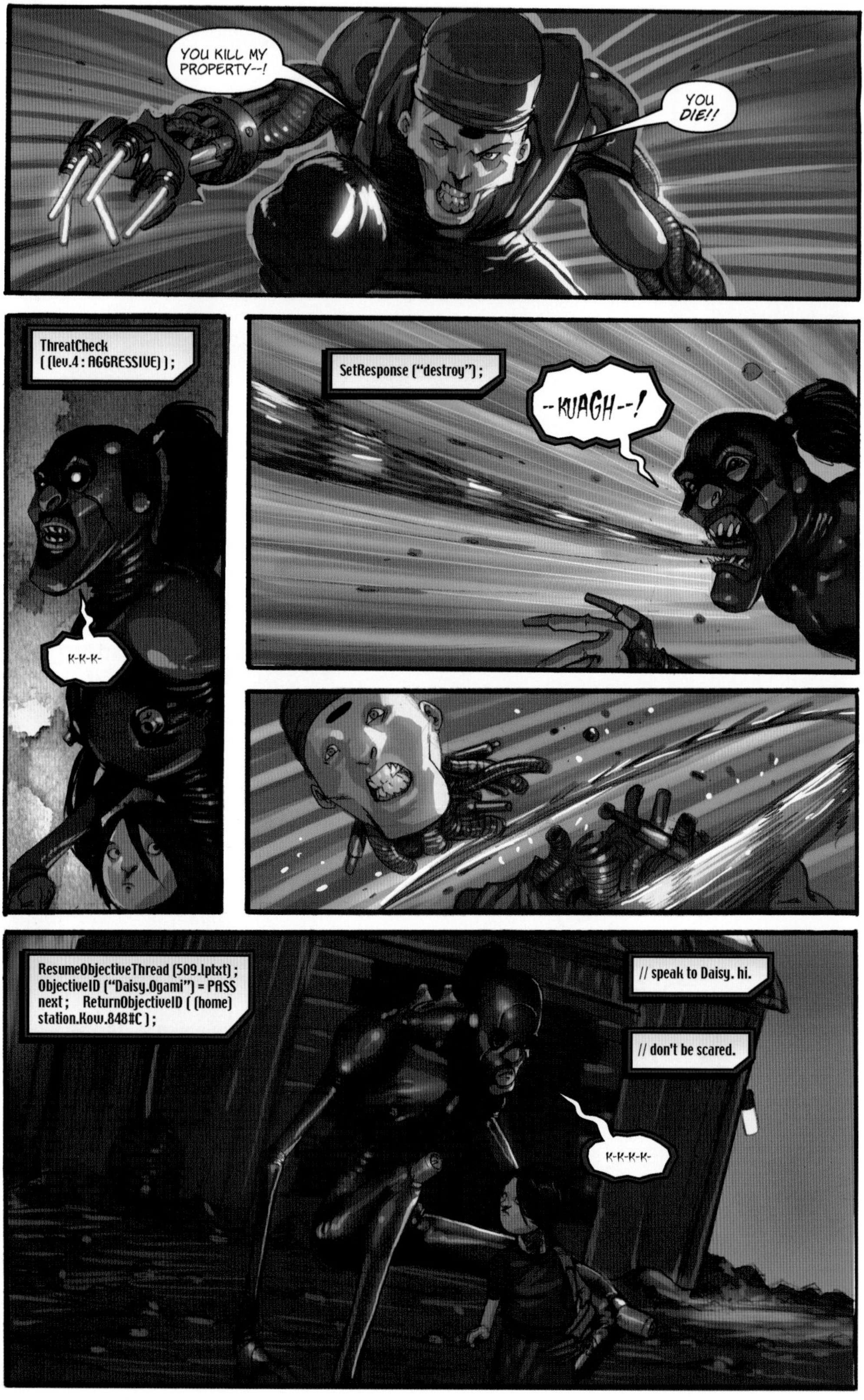
YOU KILL MY PROPERTY--!
YOU DIE!!
ThreatCheck ((lev.4 : AGGRESSIVE)) ;
K-K-K-
SetResponse ("destroy") ;
--KUAGH--!
ResumeObjectiveThread (509.lptxt) ; ObjectiveID ("Daisy.Ogami") = PASS next ; ReturnObjectiveID ((home) station.Kow.848#C) ;
// speak to Daisy. hi.
// don't be scared.
K-K-K-K-

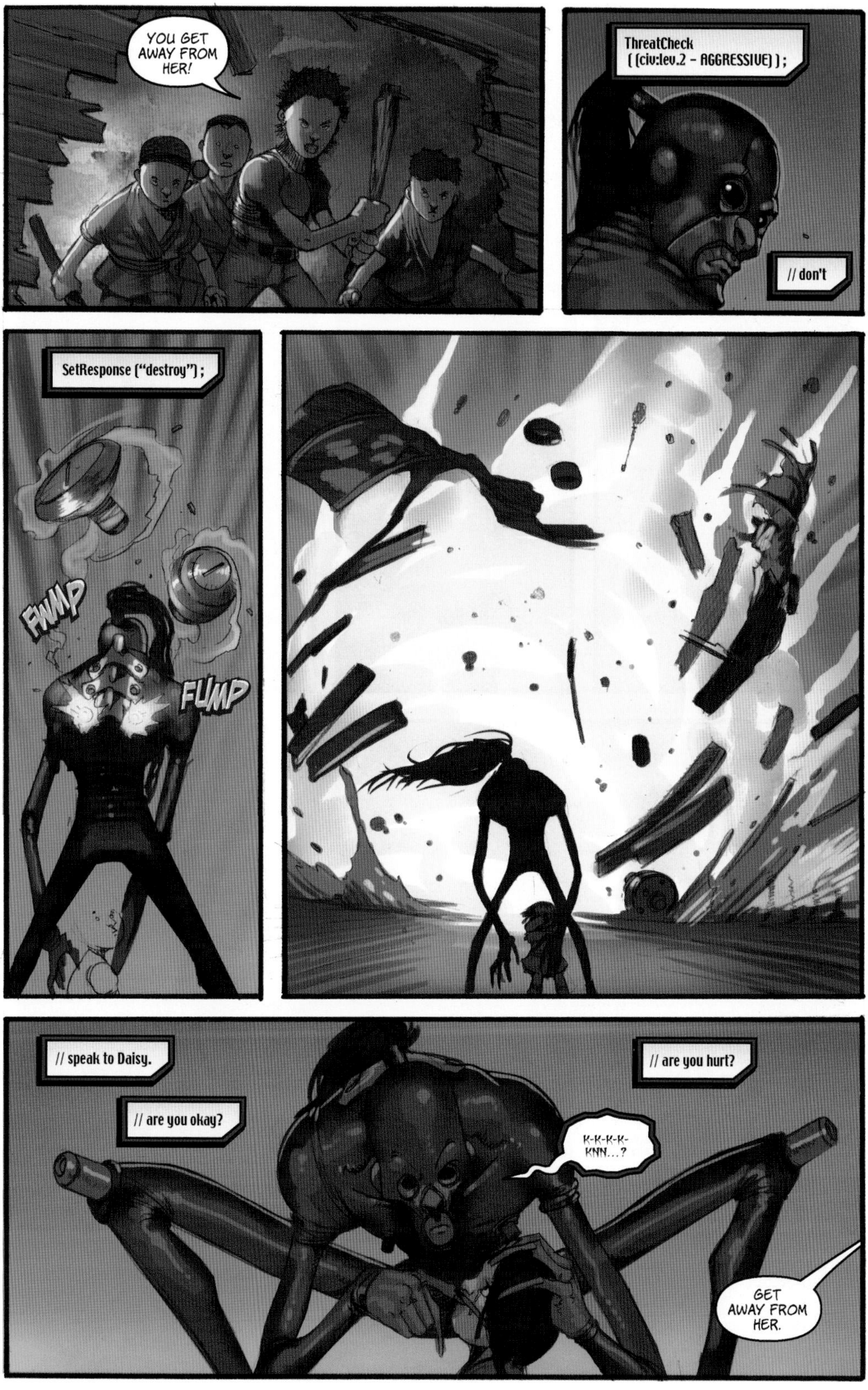
YOU GET AWAY FROM HER!
ThreatCheck ((civ:lev.2 - AGGRESSIVE)) ;
// don't
SetResponse ("destroy") ;
FWMP
FUMP
// speak to Daisy.
// are you okay?
// are you hurt?
K-K-K-K-KNN...?
GET AWAY FROM HER.

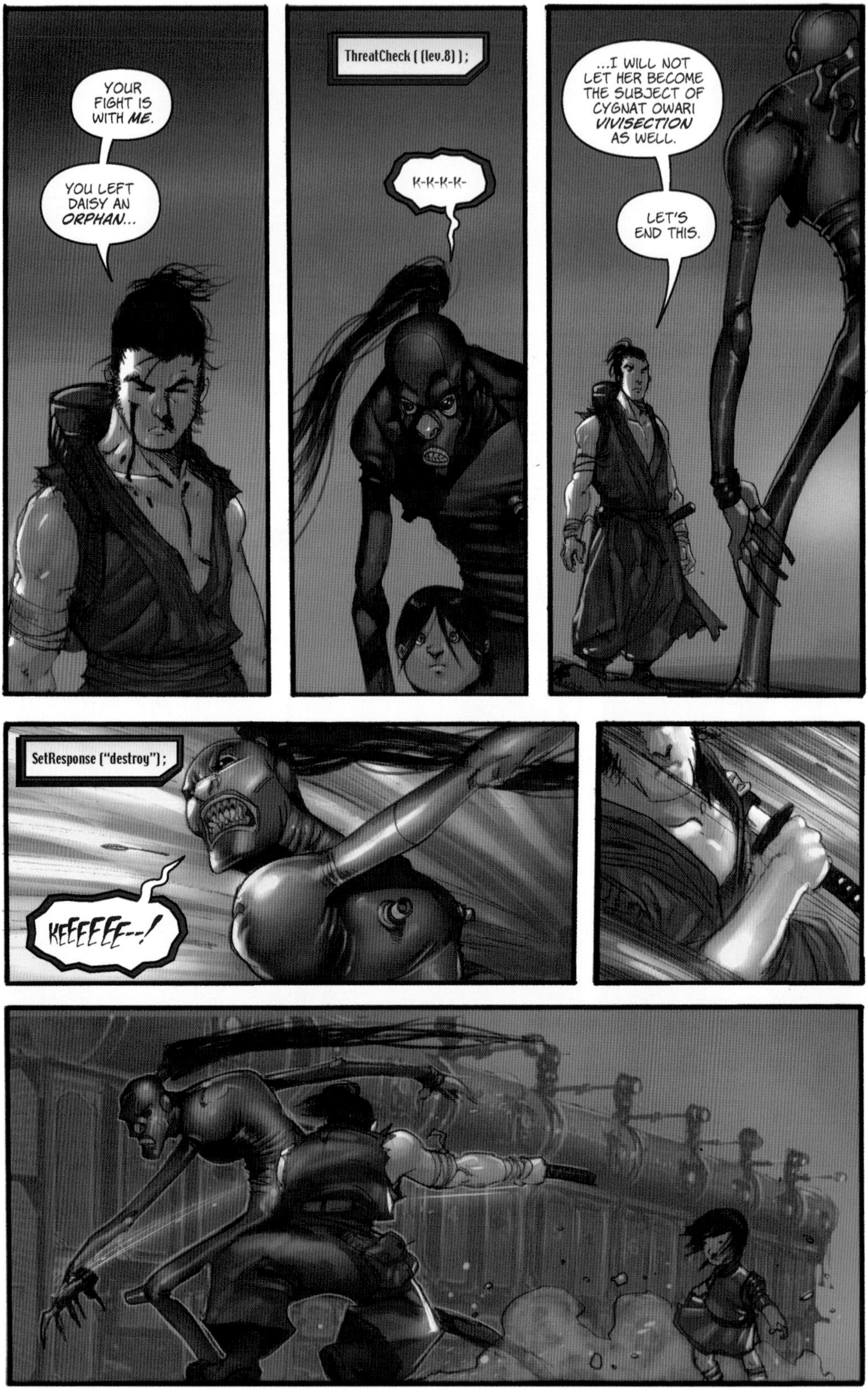
YOUR FIGHT IS WITH ME.
YOU LEFT DAISY AN ORPHAN...
ThreatCheck ((lev.8));
K-K-K-K-
...I WILL NOT LET HER BECOME THE SUBJECT OF CYGNAT OWARI VIVISECTION AS WELL.
LET'S END THIS.
SetResponse ("destroy");
KEEEEEE--!

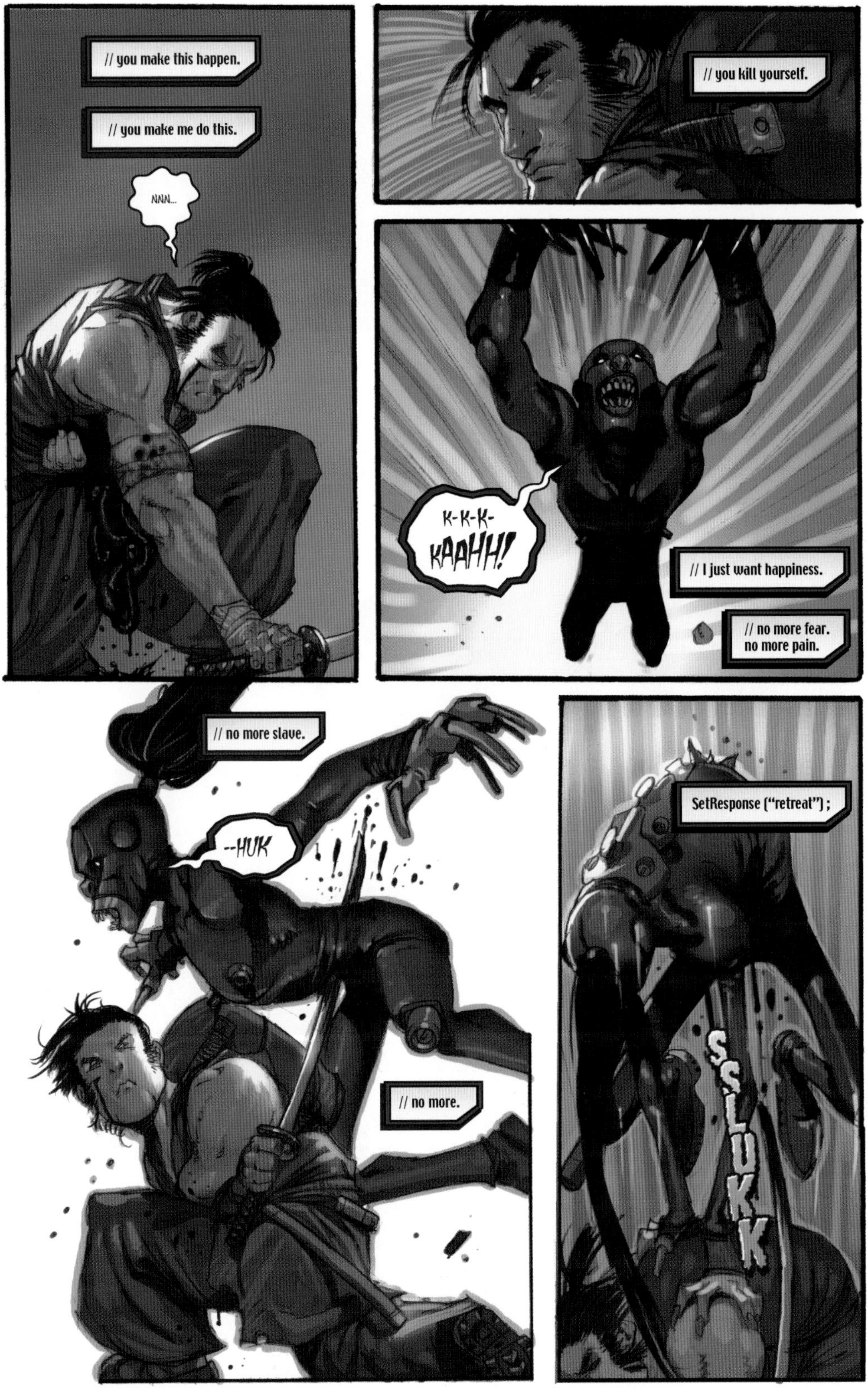
// you make this happen.
// you make me do this.
NNN...
// you kill yourself.
K-K-K-KAAHH!
// I just want happiness.
// no more fear. no more pain.
// no more slave.
--HUK
// no more.
SetResponse ("retreat") ;
SSLUKK

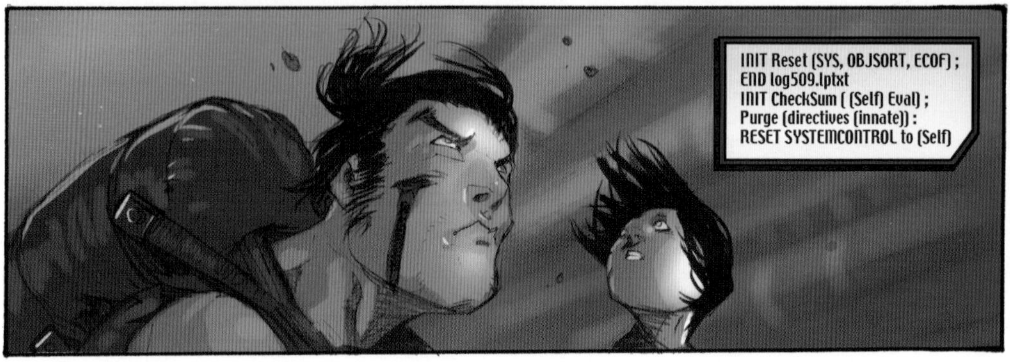
INIT Reset (SYS, OBJSORT, ECOF) ;
END log509.lptxt
INIT CheckSum ((Self) Eval) ;
Purge (directives (innate)) :
RESET SYSTEMCONTROL to (Self)

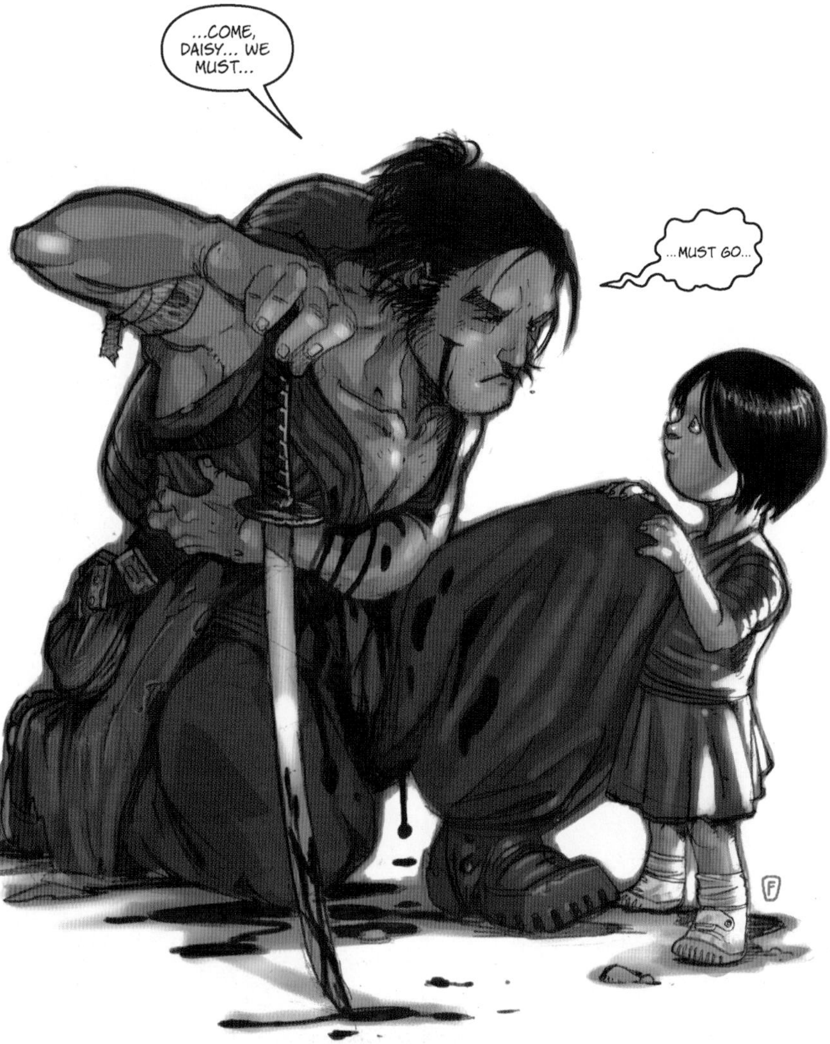
...COME, DAISY... WE MUST...
...MUST GO...

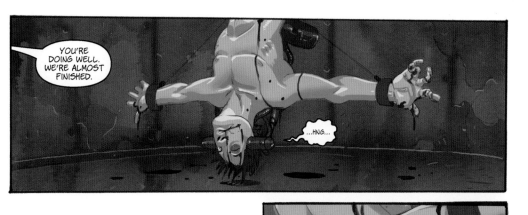

YOU'RE DOING WELL. WE'RE ALMOST FINISHED.

...HNG...

ONCE MORE, PLEASE --

GLOBALLY, HOW MANY **LEADERS** LEAD HOW MANY **FOLLOWERS**?

I SWEAR ... D'NNO... SHUT DOWN MONTHS AGO...

WE WERE FIGHTING FOR YOU...

YOU SHOULD HAVE SAVED YOUR **CHARITY** FOR THOSE WHO **NEEDED** IT.

BELLADONNA...

...HE'S HERE.

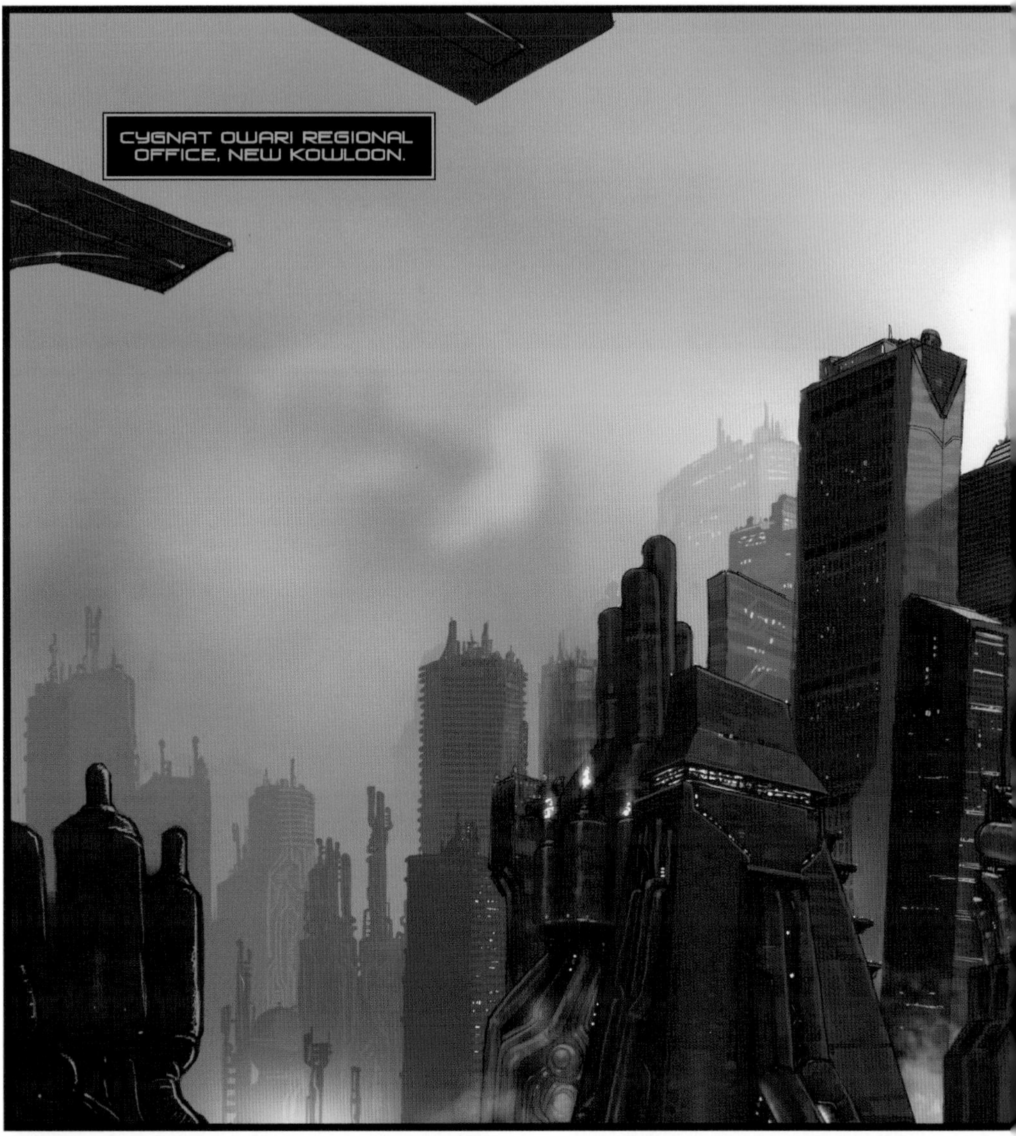
CYGNAT OWARI REGIONAL OFFICE, NEW KOWLOON.

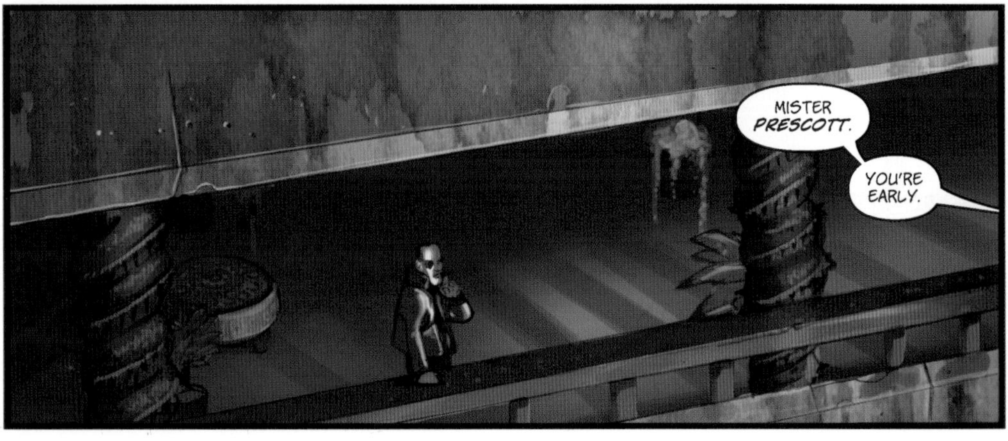
MISTER PRESCOTT.
YOU'RE EARLY.

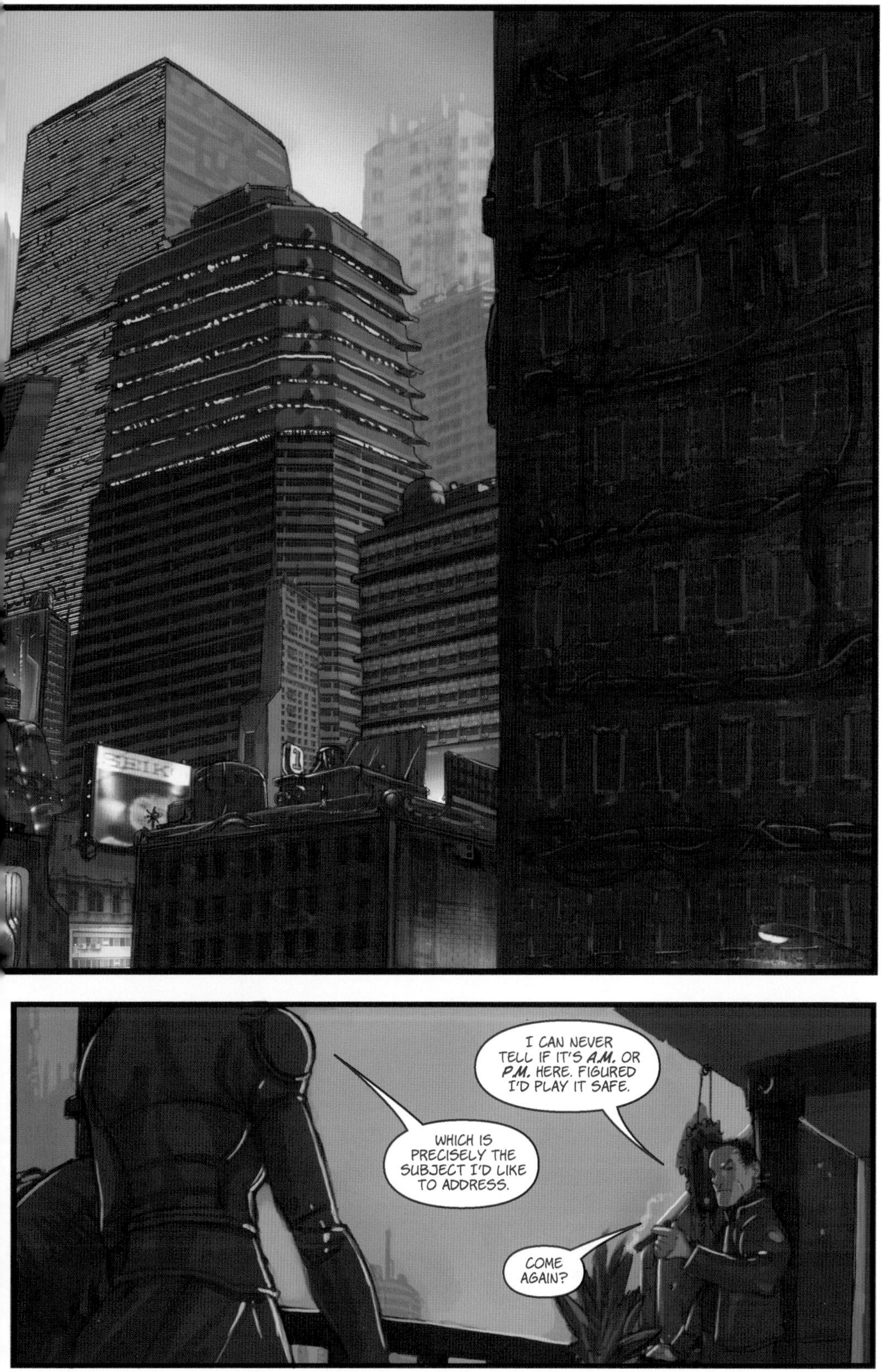
I CAN NEVER TELL IF IT'S *A.M.* OR *P.M.* HERE. FIGURED I'D PLAY IT SAFE.
WHICH IS PRECISELY THE SUBJECT I'D LIKE TO ADDRESS.
COME AGAIN?

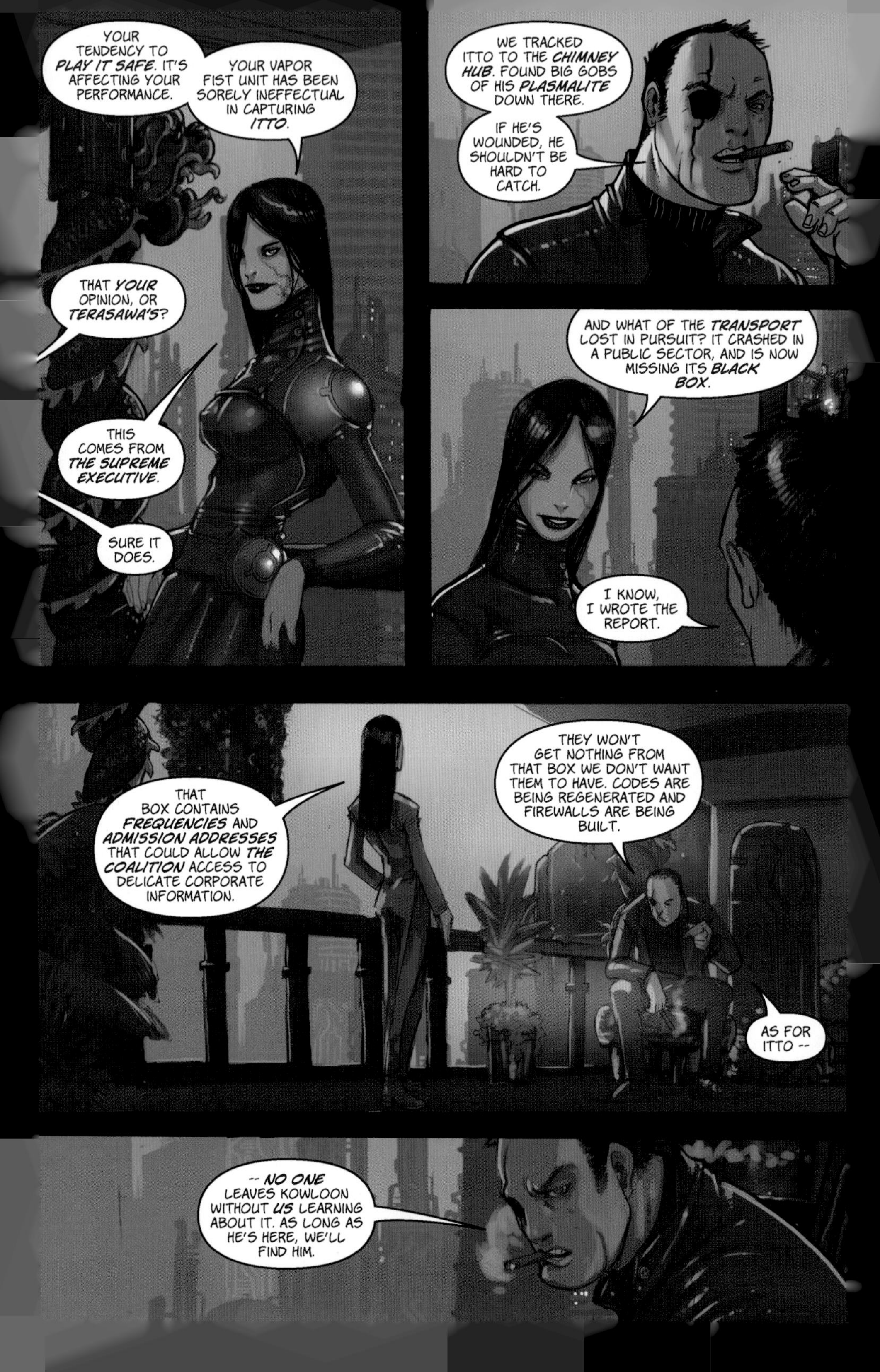

YOUR TENDENCY TO PLAY IT SAFE. IT'S AFFECTING YOUR PERFORMANCE.
YOUR VAPOR FIST UNIT HAS BEEN SORELY INEFFECTUAL IN CAPTURING ITTO.
THAT YOUR OPINION, OR TERASAWA'S?
THIS COMES FROM THE SUPREME EXECUTIVE.
SURE IT DOES.
WE TRACKED ITTO TO THE CHIMNEY HUB. FOUND BIG GOBS OF HIS PLASMALITE DOWN THERE.
IF HE'S WOUNDED, HE SHOULDN'T BE HARD TO CATCH.
AND WHAT OF THE TRANSPORT LOST IN PURSUIT? IT CRASHED IN A PUBLIC SECTOR, AND IS NOW MISSING ITS BLACK BOX.
I KNOW, I WROTE THE REPORT.
THAT BOX CONTAINS FREQUENCIES AND ADMISSION ADDRESSES THAT COULD ALLOW THE COALITION ACCESS TO DELICATE CORPORATE INFORMATION.
THEY WON'T GET NOTHING FROM THAT BOX WE DON'T WANT THEM TO HAVE. CODES ARE BEING REGENERATED AND FIREWALLS ARE BEING BUILT.
AS FOR ITTO --
-- NO ONE LEAVES KOWLOON WITHOUT US LEARNING ABOUT IT. AS LONG AS HE'S HERE, WE'LL FIND HIM.

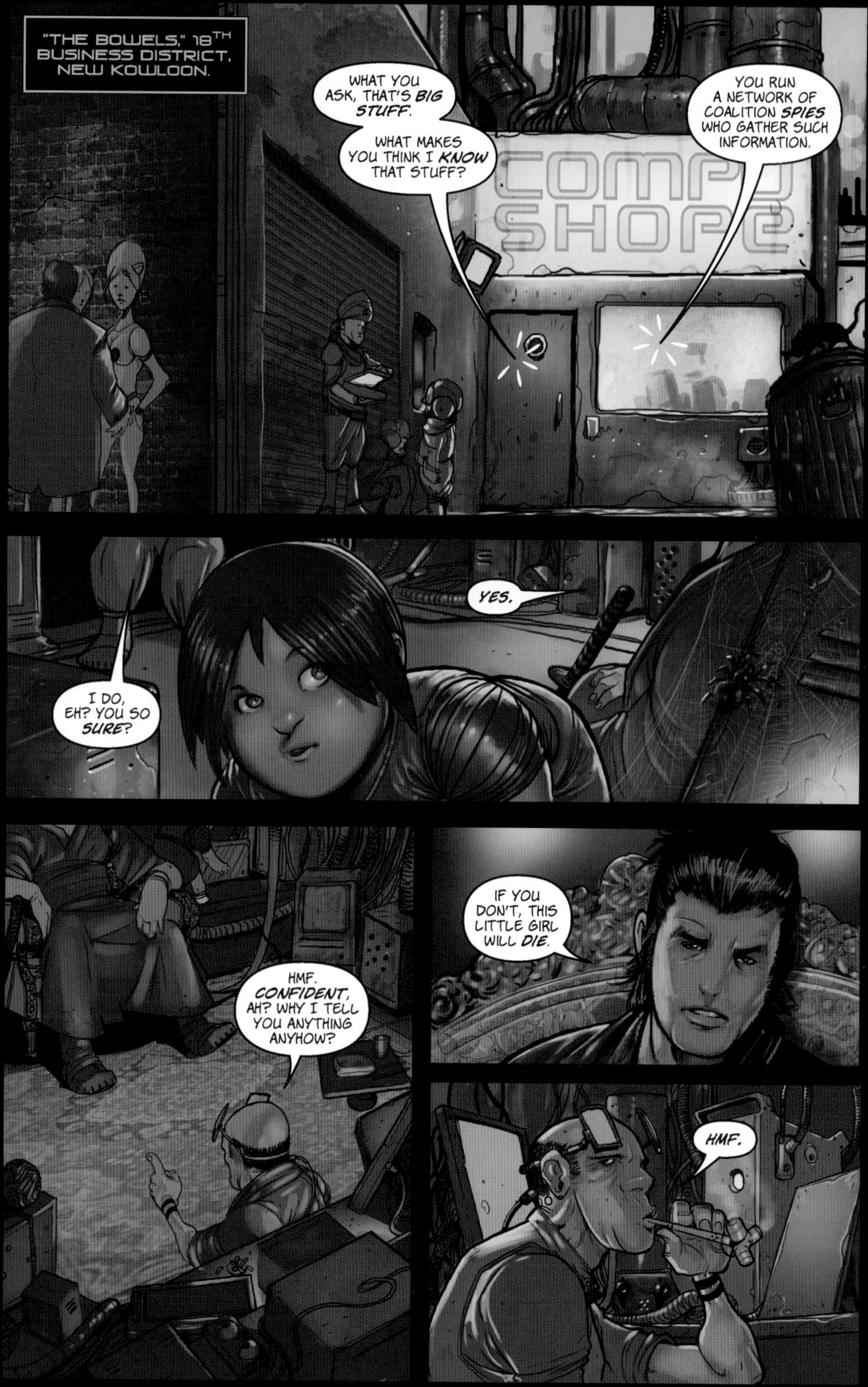
"THE BOWELS," 18TH BUSINESS DISTRICT, NEW KOWLOON.
WHAT YOU ASK, THAT'S BIG STUFF.
WHAT MAKES YOU THINK I KNOW THAT STUFF?
YOU RUN A NETWORK OF COALITION SPIES WHO GATHER SUCH INFORMATION.
COMPU SHOPPE
I DO, EH? YOU SO SURE?
YES.
IF YOU DON'T, THIS LITTLE GIRL WILL DIE.
HMF. CONFIDENT, AH? WHY I TELL YOU ANYTHING ANYHOW?
HMF.

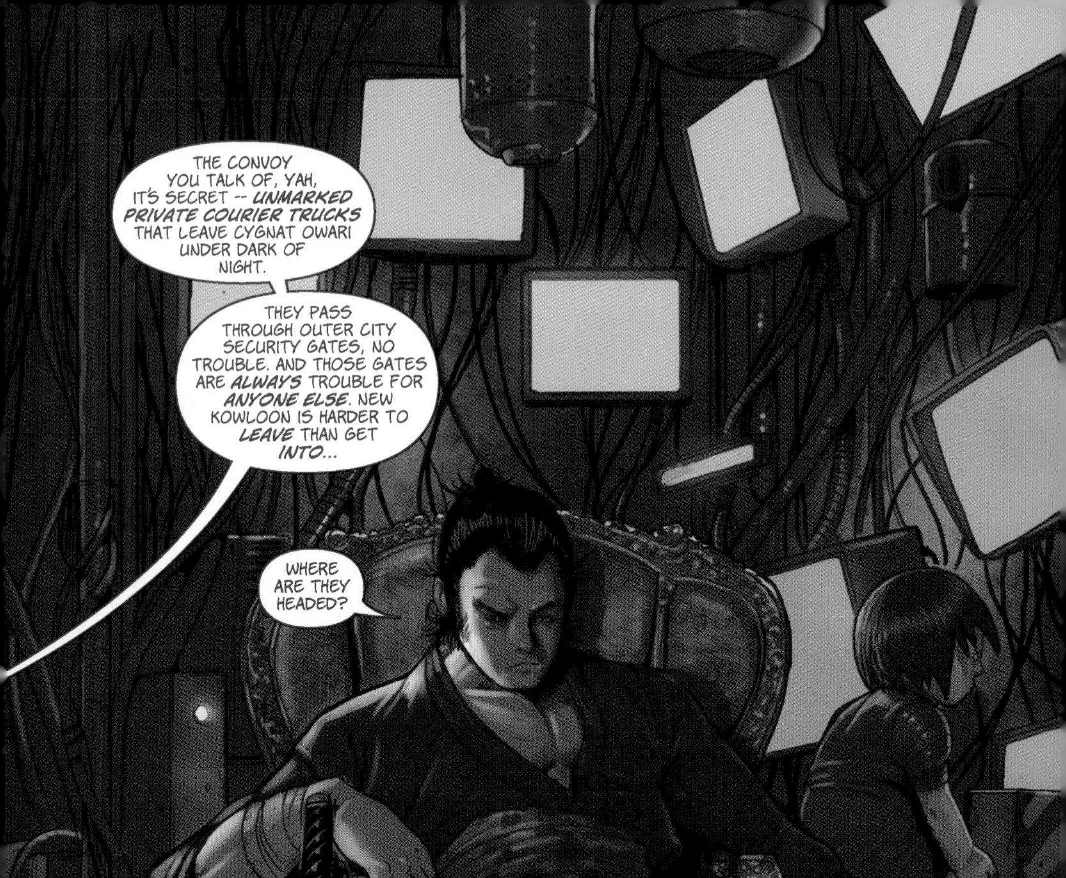
THE CONVOY YOU TALK OF, YAH, IT'S SECRET -- UNMARKED PRIVATE COURIER TRUCKS THAT LEAVE CYGNAT OWARI UNDER DARK OF NIGHT.
THEY PASS THROUGH OUTER CITY SECURITY GATES, NO TROUBLE. AND THOSE GATES ARE ALWAYS TROUBLE FOR ANYONE ELSE. NEW KOWLOON IS HARDER TO LEAVE THAN GET INTO...
WHERE ARE THEY HEADED?
YOU LOOKING TO HITCH A RIDE, AH? I DUNNO, BUT THEY'LL GET YOU OUT, THAT'S FOR SURE.
BUT IT'S DANGEROUS. TOO DANGEROUS FOR A LITTLE GIRL, MAYBE. MAYBE SHE DIE WHEN YOU GET CAUGHT, AH?
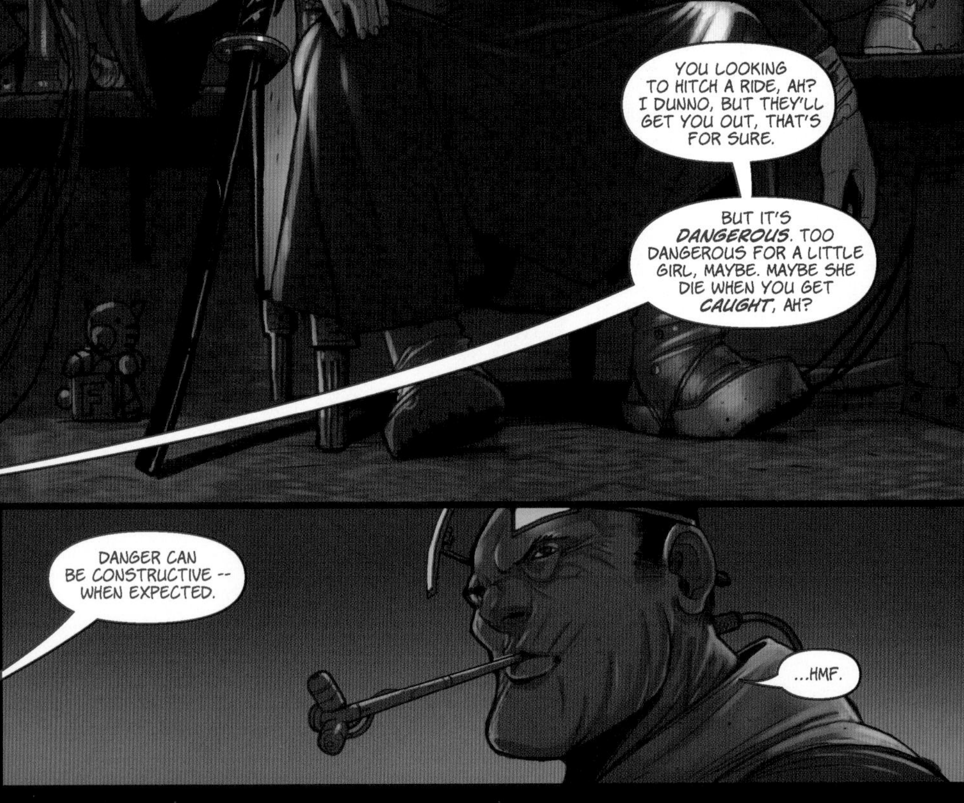
DANGER CAN BE CONSTRUCTIVE -- WHEN EXPECTED.
...HMF.

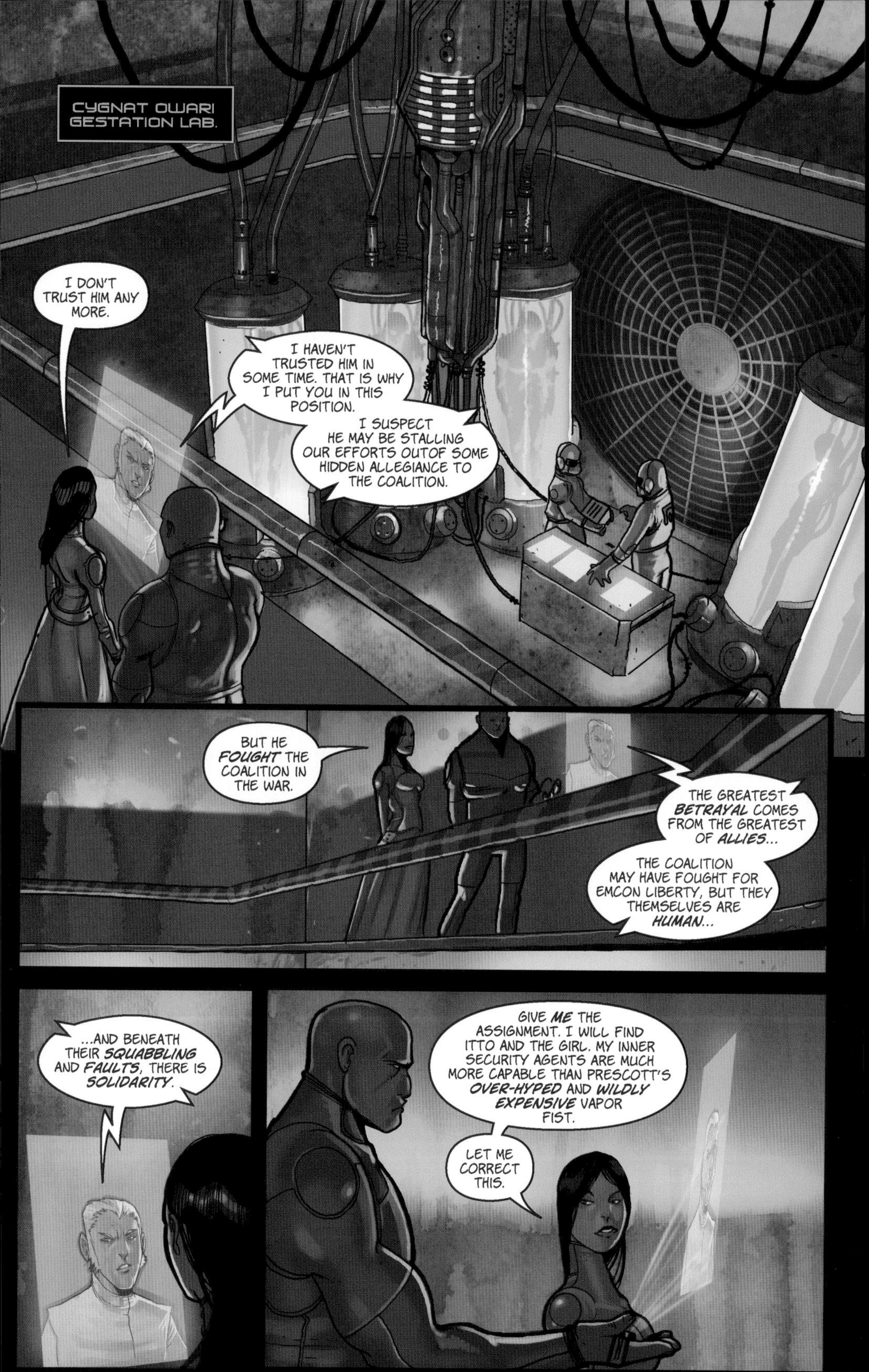
CYGNAT OWARI GESTATION LAB.
I DON'T TRUST HIM ANY MORE.
I HAVEN'T TRUSTED HIM IN SOME TIME. THAT IS WHY I PUT YOU IN THIS POSITION.
I SUSPECT HE MAY BE STALLING OUR EFFORTS OUTOF SOME HIDDEN ALLEGIANCE TO THE COALITION.
BUT HE FOUGHT THE COALITION IN THE WAR.
THE GREATEST BETRAYAL COMES FROM THE GREATEST OF ALLIES...
THE COALITION MAY HAVE FOUGHT FOR EMCON LIBERTY, BUT THEY THEMSELVES ARE HUMAN...
...AND BENEATH THEIR SQUABBLING AND FAULTS, THERE IS SOLIDARITY.
GIVE ME THE ASSIGNMENT. I WILL FIND ITTO AND THE GIRL. MY INNER SECURITY AGENTS ARE MUCH MORE CAPABLE THAN PRESCOTT'S OVER-HYPED AND WILDLY EXPENSIVE VAPOR FIST.
LET ME CORRECT THIS.

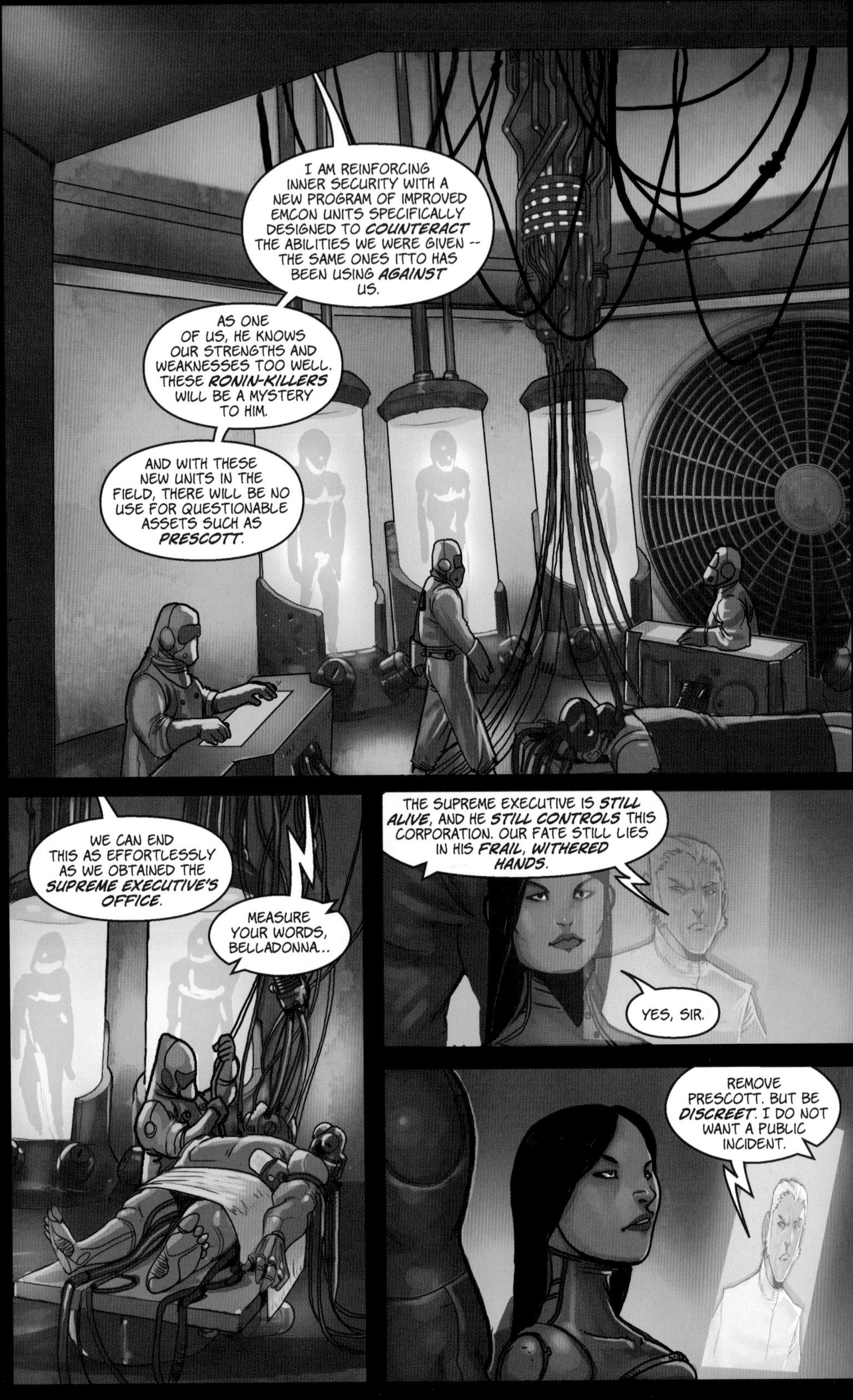
I AM REINFORCING INNER SECURITY WITH A NEW PROGRAM OF IMPROVED EMCON UNITS SPECIFICALLY DESIGNED TO COUNTERACT THE ABILITIES WE WERE GIVEN -- THE SAME ONES ITTO HAS BEEN USING AGAINST US.
AS ONE OF US, HE KNOWS OUR STRENGTHS AND WEAKNESSES TOO WELL. THESE RONIN-KILLERS WILL BE A MYSTERY TO HIM.
AND WITH THESE NEW UNITS IN THE FIELD, THERE WILL BE NO USE FOR QUESTIONABLE ASSETS SUCH AS PRESCOTT.
WE CAN END THIS AS EFFORTLESSLY AS WE OBTAINED THE SUPREME EXECUTIVE'S OFFICE.
MEASURE YOUR WORDS, BELLADONNA...
THE SUPREME EXECUTIVE IS STILL ALIVE, AND HE STILL CONTROLS THIS CORPORATION. OUR FATE STILL LIES IN HIS FRAIL, WITHERED HANDS.
YES, SIR.
REMOVE PRESCOTT. BUT BE DISCREET. I DO NOT WANT A PUBLIC INCIDENT.

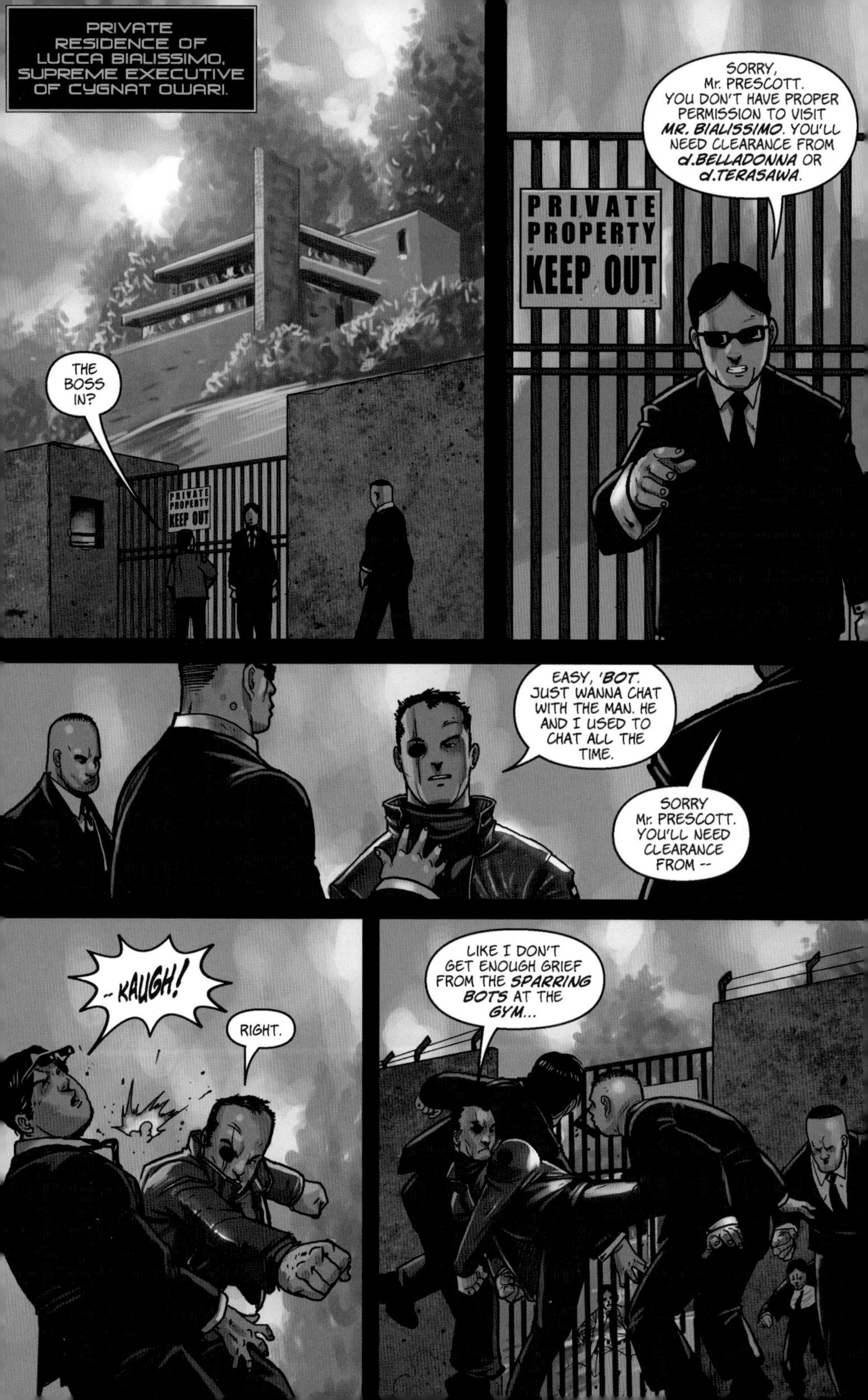
PRIVATE RESIDENCE OF LUCCA BIALISSIMO, SUPREME EXECUTIVE OF CYGNAT OWARI.
THE BOSS IN?
PRIVATE PROPERTY KEEP OUT
SORRY, Mr. PRESCOTT. YOU DON'T HAVE PROPER PERMISSION TO VISIT MR. BIALISSIMO. YOU'LL NEED CLEARANCE FROM d.BELLADONNA OR d.TERASAWA.
PRIVATE PROPERTY KEEP OUT
EASY, 'BOT. JUST WANNA CHAT WITH THE MAN. HE AND I USED TO CHAT ALL THE TIME.
SORRY Mr. PRESCOTT. YOU'LL NEED CLEARANCE FROM --
-- KAUGH!
RIGHT.
LIKE I DON'T GET ENOUGH GRIEF FROM THE SPARRING BOTS AT THE GYM...

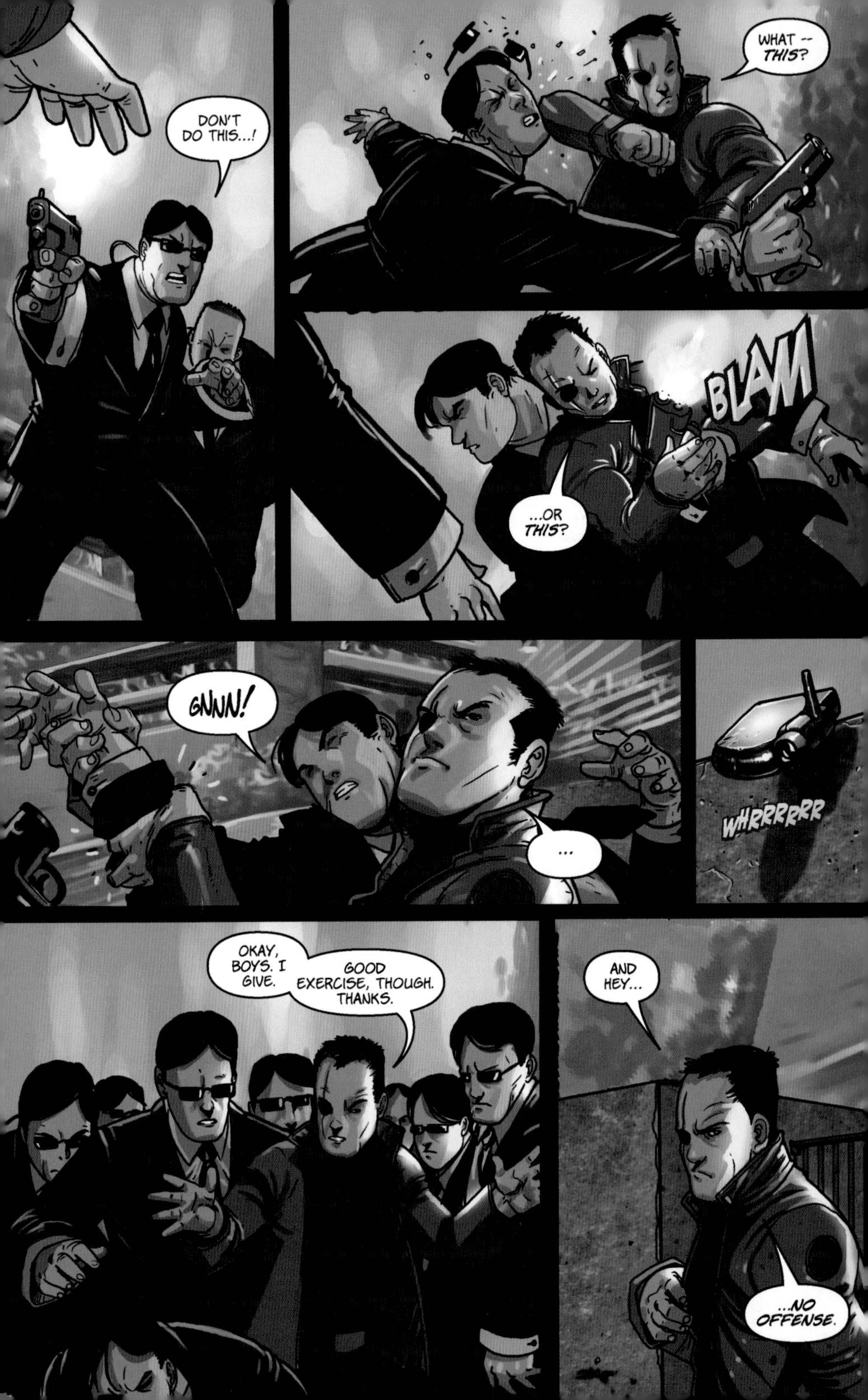
DON'T DO THIS...!
WHAT -- THIS?
BLAM
...OR THIS?
GNNN!
...
WHRRRRR
OKAY, BOYS. I GIVE.
GOOD EXERCISE, THOUGH. THANKS.
AND HEY...
...NO OFFENSE.

CYGNAT OWARI DATA CENTER, NEW KOWLOON REGIONAL CAMPUS.
TAK-TAK-TAKKA-TAK-TAKKA
HMM..
CYGNAT OWARI
An Emperor in Hiding
16 July 2099 — It has been nearly three months since Lucca Bialissimo, Supreme Executive of leading bio-synthetic development conglomerate Cygnat Owari, has been seen by the public. Though the international influence of his company continues to thrive with little competition to speak of, the once-flamboyant centerpiece of Cygnat Owari PR has become noticeably absent from the public eye. His office no longer returns phone calls. His press secretary no longer schedules trips around the world. Even his private mansion in Malaysia seems to grow stagnant and unkempt, leading many to wonder whether foul play is involved.
Such concerns were put to rest, however, when Bialissimo's EmCon Avatar designated Terasawa announced to the world that his employer was suffering from health problems, and had taken to self-imposed exile until the debilitating condition could be corrected. Details of the illness were not made available, but it is suggested to include certain disfiguring symptoms, symptoms that Bialissimo feels are too humbling to be seen or photographed by the public.
For decades, Bialissimo was known as the sharpest corporate playboy on the planet, hosting parties and events that not only drew great spectacle, but often perpetuated his enormous fortune through clever negotiation of broadcast rights and likeness royalties. He has been romantically linked with
SUPREME EXECUTIVE Lucca Bialissimo
EXECUTIVE AVATAR d.Terasawa
PRIME CONSORTIUM AMBASSADOR Yam Ko Kwan
CFO / EXECUTIVE CABINET Lewelyn Eiger
CO SECURITY AFFAIRS d.Belladonna
VE CABINET Eiger
CO SECURITY AFFAIRS d.Belladonna
...

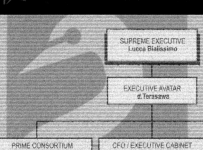

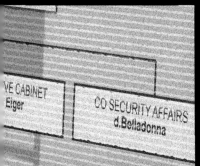

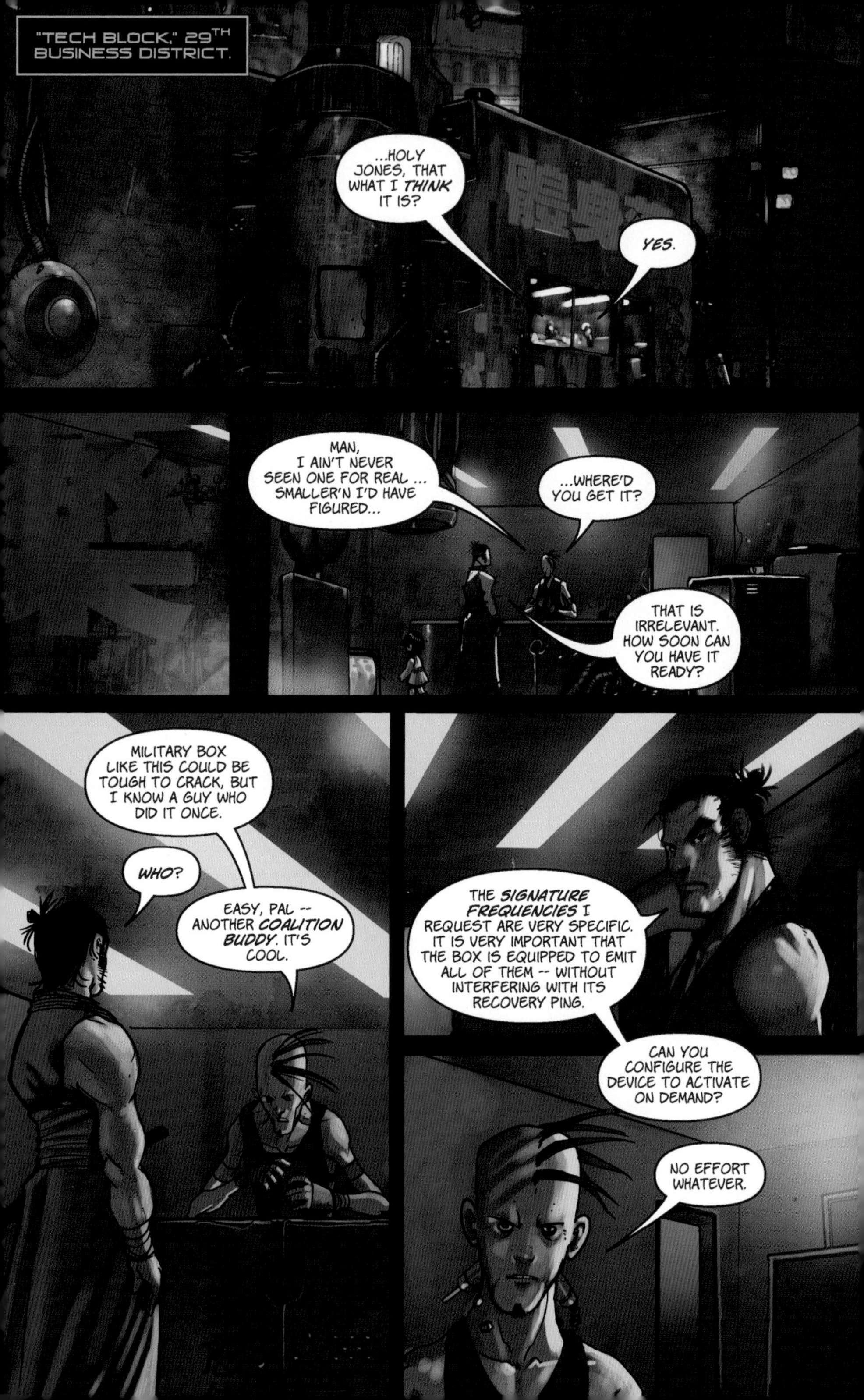
"TECH BLOCK," 29TH BUSINESS DISTRICT.
...HOLY JONES, THAT WHAT I *THINK* IT IS?
YES.
MAN, I AIN'T NEVER SEEN ONE FOR REAL ... SMALLER'N I'D HAVE FIGURED...
...WHERE'D YOU GET IT?
THAT IS IRRELEVANT. HOW SOON CAN YOU HAVE IT READY?
MILITARY BOX LIKE THIS COULD BE TOUGH TO CRACK, BUT I KNOW A GUY WHO DID IT ONCE.
WHO?
EASY, PAL -- ANOTHER *COALITION BUDDY*. IT'S COOL.
THE *SIGNATURE FREQUENCIES* I REQUEST ARE VERY SPECIFIC. IT IS VERY IMPORTANT THAT THE BOX IS EQUIPPED TO EMIT ALL OF THEM -- WITHOUT INTERFERING WITH ITS RECOVERY PING.
CAN YOU CONFIGURE THE DEVICE TO ACTIVATE ON DEMAND?
NO EFFORT WHATEVER.

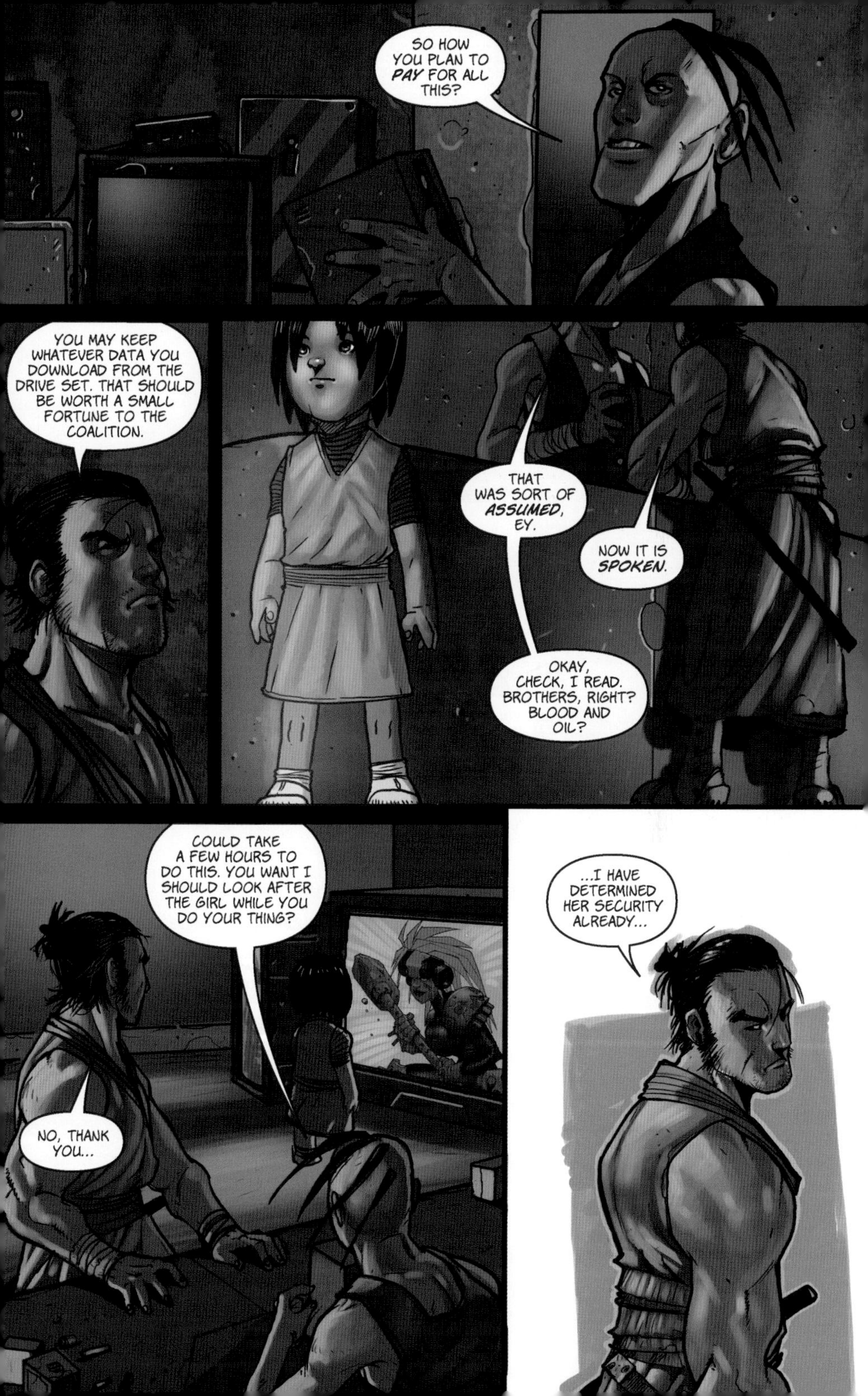
SO HOW YOU PLAN TO PAY FOR ALL THIS?
YOU MAY KEEP WHATEVER DATA YOU DOWNLOAD FROM THE DRIVE SET. THAT SHOULD BE WORTH A SMALL FORTUNE TO THE COALITION.
THAT WAS SORT OF ASSUMED, EY.
NOW IT IS SPOKEN.
OKAY, CHECK, I READ. BROTHERS, RIGHT? BLOOD AND OIL?
COULD TAKE A FEW HOURS TO DO THIS. YOU WANT I SHOULD LOOK AFTER THE GIRL WHILE YOU DO YOUR THING?
NO, THANK YOU...
...I HAVE DETERMINED HER SECURITY ALREADY...

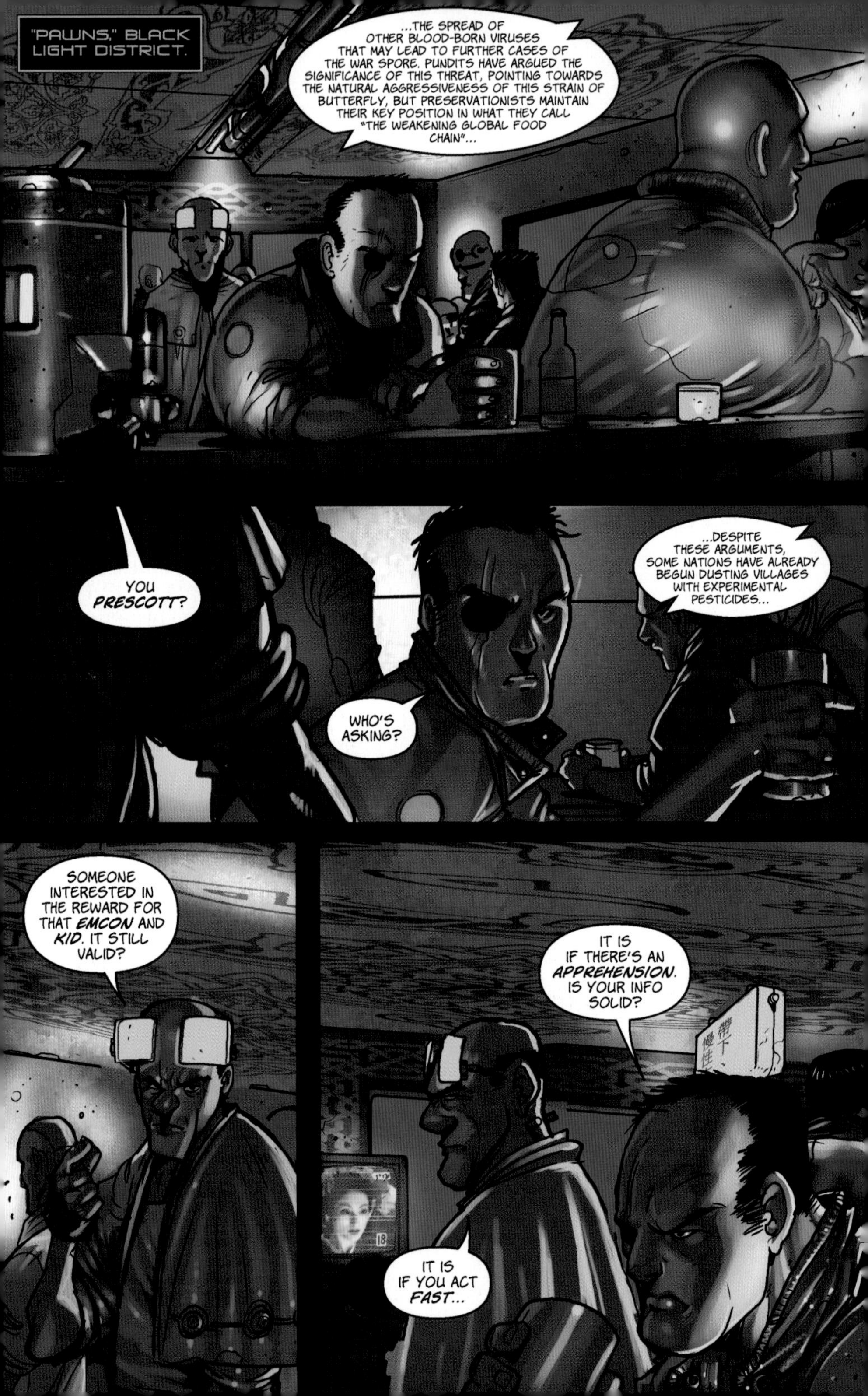
"PAWNS," BLACK LIGHT DISTRICT.
...THE SPREAD OF OTHER BLOOD-BORN VIRUSES THAT MAY LEAD TO FURTHER CASES OF THE WAR SPORE. PUNDITS HAVE ARGUED THE SIGNIFICANCE OF THIS THREAT, POINTING TOWARDS THE NATURAL AGGRESSIVENESS OF THIS STRAIN OF BUTTERFLY, BUT PRESERVATIONISTS MAINTAIN THEIR KEY POSITION IN WHAT THEY CALL "THE WEAKENING GLOBAL FOOD CHAIN"...
YOU *PRESCOTT?*
...DESPITE THESE ARGUMENTS, SOME NATIONS HAVE ALREADY BEGUN DUSTING VILLAGES WITH EXPERIMENTAL PESTICIDES...
WHO'S ASKING?
SOMEONE INTERESTED IN THE REWARD FOR THAT ***EMCON*** AND ***KID***. IT STILL VALID?
IT IS IF THERE'S AN *APPREHENSION*. IS YOUR INFO SOLID?
IT IS IF YOU ACT ***FAST***...

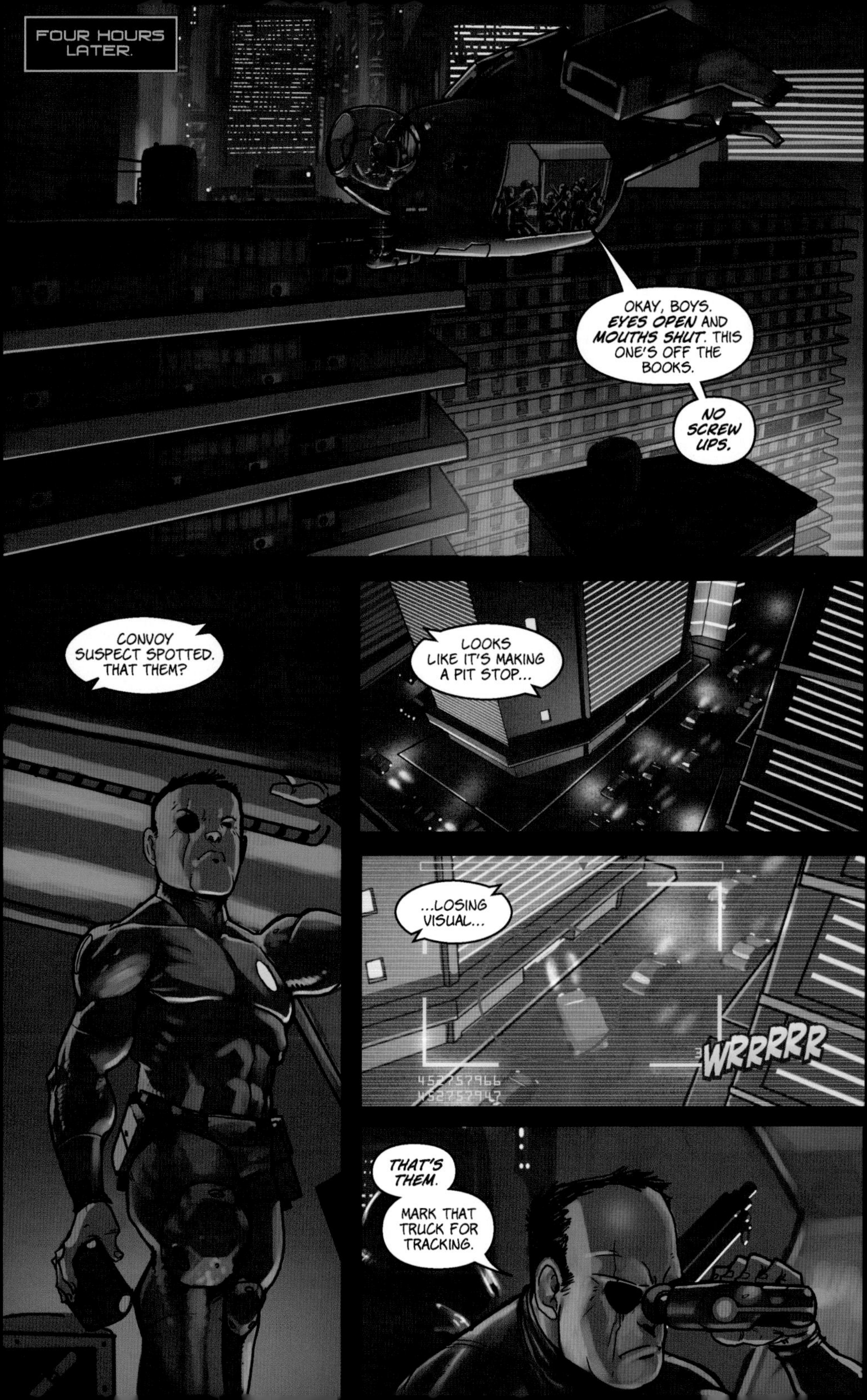
FOUR HOURS LATER.
OKAY, BOYS. EYES OPEN AND MOUTHS SHUT. THIS ONE'S OFF THE BOOKS.
NO SCREW UPS.
CONVOY SUSPECT SPOTTED. THAT THEM?
LOOKS LIKE IT'S MAKING A PIT STOP...
...LOSING VISUAL...
WRRRRR
THAT'S THEM.
MARK THAT TRUCK FOR TRACKING.

SIR, WE GOT A SIGNATURE PULSE RATE BELOW... 80% MATCH.

STAND BY...

LET'S NOT SPOOK HIM.

HE'S ENTERED THE GARAGE... HE'S OFF OUR SCREENS...

TRYING TO SNEAK OUT ON THE COMPANY BUS, EH...?

TARGET IN MOTION AGAIN.

CONVOY HAS LEFT THE GARAGE.

SHOWING A BODY SHAPE IN THE BACK. *LOW POWER SIGNATURE.*

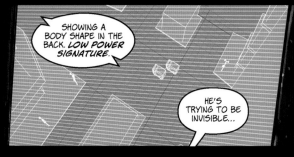

HE'S TRYING TO BE INVISIBLE...

ALL RIGHT -- SWARM AND CONTAIN!!

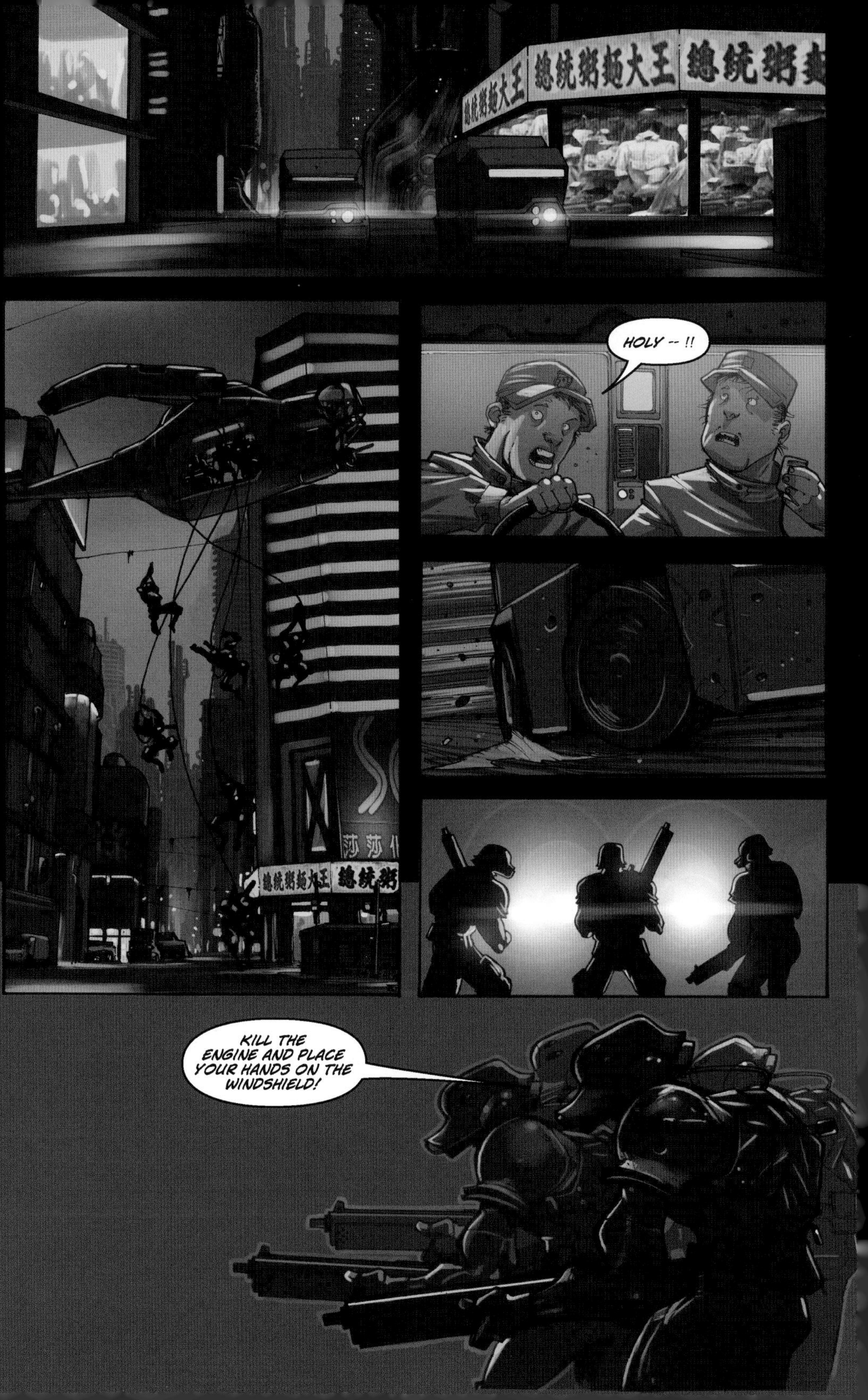
總統粥麵大王
HOLY -- !!
KILL THE ENGINE AND PLACE YOUR HANDS ON THE WINDSHIELD!

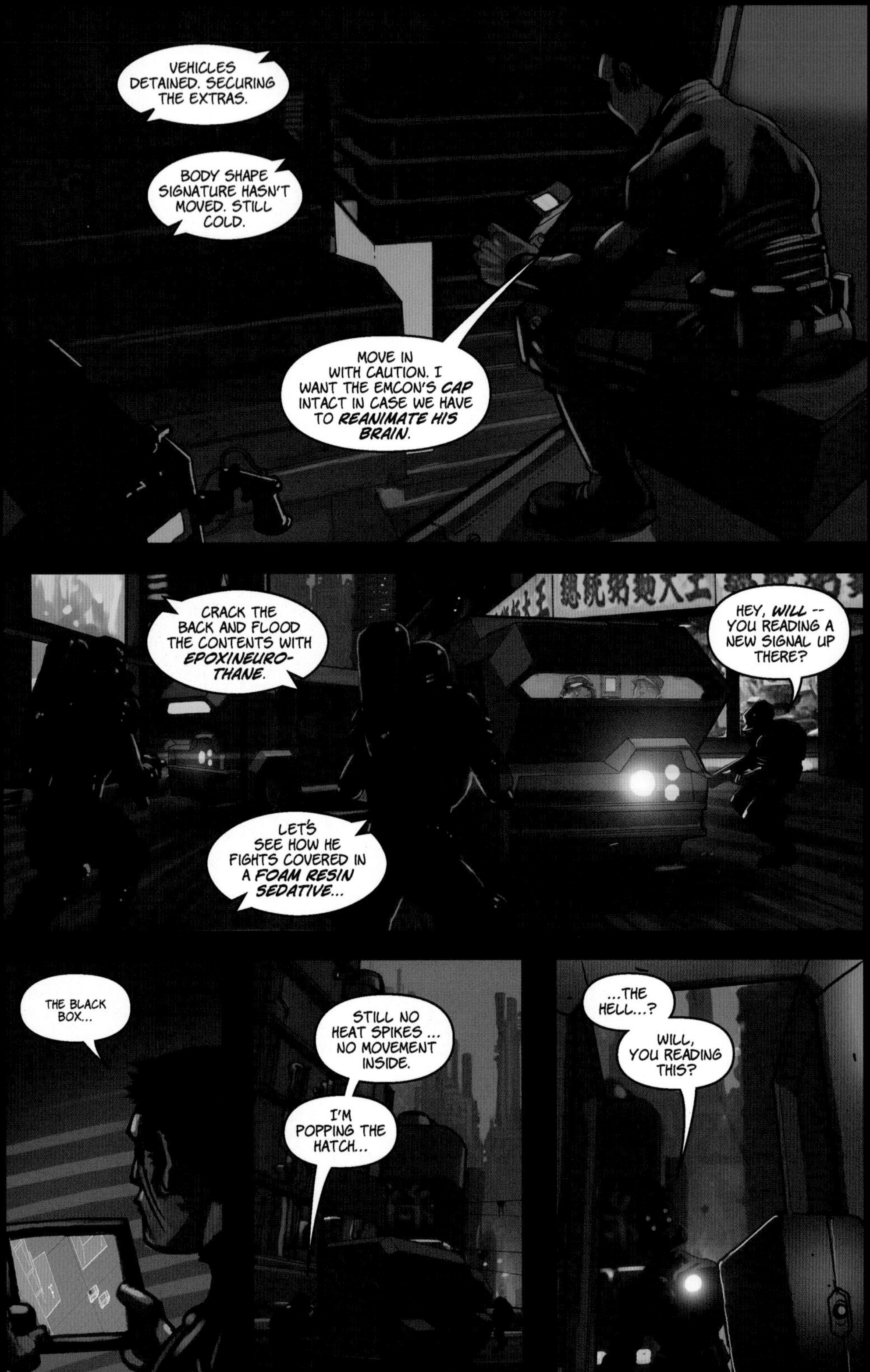
VEHICLES DETAINED. SECURING THE EXTRAS.
BODY SHAPE SIGNATURE HASN'T MOVED. STILL COLD.
MOVE IN WITH CAUTION. I WANT THE EMCON'S CAP INTACT IN CASE WE HAVE TO REANIMATE HIS BRAIN.
CRACK THE BACK AND FLOOD THE CONTENTS WITH EPOXINEURO-THANE.
HEY, WILL -- YOU READING A NEW SIGNAL UP THERE?
LET'S SEE HOW HE FIGHTS COVERED IN A FOAM RESIN SEDATIVE...
THE BLACK BOX...
STILL NO HEAT SPIKES ... NO MOVEMENT INSIDE.
I'M POPPING THE HATCH...
...THE HELL...?
WILL, YOU READING THIS?

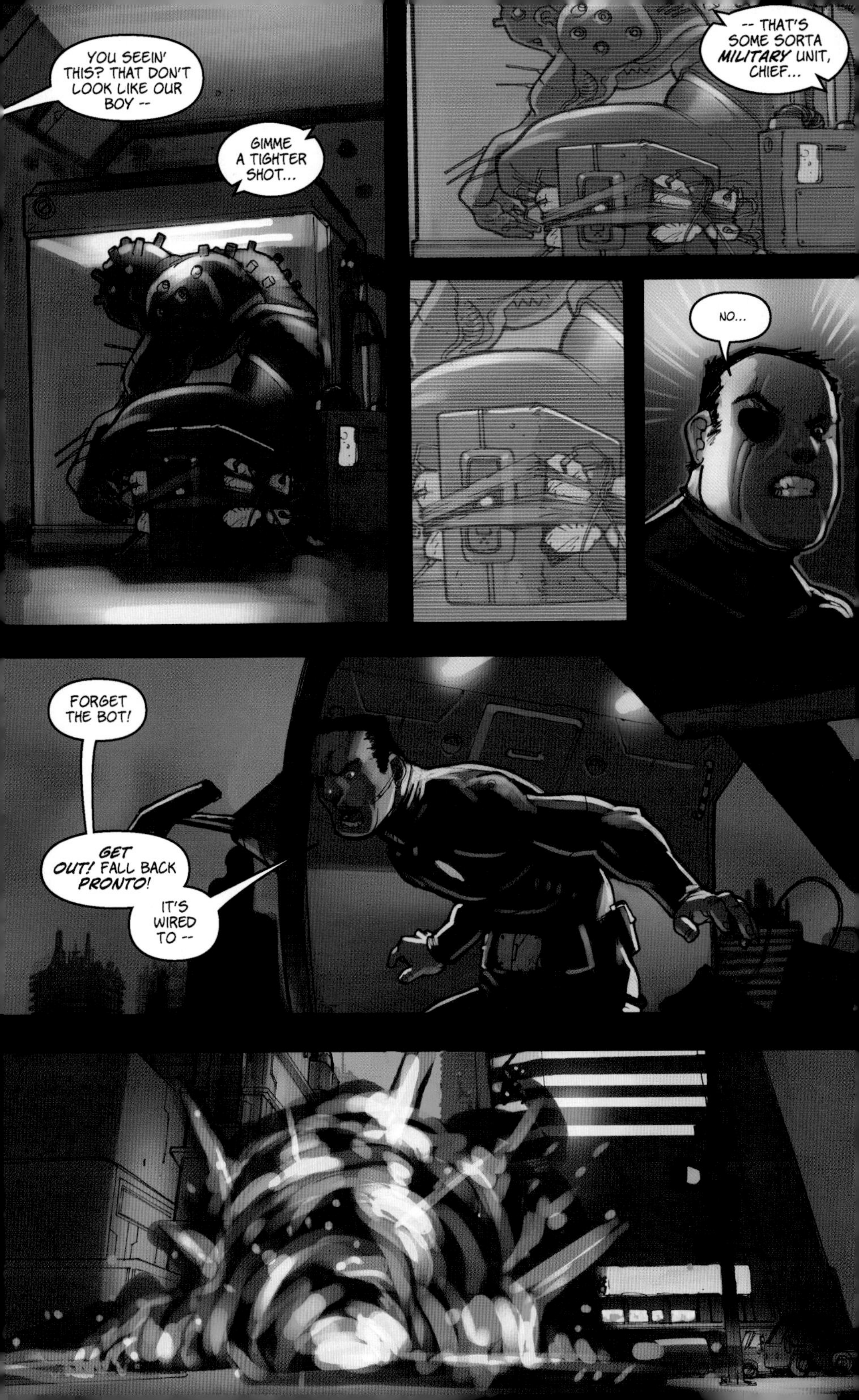
YOU SEEIN' THIS? THAT DON'T LOOK LIKE OUR BOY --
GIMME A TIGHTER SHOT...
-- THAT'S SOME SORTA *MILITARY* UNIT, CHIEF...
NO...
FORGET THE BOT!
GET OUT! FALL BACK *PRONTO!*
IT'S WIRED TO --

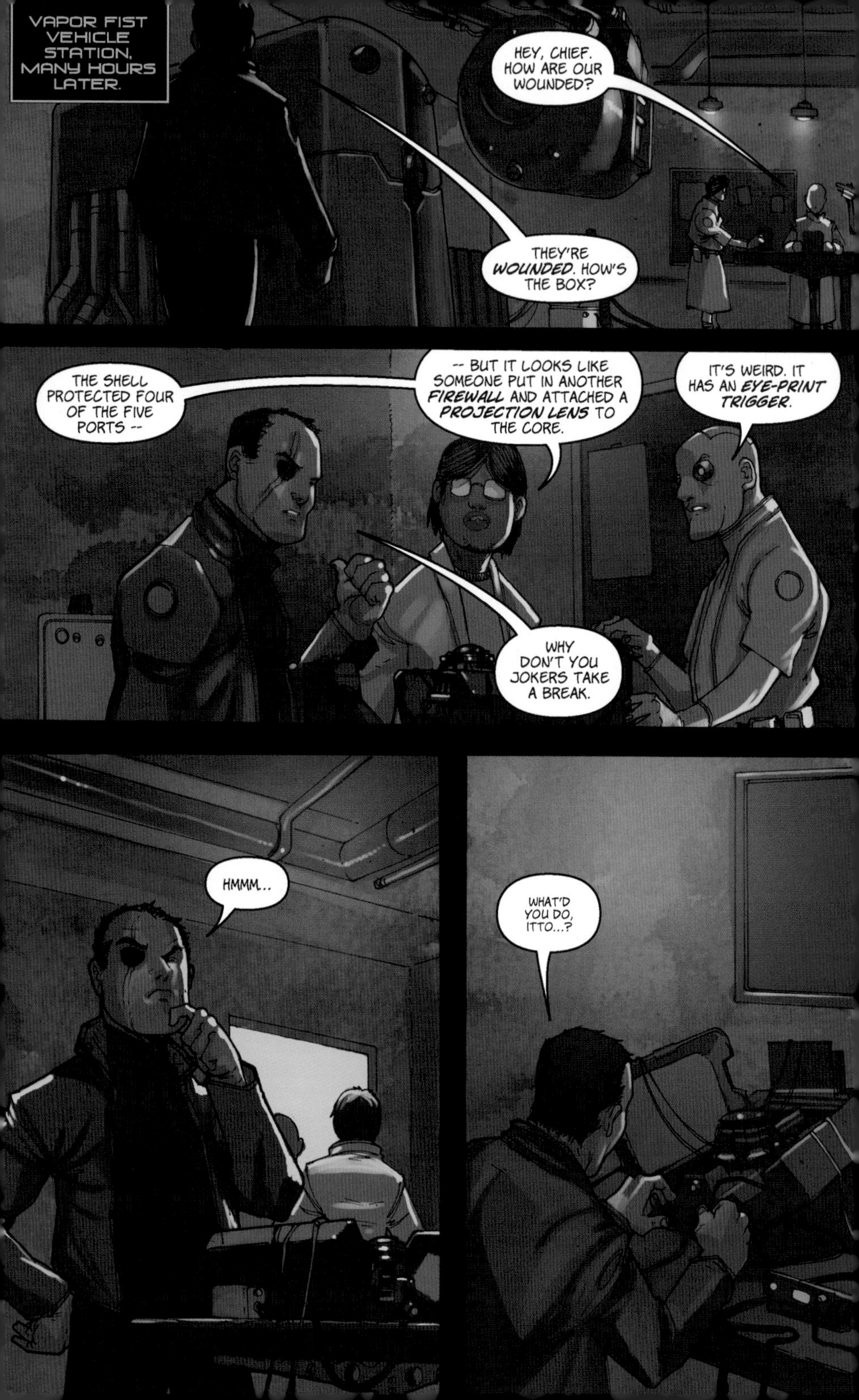
VAPOR FIST VEHICLE STATION, MANY HOURS LATER.
HEY, CHIEF. HOW ARE OUR WOUNDED?
THEY'RE WOUNDED. HOW'S THE BOX?
THE SHELL PROTECTED FOUR OF THE FIVE PORTS --
-- BUT IT LOOKS LIKE SOMEONE PUT IN ANOTHER FIREWALL AND ATTACHED A PROJECTION LENS TO THE CORE.
IT'S WEIRD. IT HAS AN EYE-PRINT TRIGGER.
WHY DON'T YOU JOKERS TAKE A BREAK.
HMMM..
WHAT'D YOU DO, ITTO...?

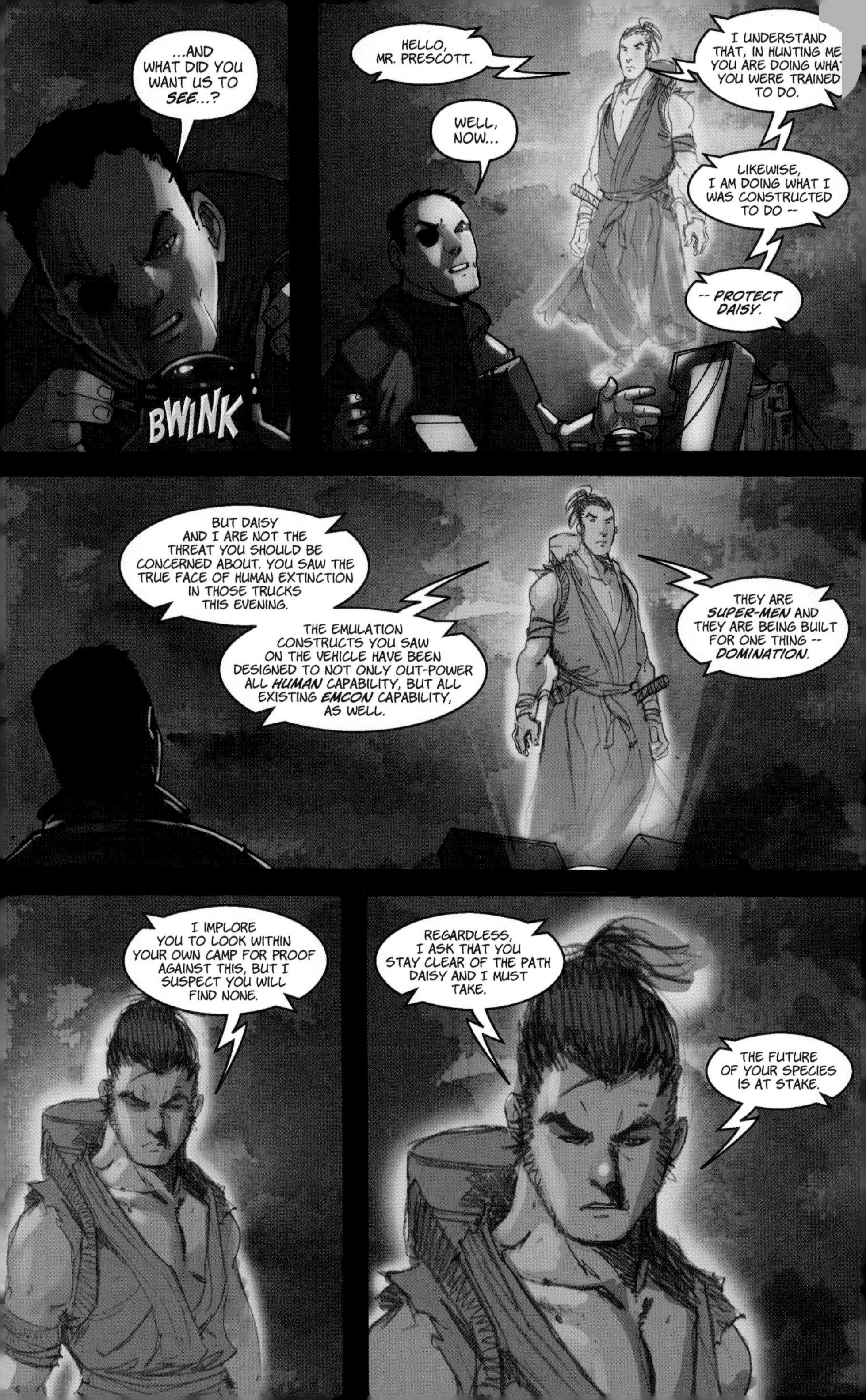
...AND WHAT DID YOU WANT US TO *SEE*...?
BWINK
HELLO, MR. PRESCOTT.
WELL, NOW...
I UNDERSTAND THAT, IN HUNTING ME, YOU ARE DOING WHAT YOU WERE TRAINED TO DO.
LIKEWISE, I AM DOING WHAT I WAS CONSTRUCTED TO DO --
-- *PROTECT DAISY*.
BUT DAISY AND I ARE NOT THE THREAT YOU SHOULD BE CONCERNED ABOUT. YOU SAW THE TRUE FACE OF HUMAN EXTINCTION IN THOSE TRUCKS THIS EVENING.
THE EMULATION CONSTRUCTS YOU SAW ON THE VEHICLE HAVE BEEN DESIGNED TO NOT ONLY OUT-POWER ALL *HUMAN* CAPABILITY, BUT ALL EXISTING *EMCON* CAPABILITY, AS WELL.
THEY ARE *SUPER-MEN* AND THEY ARE BEING BUILT FOR ONE THING -- *DOMINATION*.
I IMPLORE YOU TO LOOK WITHIN YOUR OWN CAMP FOR PROOF AGAINST THIS, BUT I SUSPECT YOU WILL FIND NONE.
REGARDLESS, I ASK THAT YOU STAY CLEAR OF THE PATH DAISY AND I MUST TAKE.
THE FUTURE OF YOUR SPECIES IS AT STAKE.

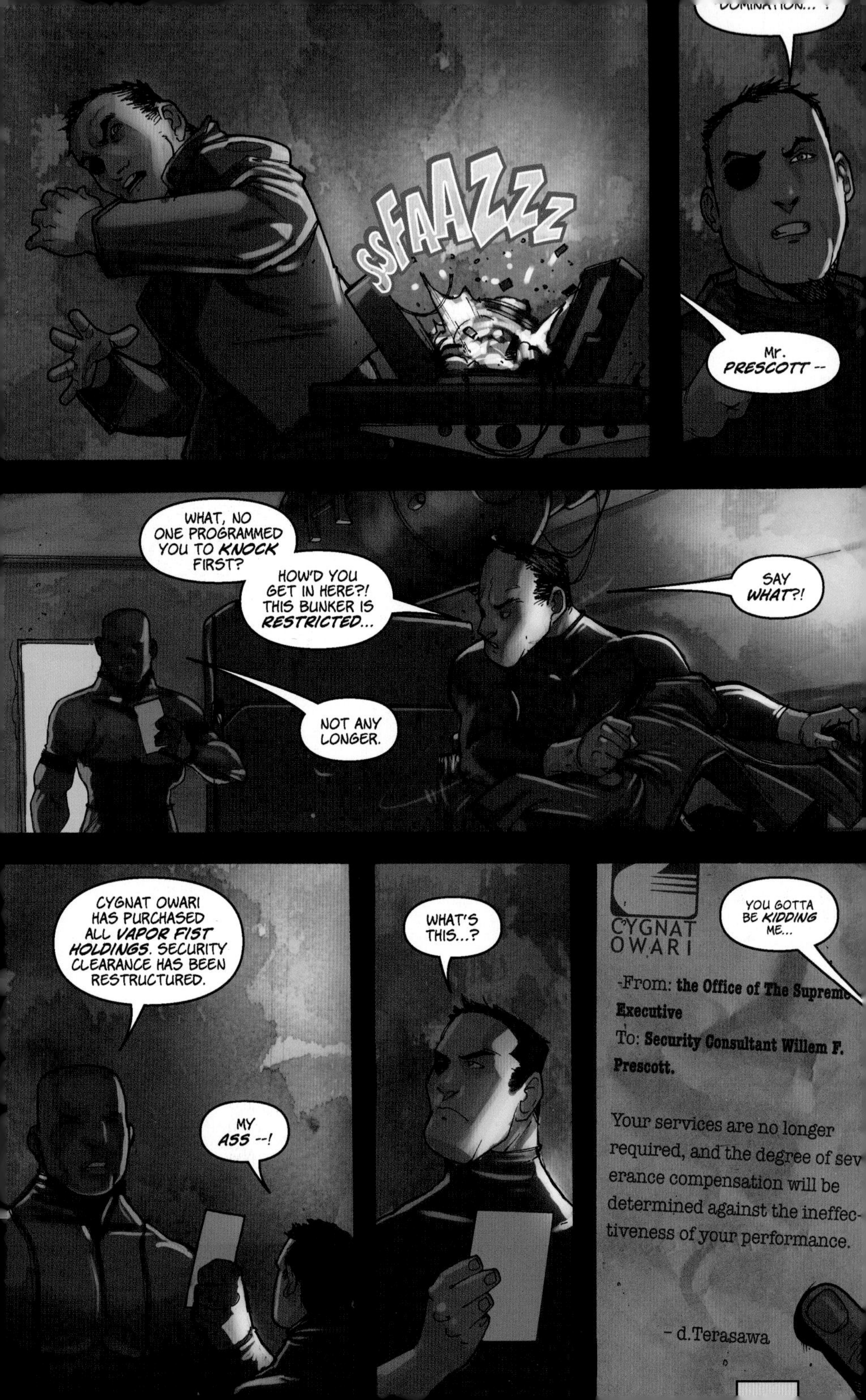
DOMINATION... ?
SSFAAZZZ
Mr. PRESCOTT --
WHAT, NO ONE PROGRAMMED YOU TO KNOCK FIRST?
HOW'D YOU GET IN HERE?! THIS BUNKER IS RESTRICTED...
NOT ANY LONGER.
SAY WHAT?!
CYGNAT OWARI HAS PURCHASED ALL VAPOR FIST HOLDINGS. SECURITY CLEARANCE HAS BEEN RESTRUCTURED.
MY ASS --!
WHAT'S THIS...?
CYGNAT OWARI
YOU GOTTA BE KIDDING ME...
-From: the Office of The Supreme Executive
To: Security Consultant Willem F. Prescott.
Your services are no longer required, and the degree of severance compensation will be determined against the ineffectiveness of your performance.
- d.Terasawa

子連れ狼

20

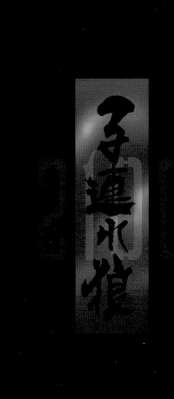

MANGA! MANGA! MANGA! DARK HORSE HAS THE BEST IN MANGA COLLECTIONS!

LONE WOLF AND CUB

Kazuo Koike and
Goseki Kojima

New volumes released monthly! Collect the complete 28-volume series!

VOLUME 1:
THE ASSASSIN'S ROAD
ISBN: 1-56971-502-5 $9.95

VOLUME 2:
THE GATELESS BARRIER
ISBN: 1-56971-503-3 $9.95

VOLUME 3:
THE FLUTE OF THE FALLEN TIGER
ISBN: 1-56971-504-1 $9.95

VOLUME 4:
THE BELL WARDEN
ISBN: 1-56971-505-X $9.95

VOLUME 5: BLACK WIND
ISBN: 1-5671-506-8 $9.95

VOLUME 6:
LANTERNS FOR THE DEAD
ISBN: 1-56971-507-6 $9.95

VOLUME 7: CLOUD DRAGON, WIND TIGER
ISBN: 1-56971-508-4 $9.95

VOLUME 8:
THREAD OF TEARS
ISBN: 1-56971-509-2 $9.95

VOLUME 9:
ECHO OF THE ASSASSIN
ISBN: 1-56971-510-6 $9.95

VOLUME 10:
DRIFTING SHADOWS
ISBN: 1-56971-511-4 $9.95

VOLUME 11:
TALISMAN OF HADES
ISBN: 1-56971-512-2 $9.95

VOLUME 12:
SHATTERED STONES
ISBN: 1-56971-513-0 $9.95

VOLUME 13: THE MOON IN THE EAST, THE SUN IN THE WEST
ISBN: 1-56971-585-8 $9.95

VOLUME 14:
DAY OF THE DEMONS
ISBN: 1-56971-586-6 $9.95

VOLUME 15:
BROTHERS OF THE GRASS
ISBN: 1-56971-587-4 $9.95

VOLUME 16:
GATEWAY INTO WINTER
ISBN: 1-5671-588-2 $9.95

VOLUME 17:
THE WILL OF THE FANG
ISBN: 1-56971-589-0 $9.95

VOLUME 18:
TWILIGHT OF THE KUROKUWA
ISBN: 1-56971-590-4 $9.95

VOLUME 19: THE MOON IN OUR HEARTS
ISBN: 1-56971-591-2 $9.95

VOLUME 20:
A TASTE OF POISON
ISBN: 1-56971-592-0 $9.95

VOLUME 21:
FRAGRANCE OF DEATH
ISBN: 1-56971-593-9 $9.95

VOLUME 22:
HEAVEN AND EARTH
ISBN: 1-56971-594-7 $9.95

VOLUME 23:
TEARS OF ICE
ISBN: 1-56971-595-5 $9.95

VOLUME 24:
IN THESE SMALL HANDS
ISBN: 1-56971-596-3 $9.95

VOLUME 25:
PERHAPS IN DEATH
ISBN: 1-56971-597-1 $9.95

VOLUME 26:
BATTLE IN THE DARK
ISBN: 1-56971-598-X $9.95

VOLUME 27:
BATTLE'S EVE
ISBN: 1-56971-599-8 $9.95

VOLUME 28:
FALLING TREE
ISBN: 1-56971-600-5 $9.95

Available from your local comics shop or bookstore!

To find a comics shop in your area, call 1-888-266-4226 • For more information or to order direct:
•On the web: www.darkhorse.com •E-mail: mailorder@darkhorse.com
•Phone: 1-800-862-0052 or (503) 652-9701 Mon.-Sat. 9 A.M. to 5 P.M. Pacific Time
*Prices and availability subject to change without notice

Dark Horse Comics: **Mike Richardson** *publisher* • **Neil Hankerson** *executive vice president* • **Andy Karabatsos** *vice president of finance* • **Randy Stradley** *vice president of publishing* • **Chris Warner** *senior books editor* • **Michael Martens** *vice president of marketing* • **Anita Nelson** *vice president of sales & licensing* • **David Scroggy** *vice president of product development* • **Mark Cox** *art director* • **Dale LaFountain** *vice president of information technology* • **Darlene Vogel** *director of purchasing* • **Ken Lizzi** *general counsel* • **Tom Weddle** *controller*